ACCLAIM FOR THE NOVELS OF
LEILA MEACHAM

TITANS

"The novel has it all: a wide cast of characters, pitch-perfect period detail, romance, plenty of drama, and skeletons in the closet (literally). Saga fans will be swooning."

—*Booklist* (starred review)

"It has everything any reader could want in a book...epic storytelling that plunges the reader headfirst into the plot... [Meacham] is a titan herself." —*Huffington Post*

"Emotionally resounding...Texas has never seemed grander... Meacham's easy-to-read prose helps to maintain a pace that you won't be able to quit, pushing through from chapter to chapter to find the next important nugget of this dramatic family tale. It is best savored over a great steak with a glass of wine and evenings to yourself." —BookReporter

SOMERSET

"Bestselling author Meacham is back with a prequel to *Roses* that stands on its own as a sweeping historical saga, spanning the nineteenth century...[Fans] and new readers alike will find themselves absorbed in the family saga that Meacham has proven—once again—talented in telling."

—*Publishers Weekly* (starred review)

"Entertaining...Meacham skillfully weaves colorful history into her lively tale...*Somerset* has its charms."

—*Dallas Morning News*

"Slavery, westward expansion, abolition, the Civil War, love, marriage, friendship, tragedy, and triumph—all the ingredients (and much more) that made so many love *Roses* so much—are here in abundance."

—*San Antonio Express-News*

"A story you do not want to miss...[Recommended] to readers of Kathryn Stockett's *The Help* or Margaret Mitchell's *Gone with the Wind. Somerset* has everything a compelling historical epic calls for: love and war, friendship and betrayal, opportunity and loss, and everything in between."

—*BookPage*

"4½ stars! This prequel to *Roses* is as addictive as any soap opera... As sprawling and big as Texas itself, Meacham's epic saga is perfect for readers who long for the 'big books' of the past. There are enough adventure, tears, and laughter alongside colorful history to keep readers engrossed and satisfied."

—*RT Book Reviews*

TUMBLEWEEDS

"[An] expansive generational saga...Fans of *Friday Night Lights* will enjoy a return to the land where high school football boys are kings."

—*Chicago Tribune*

"Meacham scores a touchdown...You will laugh, cry, and cheer to a plot so thick and a conclusion so surprising, it will leave you wishing for more. Yes, Meacham is really that good. And *Tumbleweeds* is more than entertaining, it's addictive."

—*Examiner.com*

"If you're going to a beach this summer, or better yet, a windswept prairie, this is definitely a book you'll want to pack."
—*Times Leader* (Wilkes-Barre, PA)

"[A] sprawling novel as large as Texas itself."
—*Library Journal*

"Once again, Meacham has proven to be a master storyteller...The pages fly by as the reader becomes engrossed in the tale."
—*Lubbock Avalanche-Journal* (TX)

ROSES

"Like *Gone with the Wind*, as gloriously entertaining as it is vast...*Roses* transports."
—*People*

"Meacham's sweeping, century-encompassing, multigenerational epic is reminiscent of the film *Giant*, and as large, romantic, and American a tale as Texas itself."
—*Booklist*

"Enthralling."
—*Better Homes and Gardens*

"The story of East Texas families in the kind of dynastic gymnastics we all know and love."
—Liz Smith

"Larger-than-life protagonists and a fast-paced, engaging plot... Meacham has succeeded in creating an indelible heroine."
—*Dallas Morning News*

"[An] enthralling stunner, a good, old-fashioned read."
—*Publishers Weekly*

"A thrilling journey...a treasure...a must-read. Warning: Once you begin reading, you won't be able to put the book down."   —Examiner.com

"[A] sprawling novel of passion and revenge. Highly recommended...It's been almost thirty years since the heyday of giant epics in the grand tradition of Edna Ferber and Barbara Taylor Bradford, but Meacham's debut might bring them back."   —*Library Journal* (starred review)

"A high-end *Thorn Birds*."   —TheDailyBeast.com

"I ate this multigenerational tale of two families warring it up across Texas history with the same alacrity with which I would gobble chocolate."
—Joshilyn Jackson, *New York Times* bestselling author of *gods in Alabama* and *Backseat Saints*

"A Southern epic in the most cinematic sense—plot-heavy and historical, filled with archaic Southern dialect and formality, with love, marriage, war, and death over three generations."
—Caroline Dworin, "The Book Bench," NewYorker.com

"This sweeping epic of love, sacrifice, and struggle reads like *Gone with the Wind* with all the passions and family politics of the South."   —*Midwest Book Review*

"The kind of book you can lose yourself in, from beginning to end."   —*Huffington Post*

"Fast-paced and full of passions...This panoramic drama proves evocative and lush. The plot is intricate and gives back as much as the reader can take…Stunning and original, *Roses* is a must-read."   —TheReviewBroads.com

"May herald the overdue return of those delicious doorstop epics from such writers as Barbara Taylor Bradford and Colleen McCullough…a refreshingly nostalgic bouquet of family angst, undying love, and 'if only's."   —*Publishers Weekly*

"Superbly written…a rating of ten out of ten. I simply loved this book."   —*A Novel Menagerie*

ALSO BY LEILA MEACHAM

Roses

Tumbleweeds

Somerset

Titans

RYAN'S HAND

Leila Meacham

GC

GRAND CENTRAL
PUBLISHING

NEW YORK   BOSTON

Copyright © 1984 by Leila J. Meacham
Author letter copyright © 2016 by Leila Meacham
Excerpt from *Titans* copyright © 2016 by Leila Meacham

Cover design by Laura Klynestra
Cover photo by Laura Stolfi/Stocksy
Cover copyright © 2016 by Hachette Book Group, Inc.

Grand Central Publishing
Hachette Book Group
1290 Avenue of the Americas
New York, NY 10104
grandcentralpublishing.com
twitter.com/grandcentralpub

Originally published in hardcover in 1984 by the Walker Publishing Company, Inc., New York, New York.

First Grand Central Publishing Edition: July 2016

Grand Central Publishing is a division of Hachette Book Group, Inc.
The Grand Central Publishing name and logo are trademarks of Hachette Book Group, Inc.

The publisher is not responsible for websites (or their content) that are not owned by the publisher.

The Hachette Speakers Bureau provides a wide range of authors for speaking events. To find out more, go to www.hachettespeakersbureau.com or call (866) 376-6591.

Permission to quote lines from "MacArthur Park" by Jimmy Webb graciously granted by Warner Bros. Music. © 1968 Canopy Music, all rights reserved, used by permission of Warner Bros. Music.

Library of Congress Control Number: 2016934480

ISBNs: 978-1-4555-4130-0 (trade pbk.), 978-1-4555-4133-1 (library edition hardcover), 978-1-4555-4131-7 (ebook)

Printed in the United States of America

RRD-C

10 9 8 7 6 5 4 3 2 1

To Arthur Richard the Third
in whom I have two kings

A Letter to My Friends, Fans, Readers of My Later-in-Life Novels, and Newcomers to the Books of Leila Meacham

Dear Ones,

I'm writing to share with you the history behind Ryan's Hand *as my first, long-ago attempt to put on paper a story of fiction and to say (caution?) that you will find this book—an out-and-out romance—a departure from the more recent historical sagas of* Roses, Tumbleweeds, Somerset, *and* Titans. *That* Ryan's Hand *and the other two romances subsequently published in the mideighties have been resurrected to a second life has both thrilled and somewhat concerned me. I am thrilled at the interest of my readership in the books that spurred their republication and concerned that the books may disappoint my readers' expectations. Therefore, without a whiff of apology, I believe a little explanation is in order.*

In 1982 I became aware of the Harlequin and Silhouette tidal wave sweeping the country, to name a couple of romance publishers in the forefront of the genre. The eye-opener happened in my classroom at a local junior high school where I was a teacher of ninth-grade English. I began to notice that many of the girls hurried to their seats to open up small, white-jacketed books to read before the bell rang. Curiosity—and the thrill of seeing my students reading something other than surreptitiously passed notes—drew me to their desks to see what had claimed their riveted attention. The handover was usually accompanied by a blush. "Ah, Mrs. Meacham, I don't know that this is the type of thing you read," my students would say, or something on that order.

To which I'd reply, "As long as you're reading, I don't care what the subject matter is." Well, of course I did, but the books—romances, they were called—seemed harmless enough.

So I decided to read several for myself, an experience that led me to express to a colleague that while I understood the allure of the books to teenage girls and the women who flocked to the well-stocked shelves in bookstores to buy them, I found the usual dissension between the main male and female characters implausible. I distinctly remember saying, "Why, their silly conflict could be settled over a cup of coffee at Denny's." To which she seriously replied, "Well, then, why don't you write one yourself and show 'em how it should be done?"

"Oh, I couldn't," I said. "I don't know the first thing about how to write a book, romance or otherwise."

"I bet you can," she said, "and I'm willing to put money on it. If you try and can't, I'll buy you a steak dinner at the San Francisco Steak House, and if you try and can, you'll buy me one."

Well, to my utter shock, considering I didn't even know how to chapter a novel, I lost the bet. That summer during school vacation, confident that my friend would be picking up the tab at the San Francisco Steak House, I sat down at my old Smith-Corona electric typewriter ('twas the predawn of the PC, and I wasn't awake yet) to give the romance genre a whirl, if for no other reason than to appreciate the writers of the category who tried and succeeded. So Ryan's Hand *was conceived. I was determined that the enmity between hero* and heroine (*who, of course, as the formula dictated, were really secretly hot for each other*) *was well deserved, and the story evolved from there. Novice that I was, I broke the cardinal rule of fiction: I wrote about what I* didn't *know. I never knew anybody the likes of Jeth and Cara, had never been to Boston, sat on a horse, twirled a rope, or been on a cattle roundup. I did, however, know about West Texas, land of sandstorms, blistering heat, pumping jacks, and fabulous people. A perfect setting where I could allow my imagination to run wild, I thought, as long as it did not stray too far from what I could see were the established guidelines of the romance.*

When the book was completed, the same colleague suggested I send it to a local literary agent, and before I knew it, six weeks later, Ryan's Hand *was acquired for publication. As a result, I was put under contract for two more romances,* Crowning Design *and* Aly's House, *which were published in the following two years. But I'd had enough of writing and publishing. I did not care for the solitary life and isolation of a writer, and I found the experience of meeting deadlines unnerving. I returned to the classroom, and my books went the dusty way of many an unknown author's first literary efforts, without my ever learning whether I had showed anyone "how it should be done" or not.*

But that was then, and this is now, thirty-two years later. In the sweeter light of now, I elected to let the books stand as they were then, warts and all. I ask only that you read with the understanding that at the time of their creation, I did not know what in the world I was doing. Please treat kindly and do be well.

Leila Meacham

RYAN'S HAND

Chapter One

In a lounge at Boston's Logan International Airport, Cara Martin waited for the newly arrived 727 to release its passengers. The sun streamed through the wide expanse of glass facing the runway, but it was a cold February day and Cara pulled her old wool coat closer as she waited eagerly for the ramp door to open. Ryan would be among the first to disembark, she knew, for he always traveled first class.

She hoped he'd been able to get some rest on this trip to Texas to visit his brother. Each evening the weather news had said that temperatures had been mild there, and maybe Ryan had had an opportunity to bask in the sun on that remote ranch of theirs. He'd looked so tired when he left Boston ten days before. He lived too hard, Cara thought. She was convinced the only times he ever relaxed from the fast pace he set for himself were these quiet Sundays they shared together.

An attendant arrived to open the door to the ramp. Cara, a thrill of excitement lighting her too-serious, violet-flecked eyes, moved to the mouth of the roped-off area that funneled passengers into the concourse, afraid that in the milling crowd Ryan might not see her. She was easy to overlook. Standing less than medium height, she was a slightly built, rather severe young woman whose faded jeans and outdated brown coat gave her a faint air of poverty. She wore no makeup to enliven the classic features of her winter-pale face, and the rich bounty of her golden hair had been sternly drawn into a ponytail at the base of her slender neck.

Suddenly the reserved features exploded with a smile as a tall, dark-blond young man, his gait self-assured and buoyant, strode through the ramp door. "Ryan!" Cara called out happily and waved to catch his eye. The smile had brought an astonishing beauty to her grave face, lighting up the violet-blue eyes, drawing the primly set lips back from her small, perfectly aligned teeth. Ryan saw her and responded with a one-sided grin, which gave his urbane good looks a boyish appeal, and lifted a slim briefcase in greeting.

Cara moved back away from the crowd so she and Ryan might have a private reunion, her joy still lighting her face. He had gotten some sun, she saw, but a pallor remained beneath the light tan. There was still that hollow look about his eyes.

She looked up at him with sudden shyness when he reached her. It was still a marvel to her that this handsome, popular, immensely wealthy, transplanted Texan had become the closest friend she had ever had. "Hi," she said. "Good trip?"

Ryan gazed down at her affectionately, one hand holding a costly leather suit bag over a well-tailored shoulder. "One to last forever. Miss me?"

"Bunches and bunches. How did you find your brother?"

"Impressive as usual. He looked great."

Cara's expression sobered slightly. "Did...he think the same about you?"

"He thought I looked a little green around the gills. Too much salt air, he said. I assured him it was nothing of the kind. Just overwork. Did you bring my car?"

"I did, but very reluctantly. The snooty beast doesn't like me, Ryan. I think it knows I drive a Volkswagen."

Ryan chuckled and let her take his briefcase. Holding hands, they strolled off down the concourse, too engrossed in conversation to be aware of the curious contrast they made.

Once outside in the unseasonably bright sunlight, Cara looked up at Ryan's drawn face with concern. "I had to park rather far away. If you want to wait here, I'll bring the car around."

"Don't be silly. My legs need a good stretch. Tell me what you have planned for us on this beautiful Sunday." He began the fast clip to which Cara had grown accustomed in the year she had known him.

"I thought we might go down to Devereux Beach and see if we can find some oak," Cara replied. "We had a nor'easter night before last, and I'm sure if any lobster traps were left in the water, they're driftwood now. We should be able to replenish our store if no one else has beaten us to them."

"You're quite a scavenger, you know that?" Ryan looked down at her indulgently.

"Part of my seafaring heritage," Cara answered, unperturbed. "Something you landlubbers wouldn't know anything about. I'll bet you don't have our kind of oak in Texas to burn in your fireplaces." She was referring to the oak sections of destroyed lobster traps that Massachusetts residents were fond of collecting from the beaches after a storm to add to their firewood. The salt lodged in the wood produced flames of brilliant hues.

"You'd get no bet from me on that, Puritan. Scrub oak is what you'd burn in Texas," Ryan commented.

"Not me." Cara shook her golden head. "I can't imagine myself ever being in Texas."

Ryan did not reply to that, and Cara began a rundown of what had transpired in Boston during his absence. Her summary included amusing gossip about the society lions with whom Ryan hobnobbed as well as some stories from the subsidiary of the Boston City Library where she was a reference librarian. She kept up a steady stream of chatter to spare Ryan the effort of talking, certain that he had come down with a severe virus, and fight it though he might, he was losing the battle. It was only as they arrived at Ryan's car, a sleek, red Ferrari, that she realized he had not been listening to a word she'd said.

"Ryan?" Cara spoke worriedly and touched his arm. "I don't want to harp, but I can tell that you don't feel well. Why don't we forget about going to the beach today? I can leave you the picnic lunch, or make you some soup and then pop on off to my apartment so you can get some rest."

Ryan looked down at the upturned face, caught once again by the sheer innocent beauty of it, which had always caused a throb deep in his heart. He longed to hold her, to pull her to him and crush her against him until the pain inside his body subsided once and for all. Now that, he thought wryly, would be the way to go.

"Not a chance, Puritan," he said easily and took the keys Cara handed him. "I'll get all the rest I need soon. I just want to go to the place and change; then we'll hit that beach."

Ryan's "place" was an elegantly masculine town house overlooking Marblehead Harbor. While he changed, Cara stood in the sparkling sunshine on his balcony and looked beyond the harbor toward the Atlantic, which her forebears had sailed. The ocean was calm today. Seagulls cried and soared against a bright blue sky, and waves played gently among the marble-like rocks that had given the harbor its name. It was one of those unexpectedly beautiful days rare to Boston in winter, and Cara was annoyed at the feeling of uneasiness that prevented her enjoyment of it.

She turned restlessly from the railing and walked through French doors into Ryan's well-appointed living room. Her eyes fell on a silver-framed, enlarged photograph of Ryan and his only brother, Jeth, whom she had never met. The young Bostonian picked up the photograph and studied the faces of the two brothers. Both were wearing Western cords and shirts, and had their backs against a corral fence, Jeth with an arm propped in casual affection on the shoulder of his brother. Their kinship was hard to discern. Ryan, elegant and slim and blue eyed, was an urbane contrast to his taller, more rugged brother. Ryan was handsomer than Jeth, but the older brother with his dark hair and eyes, his strong, masculine features only slightly relieved by a smile for the camera, dominated the photograph. Cara would never tell Ryan that she didn't think she would like Jeth. The older brother looked the epitome of what he was: a feudal rancher living in the remote reaches of West Texas, where he was a law unto himself. He would be a man whose heart would be hard to penetrate, the kind of man who would have held her family in contempt.

Cara replaced the photograph in its position of prominence on the mantel, aware that Ryan was standing in the doorway of the living room watching her. She turned with a smile and surveyed him. "You look better, but are you sure you want to tackle the beach? Even on a day as fine as this one, it's bound to be blustery."

Barefoot, Ryan came into the room carrying thick socks and fleece-lined boots. He had changed into a heavy sweater and down-filled pants. With a start, Cara noticed that he had lost quite a bit of weight in the last few weeks. "Did you fellows eat anything this last week," she asked, "or did you simply drink your meals?"

Ryan chuckled as he sat down in a leather chair near her and began pulling on the socks and boots. "What foolish notions you have about us bachelors. Why do you ask?"

"Because you've lost so much weight, Ryan." Cara looked down at the bent head, at the slim fingers busy with laces, and a wave of affection rushed through her. She knelt down in front of him and covered his hands with hers. "Ryan, what's wrong? Is your brother all right? Is everything okay at the ranch? You didn't quarrel, did you?"

"Whoa, Puritan!" Ryan laughed into the bright eyes that at times seemed to have stars behind them. "Your concern is sweet, but it's unfounded—"

"No, it isn't, Ryan!" Cara argued. Earnestly, her hands went to his shoulders and found them startlingly thinner than she remembered. "You don't look well, my friend. You obviously haven't been eating or getting enough rest. You've been such a compassionate ear for me this year, so please let me do the same for you. Tell me what's wrong."

Ryan lay back in his chair with a sigh and studied her from under his thick, sandy lashes. "Okay," he said cryptically, "I'll come clean if you'll do one thing for me."

"What's that?"

"Take off that monk's cassock."

Cara looked down in surprise at her coat, then back at Ryan with a grin. "Am I to assume that you do not appreciate old faithful here? I'd like to remind you that this is the only coat still around from my more affluent days."

"Fidelity has not improved its appearance, love."

"Oh, all right!" She shrugged out of the coat, letting it fall behind her, and settled on the floor at Ryan's feet. Her over-large thick gray sweater hung from the shoulders but roundly molded the high fullness of her breasts. "Now shoot," she ordered, giving Ryan her attention, unaware of the flicker that had appeared briefly in his blue eyes.

Ryan rested his head on the high back of the chair and pondered the ceiling for a few seconds before speaking. Then he admitted, "I have been ill lately. I've been battling a stomach virus for nearly a month. That's why I've lost weight and look a bit drawn. It's nothing serious, but it is debilitating."

"Have you been to a doctor?"

"Yes," Ryan said shortly, his tone implying that the subject of his health was closed. "Also"—he turned his head to the photograph on the mantel—"I can't help but worry about that rawhide-tough brother of mine. Jeth seems so alone to me. The big house is as empty and quiet as a tomb. With all that gray tile Jeth chose for the floors, it looks like one, too. Our mother never had a chance to decorate the house. Only the construction was finished when she and Dad were killed in that plane crash. I'd like to see Jeth marry a wonderful woman who will give him children to make that house a home."

"Then why doesn't he?" Cara asked. "He certainly can't be without choices."

"He has those, for sure. But Jeth thinks the kind of woman he'd want to share his life with doesn't exist."

"Perfection rarely does," Cara commented dryly, then felt herself flush as Ryan lifted his head to look down at her quizzically. "I'm sorry. I shouldn't have said that. I've no business passing judgment on your brother." Cara slipped her hand into his. "Please go on, Ryan."

"The kind of woman Jeth needs would have to be special, not perfect," Ryan explained patiently. "She'd have to be the kind of woman who could love the land like he does, accept its demands and flaws—the heat and wind and sandstorms and isolation. She'd have to respect its people too, all the different breeds and cultures of them. And she'd have to love Jeth, really love him, not his fortune or his power or his empire, but the man who lives behind that rock-hard exterior of his that's gotten thicker through the years."

"That's quite an order," Cara said softly. "Ryan, have you never thought of marrying and having those children to make that house a home? I'd hate to lose the best friend I'll ever have"—she smiled wistfully—"but still that's a possibility. The ranch belongs equally to both of you, doesn't it?"

Ryan shook his head. "On paper, yes, but the land, the house, the oil, the cattle—they really belong to Jeth. He has a philosophy that land, like horses—anything wild held captive by man—must be cared for or he has to let it go. I remember the day he demonstrated that to me. I was eighteen that summer. I'd been so busy studying for the entrance exams for Harvard I'd completely withdrawn from the ranch's operation. One day Jeth asked me to go out to the stables with him. Texas Star, my horse, was snorting around the corral, and I realized then what was on Jeth's mind. He'd found out that one of the hands had been taking care of him. At La Tierra, a man takes care of his own horse. He asked me how long it had been since I'd ridden Texas, and I had to confess I couldn't remember. I could see that he was reverting to the wild stallion he'd been when I captured him for the roundup…"

"So what happened?" Cara urged as Ryan paused.

"Jeth walked over to the corral gate and opened it. Then he slapped Texas's flank, and my horse took off for the mountains where I'd found him."

"But that was cruel!" she gasped.

"It was *kind*, Cara! Don't you see? Texas could never belong to anyone else, and he didn't belong to me anymore, so he had to be set free. I can still see that horse. He was a three-year-old palomino and at the base of his mane was a perfectly formed white star. He raced off for a distance, then he stopped and looked back. I started to go after him, but Jeth stopped me by saying something I've never forgotten..."

Wide-eyed, Cara prompted on held breath, "What was it?"

"He said that I should never tame anything I wasn't prepared to love."

Ryan's eyes closed tiredly, and there was silence in the room except for the faraway cries of the seagulls and the opulent sound of a fine antique clock ticking on the mantel. The sunlight filtering through the French doors did little to dispel the sudden chill that had crept into the room.

"I understood what he was telling me." Ryan spoke again, laying his head back. "The name of our ranch, you know, is La Tierra Conquistada. Translated, that means The Conquered Land. I suppose that after four generations, the land can be considered conquered, but it wouldn't stay that way long without care and dedication. Jeth was saying I had to let it go. I couldn't divide my loyalties."

"And so you left to study law," Cara stated quietly.

"Yes, I went away to Harvard that fall, and I never went back to stay. We both knew that I was never cut out to be a rancher. Jeth was. I had the blood of my music-loving, aesthetic mother in me; Jeth had our father's. My brother has always insisted that the ranch was as much mine as his, but also that it couldn't be run from a distance. He's made all the decisions concerning La Tierra, scrupulously dividing the profits. He's made me a very rich man."

"You could have done that for yourself even without your brother," Cara said warmly. "You're a brilliant lawyer!"

Ryan opened his eyes to stare down at her in amusement. "What is there about Jeth that nettles you so, Puritan?"

Cara reddened in embarrassment and withdrew her hand. "Forgive me again, Ryan. It's just that your brother sounds so...so high-handed. I've always been a little prickly about arrogance of that kind."

"Arrogance is often the unavoidable twin of power, Cara, and Jeth never had a chance to be anything but what he became: a very powerful man. When our parents were killed, I was eleven and Jeth eighteen. He had a very different kind of dream then; he wanted to be an Olympic swimmer. That ended when he had to take over the reins of La Tierra. There was no one to help him. The very men he thought he could trust—lawyers, bankers, other ranchers—proved to be the most unscrupulous. They saw a chance to get their hands on La Tierra and they tried every conceivable chicanery to do it. But they didn't figure on Jeth's brains and guts. He proved too smart for them and too tough. He wasn't a compassionate winner, either. Every one of those men lived to regret the day he ever crossed Jeth Langston." Ryan paused to give Cara his crooked grin. "I guess I do make the guy sound high-handed and hard-nosed, don't I?"

"I think you're worrying about him unnecessarily," she said. "He sounds like a completely self-sufficient man who will marry when he feels ready to. Besides, he's young yet, only thirty-four. I'm surprised he doesn't have to fight the women off. He has a...certain virility that's very attractive to most women."

"But not to you?" Ryan queried, and laughed when her eyes dropped in discomfort. "Don't be embarrassed, Puritan. You're right in thinking that the two of you would lock horns—at least at first." He sat up suddenly and shook his head as if tired of his thoughts. "Come on," he said, hoisting Cara to her feet. "Let's go down to the beach before the light begins to fade."

Devereux Beach, a thin neck of land separating Marblehead

Harbor from the Atlantic Ocean, was a favorite Sunday spot for Cara and Ryan. On the first Sunday after they met, Cara had taken the handsome Texan beachcombing there. It had been a blustery day in February almost a year before. They had arrived to find the beach deserted except for the seabirds that scurried about on the wet sand and cawed their plaintive cries overhead. Cara had explained to a curious Ryan that the salt-logged oak burned in spectacular colors. "I'll show you this evening," she promised.

They had made quite a haul and finished the day at Cara's modest one-room flat, which was perched atop a three-story house. The room featured a widow's walk, a narrow balcony facing the Atlantic where seamen's wives of old would go to watch for their husbands' ships returning from the sea. While a casserole bubbled deliciously in the oven and she opened a bottle of wine, Ryan had stretched his legs out on the floor before the old stone fireplace, fascinated by the brilliant colors in the leaping flames. "You've made a believer out of me," he remarked as he accepted a goblet of chilled wine.

"You must take home half of what we collected today," Cara said, sipping her wine comfortably beside him. "These colors will be dramatic in your white marble fireplace."

"Only if you promise to come to my town house next Sunday and share the fire with me. I won't promise to cook, but I know an excellent caterer."

Cara had been surprised that Ryan would extend an invitation to her so soon. He was in great demand by Boston society hostesses, and she was also aware of his reputation as a ladies' man. She was definitely not in his social circle, nor was she like the glamorous, leisured women he was accustomed to seeing. They had met when Ryan came into the library to research a legal matter.

She had recognized him immediately as the popular young attorney the society columns linked with the names of some of her former school friends. She supposed it was a form of self-torture, but she could not resist reading the social news that not so long ago had occasionally featured the names of her own family members.

When Ryan Langston asked at the reference desk for help in finding a certain volume, Cara had been impressed by his manners, his soft Texas drawl, and his clean-cut, boyish good looks. She went off duty at five o'clock, and, as she came out of the library, the sleek red Ferrari parked next to her secondhand Volkswagen told her that Ryan Langston was still inside working on his research.

Cara did not notice that her right front tire was flat until she attempted to drive out of the parking space. There was no mistaking the significance of the peculiar list on the right side, so she reparked to assess the damage.

By the time she had cut the motor, Ryan was standing beside his Ferrari. "You have a little problem there, I see," he said, indicating the tire. "Do you have a jack?"

Cara not only did not have a jack, she did not have a spare tire.

It had been one of those days when everything had conspired to remind her of the losses she had suffered in her short twenty-four years. She longed to put an end to the day, to get to her apartment and build a fire, have a light supper, and maybe play the piano until she was too sleepy to lie awake with her memories.

Now, sitting behind the wheel of her shabby car, hearing the voice of a man who had easy access to the world that had turned its back on her, she felt the sudden horrifying urge to burst into tears. She controlled her emotions by rigidly gripping the wheel and staring straight ahead, but the handsome dark-blond head of the man had bent down to peer at her through a closed window. "Are you all right?" he asked, and she could hear the sincere concern in his voice.

She had swallowed hard and given him a polite smile while praying that she wouldn't cry in front of a stranger, especially not *this* stranger.

"I'm fine," she assured him, opening her door. The night had folded about the neighborhood very thick and cold, and she drew her brown coat closer. "I thank you for your concern," she said to Ryan, "but you needn't bother. I'll go back inside and call a garage." Not for the world would she have him know that she did not have a spare tire or money to buy one. She would figure out what to do when she got rid of him.

"That won't be necessary," he insisted, looking very affluent in his tailored overcoat. "I can have the tire changed in a jiffy. If you'll just open the trunk—"

"No, please—" she protested, raising delicate hands in a gesture of panic.

"Look, young lady," Ryan said, brushing aside her protests. "I'm not about to let you wait alone in this parking lot when I can change that tire for you in a few minutes!"

There was nothing to do but yield as gracefully as possible. "Well, but you see, I...don't have a spare tire—" She could feel the heat flooding her face.

"I see..." He spoke softly, and she could tell from the almost imperceptible flick of the blue eyes over her worn coat that he understood the nature of her embarrassment. "Well, in that case, you must let me take you home."

"Oh, no, I couldn't!"

"My name is Ryan Langston," the tall young man said calmly. "I am an attorney practicing here in Boston, and I assure you you're far safer with me than waiting for a bus or a taxi on a street corner." He reached inside a breast pocket for a narrow, tan wallet. Cara saw some kind of gold insignia discreetly embossed on one corner. He extracted a card and handed it to her. "I think there's enough light for you to read that I am who I say I am. You must let me take you home."

Cara glanced at the card. It wasn't necessary since she knew who he was. "Yes, I see that. You are kind to trouble with me. I'll get my bag."

The next day Cara had shared a ride to the library with a colleague. As she arrived at the parking lot, her mouth had dropped open when she saw that the flat tire on her Volkswagen had been replaced with a new one. Opening the trunk, she found that the old tire had been mended and beside it lay a new jack.

"Mr. Langston, you were kind to bother with my car," Cara said when she got a line through to him at the law firm. "I will mail you a check first thing in the morning for the items you purchased." She spoke confidently, thinking of several pieces of sterling still to sell.

Ryan did not reply immediately. Presently he asked, "Miss Martin, you're a native Bostonian, aren't you?"

"Yes."

"Would you be willing to trade your time as a tour guide for the money you feel you owe me?"

"I beg your pardon, Mr. Langston?"

"I would like to see Boston through the eyes of a proper Bostonian, Miss Martin." Cara wondered if he were laughing at her. Proper Bostonian, indeed! But he continued, "I've been here a number of years now, but I've yet to see the city the way I want to see it. From the short time I spoke with you last night, I could tell that you have a thorough knowledge of the nooks and crannies of the area, the kind of thing you don't read about in tour books."

Cara hesitated. He wanted to see her. The tour-guide business was a line, fed to her with subtle good humor, if she had been any judge of the young Texan. And suddenly she wanted to see him. It had been so long since she had enjoyed the company of someone like Ryan Langston.

"It seems to me, Mr. Langston," Cara replied, "that you are making a poor trade. However, I would enjoy showing Boston to you, and I dislike debts. When shall we begin?"

He had surprised her by saying, "This evening, Miss Martin, if you have no objection. I'll pick you up at your apartment at six o'clock."

Ryan had allowed her a brief moment to refuse, then wished her good morning and hung up. That evening at six, the Ferrari swung into the drive before her private entrance. Still in business suit and overcoat, Ryan looked at her casual slacks and sweater and remarked that he'd like to go home first so that he might change. "Tell me where we're going," he said, "so that I can dress for it."

They were going for an evening of chowder and cards with an old sea captain friend of her late grandfather's. "He's a widower," Cara enlightened Ryan in the living room of his town house. "You'll like him. He can remember when the people of Boston depended upon the sea for a living." While Ryan dressed, she wandered admiringly around the beautiful room, resisting the urge to try the baby grand piano that filled a corner of it.

At the end of the evening when Ryan brought her to her door, they shook hands and agreed to meet again on Sunday. This time, Cara told him, he must allow her to prepare a meal for him as a small token of gratitude for the car.

After their next meeting they fell into the habit of seeing each other regularly on Sundays, and a surprising relationship evolved that satisfied them both. Ryan referred to her as his "Sunday girl" and called her "Puritan" after her New England ancestors, or so he said. But Cara suspected that in his experienced, man-of-the-world way, Ryan knew that she was still a virgin. She was relieved that he preferred and needed her only as a friend. She could not become involved with anyone until her family's debts were paid. There were other women in his life, she knew—beautiful women he squired around to the expensive, public haunts he never suggested taking her. Cara feared he might be ashamed of her. Her clothes were abysmally old, her hair unfashionably long. But in time she realized that Ryan would never be ashamed of a friend. For her sake their Sundays were confined to picnics or walks on the beach, to country drives and out-of-the-way, nose-poking places. With typical compassion, Ryan had known that she did not want to be seen by her former crowd, to once again become the subject discussed over teacups or martini glasses.

Cara found it a release to be able at last to confide in someone of Ryan's sensitivity the series of events that led to her living a solitary existence in near poverty. As she came to trust Ryan, she revealed that she was a direct descendant of one of the first ship-building magnates to settle in Boston. He had built the fine mansion where she had spent carefree years growing up as an only child. Through succeeding generations, the fortune had dwindled, but there had been enough money to sustain the family in the highest echelons of Boston society, and for Cara's father to pursue his literary career without the need to work for a living. His written histories of the Boston area achieved for him a modest fame but little remuneration. There had been enough money for Cara to attend the Juilliard School of Music in New York with hopes of becoming a concert pianist. And then, in the second year of her studies, her mother's heart stopped one day in the garden as she bent to welcome the first crocus peeping through the snow.

Cara flew home often that year, and each visit she found her father looking more feeble, more lost and bewildered. Because he seemed to be rapidly losing his grip on reality, she took it upon herself to sort through the family's financial records, and made a shocking discovery. There was no money and had not been for some time. The mansion had been mortgaged to subsidize her father's latest literary effort and to provide money for her Juilliard education. Insurance premiums had been allowed to lapse. Even her mother's funeral expenses had not been paid.

"What are we going to do?" she asked her family's lifelong attorney after he had read the long list of outstanding debts.

"Declare bankruptcy, of course," he advised smoothly. "You've no other choice."

Cara had left her father sleeping in a deck chair on the porch that caught the sea breezes from the Atlantic. "Dad." She shook him gently, determined that he would not be evicted from his home. His thin, blue-veined hand fell lifelessly from his lap, and with a cry Cara knew that he had been spared.

After seeing her father buried beside her mother, Cara had gone away to analyze the numbing realities of her situation. Her family was gone. The world she had once known was closed to her—she refused to live in it on credit—and a mountain of debts remained to be paid.

She would pay them. That decision made, Cara withdrew from Juilliard, then went to each creditor and pleaded for time. She could not declare bankruptcy, she explained. She considered it immoral not to pay back what had been loaned her father in good faith. Could they extend her time to earn a degree in library science—at a cheaper, state-supported university—which would then give her greater financial opportunity to settle the debts?

The creditors, themselves of the same Puritan stock as she, recognized her plea for what it was: the cry of her Yankee pride to clear her family's name and salvage her self-respect. They agreed. Cara sold the house and auctioned its furniture, including the treasured Steinway that had been the joy of her life. Except for a strand of pearls that had been her mother's and a gold chain her parents gave her the day she had been accepted at Juilliard, all of Cara's personal possessions went on the block. By the time Ryan came into her life, she had been out of college three years, subsisting on a shoestring budget that had allowed for only the two luxuries of a small piano for her one-room apartment and a good pair of fleece-lined boots for walking the beaches. She had totally withdrawn from her former world, knowing that she was regarded, if remembered, as an object of pity and condescension.

Chapter Two

Oh, look, Ryan!" Cara exclaimed as they drove into the sandy parking area that led to the beach. "We have the place to ourselves."

"Let's get cracking, then," Ryan said. "The light will be gone in no time."

His skin still had an unhealthy pallor, and Cara had some misgivings about her suggestion to come here today. She reached for his gloved hand, and his fingers curled tightly around hers. Ryan looked down at her and smiled, and she smiled back. Then they began to walk toward the beach, Cara swinging the canvas bag she always brought along for what Ryan called her loot.

They unearthed quite a number of broken sections of oak, one piece a foot long. In addition Cara found several pieces of "bottle glass," broken portions of bottles that the salt had imbued with delicate color and whose edges the seas had worn smooth.

"You must have a bag of that by now," Ryan commented when she held up the broken neck of a bottle for him to examine. "What are you going to do with it all?"

"I don't know yet. But I'll think of something special—you'll see."

"Maybe," said Ryan unexpectedly, and turned away from her to walk farther up the beach, having spied something that drew his attention.

Cara looked after him. A funny chill played round her heart. What did he mean by that? she wondered. Surely he wasn't leaving Boston, going back to Texas after all? He had become such an integral part of her life. She had only realized how much this last week when she had been almost bereaved by his absence. The prospect of Sundays without Ryan would be unbearable. He meant everything to her. Surely he wasn't planning on leaving?

"What are you staring at?" Ryan asked as he returned to her. She gazed up at him, her violet eyes catching the glow of the sunset. He was so tall, and even on a day as blustery and cold as this one, he refused to wear a head covering of any kind. The wind lifted his sandy hair and played with it. The dying sun shadowed the gaunt concaves of his cheeks. Her heart contracted with a kind of fear, and she faltered, "Ryan, I—"

"What is it, love?" His voice was gentle and very kind.

"Ryan, I am very fond of you."

He drew her into his arms. "I know that. I am of you, too, Cara." He tilted her chin and searched her disturbed eyes with tender amusement. "You look sad. Don't be." But the lips he pressed to her forehead for reassurance were as cold as death.

Later, in the town house, they picnicked on the floor before the fire, and afterward, with their legs stretched out side by side and their backs against the davenport, Ryan spoke of his brother again.

"When Jeth graduated from high school, my father presented him with a gold wristwatch. On the back of the watch he'd had inscribed, 'To my beloved son in whom I am well pleased.' That watch and inscription meant the world to Jeth. It was Dad's way of telling him that he approved his dream of becoming an Olympic swimmer.

"The night before I left for Harvard, Jeth and I had a last drink together in the study. I was feeling pretty low. I felt as if I were deserting my heritage, disavowing my Langston blood, not to mention leaving Jeth alone to run the ranch at a time when he really needed me. The only people left that he could count on were Fiona and Leon. They're our housekeeper and ranch cook, who have been at La Tierra since before Jeth was born.

"Jeth handed me a small wrapped box. 'If Dad were here,' he said, 'he would have given this to you.' I unwrapped it and removed the lid. Inside the box was Jeth's gold watch."

Cara remained silent, too moved by the simple story of brotherly love to comment. She watched him stroke the face of the gold watch encircling his arm, his expression slack in the firelight.

"It was a fine moment between us," he continued. "Jeth couldn't have given his blessing more eloquently—or magnanimously. He stood awfully tall to me in that moment."

She said softly, "You love him very much, don't you?"

"Yep," Ryan said, rising to his lanky height. "He's still the tallest man I'll ever know. I'll get us some more wine."

He had been gone for a while before her thoughtful state was penetrated by the sound of retching from the bathroom. She sat up, alarmed. "Ryan!" she exclaimed, getting up. "Ryan!" She found him doubled over the basin, holding a wet cloth to his mouth. His face was ghostly gray. "My God, Ryan, what is it?"

"It's nothing to worry about," Ryan gasped between heaves. "Just this stomach virus."

"Let me call your doctor!"

"No, there's nothing he can do. I'll be all right in a few minutes. Just get me a glass of cold water, will you?"

She did as he asked and watched as he took a couple of pills. "Get ready for bed," she ordered. "Right now."

Ryan didn't argue. While he was in the bathroom, Cara turned down the covers and switched on the electric blanket. She filled a glass with fresh water and placed it on his nightstand. Ryan came out of the bathroom a few minutes later wearing pajamas. "These pj's are for your benefit, I want you to know."

"Come on," she said, holding the covers for him to slip under. His sick pallor frightened her.

"You won't get any argument from me." He attempted a grin, and Cara tried to smile back.

"Do I sound bossy?" she asked.

"Yes, but I like it," Ryan murmured as she pulled the covers up to his chin.

"Is there anything I can do for you before I leave?"

Ryan's sandy lashes fluttered sleepily. The pills had been sedatives. "If you'll just open the blinds to let the moonlight in. Thanks for a great day, Puritan."

"Thank *you*, Ryan." She stooped to kiss his forehead. "Sleep well."

"No fear of that," he mumbled drowsily as his face closed in sleep.

Cara looked down at the ashen face and wished suddenly, inexplicably, for this man's brother. The strange desire persisted when she went downstairs into the cold February night to her Volkswagen, parked beside the red Ferrari. "If you two aren't a classic example of Lady and the Tramp!" she observed in wry amusement.

She drove out of the parking lot into the evening flow of traffic toward Boston, hardly aware of the other motorists. Images of the day, scraps of remembered conversation floated like random leaves in her mind. The chill around her heart would not go away. The familiar taste of loss was in her mouth. Ryan's response to her query about his trip came back to her. "One to last forever," he had said—almost as if he had no plans to go again. Other phrases floated disjointedly, lazily, teasing at her memory like a haunting concerto whose name eluded her. "I'll get all the rest I need soon…" "Let's go before the light begins to fade…"

Suddenly her foot slammed down on the brake pedal. The small tires squealed in protest at the suddenness of the illegal U-turn in the middle of the street. Cara barely heard them. The sound of her own cry had filled her ears.

Under the covered parking ramp the Ferrari seemed to be waiting for her, as if it had expected her return. Cara fumbled in her purse for the key to the town house that Ryan had insisted she have. She let herself in, listening. Then she walked to the door of Ryan's bedroom. A band of moonlight, like a mask, lay across his eyes. They were open and observed her standing in the doorway without surprise or alarm. The rest of his face was in shadow. "Hello again," he said softly, and Cara thought he smiled in the darkness. "Why did you come back?"

"You know why, Ryan."

"And why is that, love?"

"I know how ill you are, Ryan. It's terminal, isn't it?" Her entire being pleaded with him to deny it, but the answering silence confirmed what she dreaded. "How much more time?" she asked, but her knees had turned to water.

"Not much. I'm living on the borrowed end of it."

Incredulous, Cara walked to the bed and gaped down at the handsome, gaunt face. "It can't be," she whispered, but the unblinking blue eyes stared the truth back at her, and the bottom fell from her heart. "Ryan..." She knelt beside the bed, next to his pillowed head. "Tell me it isn't true."

When he did not reply, tears slowly welled in her disbelieving eyes and began to slip unchecked down her cheeks. "Ah, love..." Ryan consoled her, drawing the golden head down to the thin hollow of his shoulder. In silence, his cheek against her hair, he held her until the first bitter wave of sobbing had ceased. Then she pulled back to look at him, her breathing erratic in the aftermath of grief. "I'm—not—leaving you, Ryan!"

"That's comforting to know. There's a set of pj's in my armoire, and I think you'll find an unused toothbrush in the medicine chest. I always keep a few on hand for...er..."

"I know, Ryan. They must think it awfully thoughtful of you." She rose on unsteady legs. "I won't be a minute."

When Cara was ready for bed, she came once again to his doorway. "I don't want to go to the guest room, Ryan." She spoke obstinately, like the child she appeared in the baggy blue pajamas, her cheeks red from the salt of sea wind and tears, her long golden hair loose about her shoulders.

Ryan studied her without expression for a long moment; then his mouth softened in a slight smile. "Come here, then, Puritan," he said, throwing back the covers on the other side of his bed. Immediately she went and crawled in beside him, snuggling close and wrapping her arms in desperate protection around him, as if to imbue his body with the health that flowed in her own. Cradled together, Ryan drifted into a peaceful sleep but Cara lay awake and vigilant throughout the long night, listening to the distant sound of the Atlantic and the precious beat of his heart.

The next morning she rose and dressed before Ryan was awake. When he awoke, she had hot tea ready, which she served to him in bed. "I've called the library to say I won't be in today," she informed him. "Is that all right with you?"

"Need you ask?" He sipped his tea. "Thanks for helping me make it through the night."

"Like the song says," she said simply.

"Well, not quite, Puritan." He laughed when he saw her blush. "This relationship of ours is really something. Who would ever believe that I slept in the arms of the most beautiful woman in Boston and nothing happened?"

"Oh, Ryan!" Cara fussed. "Your fondness for me has affected your objectivity. I'm not in the least beautiful."

"You've just forgotten you are. You probably haven't really looked at yourself in years."

"There's no reason to. I can't afford cosmetics and clothes, and my job doesn't require them. Someday I'll be in a position to let my appearance matter again."

"But I want your appearance to matter now, Cara. Do something for me?"

Cara looked at him curiously, realizing he was serious. "Why, of course, anything."

"I would like for you to buy yourself a new wardrobe. Also a new hairstyle, cosmetics, anything that will show off that beauty of yours to its best advantage."

Cara tried not to show her shock. She said gently but firmly, "Ryan, you know I can't do that."

"You said anything for me, remember? Surely you can shelve that Yankee pride of yours to indulge a dying man's request. Besides, it's all been arranged anyway. I knew you would balk at charging anything to me, so I've had money transferred to your account. Please don't refuse what I ask, Cara." Ryan's blue eyes were imploring.

"But, Ryan—"

"I took the liberty of making the first purchase for you. Will you look on the top shelf of that closet?"

Reluctantly, apprehensively, Cara went to the closet door and opened it. On the top shelf was a large silver box. Her breath stopped when she hauled it down and recognized on the cover the embossed name of a furrier her mother had once patronized. She threw Ryan an alarmed look. "What have you done?"

"Open it, love."

Cara slowly removed the ribbon, lifted the lid, and pulled aside the silver tissue paper. Her mouth parted in awe as she drew out a superbly cut raincoat the color of pearls, fully lined in sable. "Oh, Ryan...it's the most beautiful thing I've ever seen!"

"Try it on, love. Let's see if I chose the right size."

"Ryan, I couldn't possibly accept this."

"Of course you can, and you will. I'm a dying man. You must humor me. Now try it on."

Cara obeyed him, and in spite of the leaden pain within her, the sensuous feel of the coat stirred long-denied memories of the pleasure of lovely clothes. "It's so light, yet so warm," she said in fascination.

"And far more suitable for you than that monk's robe." Ryan held out a hand to her, and she took it and sat beside him on the bed. "Now about the rest of the things you'll need—"

"That I'll need, Ryan?"

"When I'm no longer here to see after you," he said reasonably. "I want you to buy clothes for every season. The cruise clothes are out now, so there should be a good choice of summer clothes. Buy lots of those."

"Ryan—" Cara stopped him determinedly. "We should concentrate on getting you ready to go home rather than having me gallivanting around buying clothes."

"I'm not going back to Texas," Ryan said quietly.

Cara stared at him. "What? You're not planning to stay in Boston, surely. What about Jeth?" Then a shocking thought struck her. "He doesn't know, does he, Ryan?"

"No. He believed I had a stomach virus and wanted to come back to Boston to see my doctor."

"You can't mean that you would keep this from Jeth! He'll be irreparably hurt, Ryan!" Cara got up from the bed abruptly and flung off the coat.

"All this concern for a man you don't even like!"

"He's your brother, Ryan! Think how you would feel!"

Ryan's features tightened stubbornly. "I know what I'm doing, Cara. You have to believe that and trust me. Someday Jeth will understand why I didn't tell him, why I didn't stay at La Tierra. Let's not discuss it anymore, if you don't mind." It was the closest they had ever come to a quarrel, and Ryan softened the atmosphere with his engaging smile. "Now get out of here and go shopping. I want to see a style show this evening."

Numbly, Cara spent the day doing as she had been ordered. She went to a dozen dress shops in order to make a dent in the staggering amount of money she had been told to spend, knowing that if she didn't, Ryan would send her out tomorrow on another expedition when all she wanted was to be with him.

By the end of the afternoon she had completed her purchases and the little Volkswagen—she had refused to drive Ryan's Ferrari—was filled to its bug top with boxes and bags. On her way back to Marblehead, she stopped by the library to speak to the woman who had been her supervisor for three years. The iron-gray head of the librarian nodded in understanding as Cara explained that she had to take emergency leave and didn't know how much time she would need. Should she resign now,

Cara wanted to know, or could she take an indefinite leave of absence and return to her job when she was free to do so?

"We don't have to decide that now," the librarian told her. "Call me at the end of the week when you have a better idea of how much time you'll need. Then we'll discuss your options."

Driving to the town house, Cara thought that she had only one option: even if she lost her job and the few remaining debts remained unpaid for a while, she was not going to leave Ryan to die alone.

That evening Cara turned and pivoted before an admiring Ryan as she modeled the dozens of dresses, separates, and suits she had purchased that day. "Tomorrow," Ryan told her tranquilly, "you're to have your hair styled. Also, afterward, you have an appointment with Boston's best makeup artist."

Cara sighed. There was no point in arguing. Ryan was clearly enjoying his benefactor's role, and if it kept his mind occupied, then she would submit to anything.

Later in the evening, Cara prepared a meal from a diet prescribed for Ryan's condition, which she had found tucked away in a kitchen drawer. After dinner, with the brilliant flames throwing their reflections on the white marble fireplace, Cara played Ryan's favorite classical selections while he listened from the leather chair that now seemed to swallow him.

Eventually she saw sleep begin to take hold of the handsome features, and, trailing her fingers off the keys, called softly, "Ryan?"

He opened heavy lids, somewhat startled that she had spoken. "Yes, love?"

"Shall I stay again tonight?"

"Need you ask? Actually, I was hoping you would move in with me until I have to go to the hospital."

Without hesitation, Cara replied, "Tomorrow I'll go get a few things from my apartment."

In the week that followed, Ryan grew weaker each day, but still he was quick with a laugh or a joke. The weather still held, and he sent Cara out on another shopping spree. When she returned, she dumped the armload of parcels on his bed where he sat propped up reading and declared, "Now, Ryan, I've gone through that money you put in my account, and I'm not spending another cent for clothes. I have enough for years!"

"Good," he said, eyeing her with approval from head to foot. Her hair had been cut shoulder-length and styled to emphasize the oval shape of her face. Artfully applied makeup enhanced her remarkable eyes, the exquisite beauty of her classic features. In the sable-lined coat she was a captivating mixture of sophistication and innocence, and Ryan said with satisfaction, "Now your appearance is worthy of you."

One afternoon while they were sitting on the balcony and Ryan was comparing the endless expanse of the Atlantic to the plains of West Texas, the phone rang. Cara answered it, and after a brief pause, a male voice, deep and unequivocal, asked to speak to Ryan Langston.

"Who's calling, please?" she asked, intrigued by the voice but not wishing to disturb Ryan for a casual caller.

"His brother—Jeth Langston."

For some reason, a chill swept her spine. "Oh!" she exclaimed involuntarily. "Just—just a moment and I'll get him."

Cara watched Ryan assume a smile before he spoke into the phone. In a jaunty voice that belied the fatigue and pain that racked his body, he chatted genially with his brother while Cara returned to the balcony. When he joined her again, she turned on him accusingly, her voice breaking. "Ryan, you still didn't tell him, did you? For God's sake, why not?"

But Ryan was unable to answer her. Clutching his stomach, he gave a cry of intense pain and slumped to the floor of the balcony.

Cara ran for blankets and pillows and made him as comfortable as possible before going to the phone to call the number she had written beside it for just this moment. Then she went back to Ryan to await the ambulance.

The next few days were a nightmare of despair for Cara as she sat beside Ryan's bed, knowing that his life was ebbing away and that there was a brother in Texas who did not know it. Her one source of comfort was the soft-spoken law partner from Ryan's firm who had arrived at the hospital shortly after his younger colleague had been admitted.

The man, who appeared to be somewhere in his midthirties, had approached Cara with deeply distressed eyes and handed her his business card. "I am Harold St. Clair," he told her, "a friend and colleague of Ryan's. His doctor had instructions to call me."

Out of the maze of grief through which she wandered during the remaining three days of Ryan's life, one fact emerged clearly: Ryan had his business affairs in order. The firm, Harold told her, had been named to handle Ryan's estate. His personal effects would be sent to his brother in Texas. The firm would take care of the disposition of Ryan's town house and furnishings. It would see to the sale of the red Ferrari, unless, of course, she wanted it. It had been a stipulation of Ryan's that she was to have anything in the town house she desired.

Cara was aghast. None of Ryan's things were hers, she made it clear to the lawyer. Then she remembered the photograph on the mantel. "There is one thing," she hurriedly amended. "A picture of Ryan and his brother. I—I'd like to have that."

"Of course," the lawyer agreed, making a note in his small leather book. He cast a contemplative glance at the averted profile of the girl. She was exquisite, no doubt about that. No wonder Ryan had completely lost his head over her.

In the three days, Ryan became lucid only once. Cara was sitting beside the bed, dozing. Harold had gone to the cafeteria for a cup of coffee. Ryan opened his eyes and looked at her. "Hi," he said, and Cara, thinking she was dreaming, lifted her blond head.

"Ryan..." She smiled and drew her chair closer to the bed. "I'm so glad you're awake."

"Thank you for not asking me how I'm feeling." He gave her his ironic grin. "I wouldn't want to lie to you."

"It's bad, is it?"

"Yes, very bad. I almost waited too late to ask you something."

Cara's throat closed painfully. She reached for Ryan's cold, inert fingers, careful not to disturb the tubes taped to the back of his hand. "Ask me what, Ryan?"

"Do you trust me, Cara?"

"With all my heart."

"Then would you promise to do something for me after I'm gone, even though I can't tell you now what it is? Think before you answer, love. I know that Yankee determination of yours well enough to know that once you give your word, the devil himself couldn't make you break it."

"Is it important to you that I do whatever it is you're asking?"

"Yes. It means that I can rest in peace."

"Well, then, I promise, Ryan."

"Thank you, Puritan. You won't be sorry. You will be at first, and your courage will try to desert you, but don't you let it. See your promise through to the end. You'll be glad you did. I am confident of that."

"How—how will I know what it is you want me to do?"

"Harold will give you an envelope after my death. I have left instructions in it. Remember always that I had only at heart the interests of those I...loved."

The words trailed off. His lids closed in quiet finality. "Ryan, dearest—" But Cara knew that Ryan had slipped forever beyond the sound of her voice. Already the beloved features had assumed an eternal stillness. Tenderly, as the tears began to come, she lifted Ryan's hand to her cheek and cradled it there for a few private seconds before the door burst open and blurred images in white surrounded the bed. Someone in a business suit spoke gently in her ear and eased Ryan's hand away, then led her from the room.

"Jeth has to be told," Cara said dazedly to the man whose arm was around her. "Someone has to tell Jeth that his brother is gone."

"Shh," Harold St. Clair spoke soothingly. "Don't concern yourself with that, Cara. The firm will inform him. It would be more appropriate for us to do so."

A week later on the first day of March, Cara sat in Harold St. Clair's office. Sleet struck the windows, making the shapes of things beyond them gray and indistinct. In her lavender wool coat, the neck designed to reveal a matching dress beneath, she was like a splash of spring in the somber office, and Harold thought that he had never seen a more beautiful woman. "How have you been this past week, Cara?" he asked, observing her with his astute eyes.

"Empty," she answered briefly. "Quite empty."

"Yes, I can understand that," the lawyer responded sympathetically, but in fact he did not understand at all. What had been the relationship of this lovely woman to Ryan? Had she been his mistress? Harold was now inclined to think not. This girl possessed an indefinable quality of sexual innocence, which made him believe that she had never warmed any man's bed. Yet Ryan had loved her above all the women in his life, of that he was certain. Why else would he have arranged his will against Harold's legal counsel and in direct defiance of his brother, whom Harold knew to be one of the most powerful men in Texas?

The lawyer's hands fidgeted with the legal document on the desk before him. Thank the saints that the two people it concerned would never meet. This fragile young thing in a clash with Jeth Langston, a man notorious for his ruthlessness, was almost obscene to contemplate. At least she would have the firm behind her as well as the courts. Together they would protect her from the vindictive rage that Jeth Langston was bound to be feeling at this moment.

"Cara," the lawyer began, clearing his throat, "did Ryan ever discuss with you the provisions of his will?"

Her large eyes regarded him in surprise. "Of course not. Why should he?"

The lawyer returned her gaze with equanimity. "Because you have been remembered very handsomely in it."

"What do you mean?" Cara was puzzled. Ryan would have known that she wanted nothing material from him.

"You have inherited Ryan's share of La Tierra Conquistada."

Cara sat like a stone figure in the chair, her eyes riveted on the man before her, hoping to see something in his face that would betray his words as a horrible joke. "You can't mean that," she said slowly in disbelief. "Ryan would never have done that to his brother."

"I'm afraid that he has," Harold answered her quietly, in that moment utterly convinced of the girl's sincerity. He would have taken bets of any amount that she had not known about the will.

"I'll give it back. I can do that, can't I?" she demanded

earnestly, her voice rising. "I don't want any part of the ranch. It belongs to his brother. I can't imagine Ryan doing such a thing!"

"Before you make any decisions about giving up your inheritance, Cara," Harold advised her, "I think you'd better read this. I was instructed to give this letter to you after I informed you of the will's contents."

Wordlessly, her heart accelerating, Cara took the envelope. "I'll leave you alone for a few minutes," the lawyer said, and pressed her shoulder as he left the room.

Her mouth dry, Cara opened the envelope and drew out a brief letter in Ryan's handwriting. She began to read:

Dear Cara,

What must you be thinking now that you have learned that you've inherited one half of La Tierra Conquistada? No doubt, knowing you, your first scandalized reaction was to tell Harold that you want the land returned to Jeth.

You cannot release the land to anyone, Puritan, not until you have lived for one full year, beginning the first day of spring, in the big house on La Tierra. At the end of that time, you may do as you wish with your inheritance.

You are not to divulge to anyone, especially not to Jeth, that I asked this of you until after your year's tenure in the house is fulfilled. This is the promise you made me, love, and the one that I trust you to keep.

Vaya con Dios,
Ryan

Cara looked up from the letter at the sleet-encrusted windows, unaware that Harold St. Clair had returned to the room.

"Cara?" He spoke her name close to her chair, and she jumped nervously. Conscious that the letter was exposed to his view, she folded it quickly and slipped it back in the envelope.

"Mr. St. Clair, does Mr. Langston, Ryan's brother, know the terms of Ryan's will?"

"I'm afraid so. I've been on the phone with his attorneys all morning. It was a great shock to him to discover that the original will had been altered in favor of someone other than himself."

"And he probably thinks I used—undue influence is the correct term, isn't it?— to get Ryan to change the will?"

"I am afraid that is his opinion."

"Can the will be contested?"

"Ryan was an attorney. He would never have drawn up a will for himself that could be contested." Seated once again at his desk, Harold assumed an expression designed to ease her misgivings. "I imagine that you wish to either sell your share of the ranch to Mr. Langston or restore it to him once the estate clears probate. The firm, of course, will take care of all the necessary transference of ownership. No need for you to concern yourself with the—er—unpleasant possibility of confronting Mr. Langston or his attorneys."

Cara Martin sat straighter in the chair and tried to sound braver than she felt. "I'm afraid I will not be able to avoid that confrontation, Mr. St. Clair. I'm going to Texas. I plan to live at La Tierra Conquistada."

Chapter Three

The silence that hung in the senior partner's office of the Dallas law firm representing the vast interests of La Tierra Conquistada was thick with tension. John Baines, the senior partner, along with another of the firm's attorneys, regarded Harold St. Clair and his mystifying client with frowning, tight-lipped censure.

Finally, the senior partner broke the silence with one last appeal. "Miss Martin, *please.* I beg of you to reconsider your decisions. Sign these papers. Mr. Langston wants back only what rightfully belongs to him. He is willing to pay you a more than fair price for the guarantee that once the estate is settled the land becomes his. Since the estate will take at least a year to go through probate, and since he is willing to pay you *now*, you must surely see how generous he is being."

Cara's reply, her face pale and set, was a negative shake of her honey-blond head.

"Miss Martin—" The frustrated attorney decided to try a different tack and left his chair to sit on the corner of his desk in cozy proximity to Cara. After all, this young woman was the same age as his youngest daughter, and from time to time, he had been able to reason with her. "Miss Martin—" He chose a soft, imploring timbre. "Surely you can imagine what Jeth Langston must think of you?"

Hearing it stated like that, Cara could not prevent the convulsive swallow from moving down her throat. "Yes," she nodded, lowering her eyes from the penetrating gaze. She had been trying to avoid thinking about that question ever since she had read Ryan's letter. If she had thought about it, she could never have resigned her job, sublet her apartment, shipped to La Tierra the belongings she would need for a year, and flown with Harold St. Clair to Texas, all in less than three weeks' time.

"Well, then." The smooth tone had an edge of exasperation to it. "Why can you not see that it is sheer madness even to consider taking up residence on La Tierra Conquistada? You will be like the biblical stranger in a strange land. You will have no protectors, no one to see after either your person or your interests—"

Cara raised her gaze to his. Her eyes darkened with some strongly felt emotion that intensified their beauty. The lawyer, nonplussed, drew back from their stunning assault as Cara said, "You paint Mr. Langston as quite a savage, Mr. Baines."

"Mr. Langston is not a savage, Miss Martin." The lawyer's patience was strained to the breaking point. "He is a fair man noted for his ruthlessness toward those who would pose any threat to La Tierra Conquistada. You must admit that you are doing that. By insisting on living under his roof, you are rubbing salt in the wounds of a man who has recently and quite unexpectedly lost his dearly loved brother, the only family he had. He believes you used your, ah, relationship with Ryan to persuade him to leave to you half an empire that has belonged to the Langstons for generations." The lawyer peered at her over his glasses, sensing the nodding agreement of his colleague. "Quite frankly, I would not wish to be in your shoes at the moment. For your own sake, I plead with you to reconsider your decisions."

Cara heard her even reply as if she were disembodied from it. "I understand what you are saying to me, and I appreciate both your advice and concern. However, my mind is made up. I will not consider any negotiations for the sale of my half of the ranch to Mr. Langston or to anyone else until the estate is settled. During that time, I choose to live at La Tierra. If Mr. Langston wants my cooperation, he will have to abide by that wish."

In the long silence that followed her little speech, Cara thought shakily that the trio of lawyers, even Harold St. Clair, was staring at her as if she were Joan of Arc just renouncing her last chance to escape the stake.

The hush was broken when the senior partner gave a defeated sigh and straightened his tall, brittle frame from the desk. He stared down at Cara coldly. "I do not know what unseemly charade you are playing here, Miss Martin, but I must make sure you understand one thing: Jeth Langston is not a man to be trifled with. You are too young and inexperienced to engage in a contest of any sort with a man of his enormous power and prerogative. He does not merely defeat his enemies—he destroys them. And you, my dear, as lovely as you are, have given him no reason whatever to make an exception of you."

The hard conviction of his words held them all enthralled. While he spoke, the color completely drained from Cara's face and her stomach began to churn. For the thousandth time she wondered what in the world had possessed Ryan to force her into such a dangerous and untenable situation.

The sudden sound of a buzzer on the desk startled them all. Leaning around, John Baines jabbed an intercom button and barked, "Yes!"

His secretary's crisp voice announced, "Mr. Langston has arrived, sir."

The senior partner, with the resignation of Pontius Pilate having washed his hands of the whole matter, spoke into the intercom. "Kindly show Mr. Langston in, Louise."

Cara was grateful that her back was to the door. Her position gave her time to try to calm her racing heart, which was threatening to burst through its walls. She heard the door open, then close with a quiet, emphatic click. A force flowed into the room, drawing the men at once to their feet. She sensed from their fixed, apprehensive gazes that the man had paused just inside the door, no doubt for dramatic effect.

John Baines did his best to smile. "Come in, Mr. Langston, come in!" he said in the hearty voice of a businessman welcoming a preferred customer. "Allow me to introduce Harold St. Clair of Boston, who was a legal partner of your late brother's, and, uh, Miss Cara Martin, also of Boston."

Cara found that her legs would not permit her to rise. She could feel the man's presence, strong and hostile. Suddenly angry and resolute, Cara stood and turned to meet the steady gaze of Jeth Langston.

The impact took her breath away. She had expected, of course, an imposing man—similar perhaps to the legendary breed who sailed her great-grandfather's ships and answered to none but the sea. But no knowledge of those long-ago sea lords, and certainly no male of her acquaintance, not even Ryan, could have prepared her for this man. He was easily the most awesome human being she had ever seen. Tall and powerfully built, he stood like a man accustomed to power—strong legs in razor-creased slacks spread imperiously apart—and took her measure from beneath the low brim of a superb fawn Stetson. His presence seemed to flow across the room, almost suffocating her with apprehension.

Looking at him, noting the narrow black band of mourning

around the soft crown of the hat, Cara was tempted to speak to him of his sorrow—of their sorrow—but the icy contempt in his eyes froze the words on her tongue. Her hammering heart pounded in her eardrums. Mute and paralyzed, she felt as helpless as a dreamer caught in an inescapable disaster. For the man had begun a slow, deliberate approach toward her, his gray eyes glacial and still. She could not find in his hard, handsome face a single similarity to the brother they both had loved.

John Baines waded into the silence by clearing his throat and saying in a tone of accusation, "Miss Martin refuses to change her mind, Mr. Langston, in spite of our reasoning."

Jeth, pausing a few feet from Cara, spoke softly. "Perhaps I can change Miss Martin's mind. Gentlemen, would you mind leaving us?"

"Not at all, Mr. Langston," acquiesced the attorney, who nervously shuffled a few papers on his desk before relinquishing his turf. He and his colleague filed past, but the Boston lawyer went to Cara's side. "If you like, I'll remain, Cara."

"That won't be necessary, Mr. St. Clair." Cara spoke for the first time and attempted a weak smile. "I'll be all right."

Harold's heart moved queerly at the sight of the brave little smile. He touched her shoulder comfortingly. "You've only to call. I'll be just outside the door." Sidestepping Jeth, he nodded to the rancher and left the two antagonists staring at each other.

As the door closed, Jeth's eyes left hers and went to her hair, his stony expression betraying nothing of his thoughts. It was the color of pure honey and framed a face that could stop the heart of any man. He had experienced many griefs, but he felt a new kind of sorrow as his gaze lowered in a merciless descent down her body. He had thought that he had known them all, had experienced every variety of alluring fortune hunter known to man, but this one was of a singular cast. He could see how Ryan had been taken in; certainly he would have been, too.

Cara drew a sharp breath and resisted the urge to cover herself from Jeth's disturbing eyes. He said slowly, "Yes...now I understand. Who would ever take a girl like you to be what you are?"

Cara could endure no more. "Jeth, I—"

"*Mister* Langston to you, lady!" The words were rapped out like gunshots. "We're going to keep this conversation on a strictly formal footing, do you understand?"

"Very clearly," Cara said with rigid dignity, determined not to give any ground during this initial, crucial interview.

Jeth regarded her in silence for a few seconds, and Cara thought she saw a flicker of surprise beneath the chilly stillness of the gray eyes. "Well, now that that's settled, let's talk, you and me." He tossed his hat to a couch and chose for himself a deep armchair to accommodate his tall frame. He had thick, dark hair, Cara noted, the kind with a tendency to curl.

Cara, following his lead, sat down in her original chair and remained waiting for him to speak, outwardly calm. "So you want to live at La Tierra, do you?" he asked conversationally, lifting brows as dark as his hair.

"Yes," she answered with as much force as her taut throat would allow. It was very difficult to meet his eyes. In all fairness, she could not blame him for thinking of her as he did. What in the world *had* Ryan been thinking to extract such a promise from her?

"Why?" Jeth asked bluntly, watching her face carefully as if he did not trust her words to reveal the truth.

"My reasons are personal."

"Ah" was Jeth's only reaction before reaching inside the inner pocket of his Western-cut leather jacket for a slim cigar case. Cara could see the same discreet insignia in gold on it that Ryan's wallet had borne, but now she knew it was the brand of La Tierra Conquistada, a *T* crossed with a *C*. Jeth selected a long, slender cigar and returned the case to his pocket.

"Ordinarily," he said, biting off the tip of the cigar with strong white teeth, "I ask a lady's permission before smoking in her presence. However…" The implication hung in the air along with the tendrils of smoke that fanned from his narrow nostrils. Cara felt a surge of heat on her cheeks. Let him insinuate anything he wished! she thought angrily. Knowing she had no cause to feel ashamed gave her inestimable strength. He could blow as much smoke as he liked!

"You've made your point, Mr. Langston," Cara stated with a trace of hauteur. "And as a matter of fact, you're not the first…"

"You'd better get used to it, Miss Martin. The kindest name I've heard in reference to you lately is Ryan's whore."

He had hurt her there, Jeth thought without pleasure, watching the blood drain quickly from her delicate face. She had to look away from him, her eyes apparently seeking refuge in a painting on a far wall. It was a seascape of sand and seagulls and ocean. *Home*, he surmised, wondering if she missed Boston, if she regretted this course upon which she was embarked. Her expression when she turned to him again was completely composed, revealing nothing. Like him, she too had learned the value of concealing her vulnerabilities.

"Now," he continued in the tone of a father who has just satisfactorily reprimanded a child, "back to my original question. Why do you want to come to La Tierra?"

Suddenly, quite thoroughly, Cara hated him. She fought to keep her body from quivering in cold anger at his overbearing manner. "Back to my original answer, Mr. Langston," she replied icily. "My reasons are my own."

"Shall I take a stab at what those reasons may be, Miss Martin?" Jeth suggested amicably, his mouth quirking in a slight smile that held no humor whatever.

You may take a straddling leap at a high fence, Cara silently suggested, but refrained from voicing her thought. "Why ask, Mr. Langston, since you intend to tell me anyway?" She squared her shoulders and raised her chin, exposing the smooth, vulnerable line of her throat. Waiting for him to continue, she willed herself not to be affected by his words, however harsh they were. You're no stranger to pain, she reminded herself. You can bear whatever *he* says!

Jeth drew on his cigar, regarding her narrowly through the smoke. For the first time she noticed the handsome, masculine ring he wore on the ring finger of his left hand. It had been designed with a black face on which was engraved the brand of La Tierra Conquistada, set in pavé diamonds. There seemed to be nothing about the man, she grudgingly admitted, that did not declare his wealth and position. The boots, which matched the tan leather of his jacket, were obviously hand sewn. The sharply creased slacks were of fine wool, the complementing beige tie of the finest silk.

"I can think of three possible reasons for wanting to ensconce yourself at the ranch," Jeth began, settling comfortably in the chair. "One, you feel that by living there for a year you will better be able to determine the true value of what you've inherited to set your price once the estate is settled. Second, I understand that you've quit your job. Without an income, you need free room and board for a year, so what better place to nip into than La Tierra? A year without having to work for a living will prepare you for the kind of life to which you anticipate becoming accustomed. How am I doing so far?"

Cara could only stare at him, too appalled to answer. She was forced at last to appreciate fully how she must appear in his eyes, in the eyes of all of those who had loved and respected Ryan. They thought her lazy and opportunistic, a fortune hunter who now had the gall to demand living accommodations under the very roof of the man it appeared she had swindled.

Why would Ryan have demanded something from her that would place her in such a light? He knew she loathed freeloading. He had often become exasperated with her because she would accept nothing from him that she could not return in kind. And she was nothing if not a hard worker. She had not wanted to give up her job, leaving unpaid for yet another year the final debts that clouded her family's name. Ryan, whom she had trusted, whom she had loved—why had he extracted a promise that would compromise her very soul in the eyes of others?

Inwardly she sighed. Now there would be another name to add to her list of debtors. She would pay Jeth Langston back for the cost of her room and board if it was the last thing she ever did!

"You mentioned a third reason," she reminded him.

"Yes," Jeth said slowly. Without hurry, he pulled toward him a bronze ashtray on the desk. The sensuous leather of his coat sleeve defined the hard, virile line of his arm. Cara sensed a sudden and dangerous change in him that made her look at him warily. When Jeth gave her his attention once again, her skin tingled with an ominous chill.

"I think that somewhere in that scheming little head of yours, you actually entertained the idea that I may be induced to pick up where Ryan left off—two halves are better than one, so to speak—"

Cara was horrified. "No!" she gasped. "What an insane idea!"

"Is it, Miss Martin?" Jeth returned with icy calm. "Unlike my brother, who preferred tall, statuesque women, I have always had an inclination toward the Dresden type, the kind who are all cool fragility without but fire and passion within—like the kind of woman I suspect you are, Miss Martin. But then you were aware of that. You probably pumped Ryan plenty before he died."

At the mention of Ryan's death, a sudden shadow flitted across Jeth's sun-browned face. For a brief moment Cara saw naked pain etched there and remembered what she had forgotten in their bitter interview—that Jeth was suffering, too. Nonetheless, she jumped to her feet, small fists clenched, instinctively knowing that she must make clear her position on this vital point or lose a foothold that she could never regain. "I knew nothing of the sort about you! I couldn't care less about your preferences in women! You are reading far too much into why I want to come to La Tierra. I can understand how you must feel about my living in—in your home, and I don't blame you, but I promise you that I will sell back to you my share—"

"*Ryan's* share," the man across from her corrected softly, the gray eyes very still.

"Ryan's share," Cara allowed. "And for a fair price."

"And what do you consider fair?"

"That will have to be discussed when the estate is settled. You have my word, though—however little it means to you—that the sum will be reasonable. In exchange—" She faltered and bit at the soft flesh of her lip, feeling herself blush.

"Yes?" Jeth pressed, with unnerving patience.

Cara drew a deep breath. "In exchange for the guarantee that I will sell to no one but you, I must have your guarantee that no harm will come to me while I am living at La Tierra."

There was a short silence, broken when Jeth instructed, "Do

sit down, Miss Martin. Your height is inadequate to provide you much advantage. Besides, you look tired enough to drop." She did, too. He had just noticed the delicate blue tinges of fatigue beneath the startling eyes. "Now tell me, why do you think you'll need my protection?"

"Mr. Langston!" Cara regarded him coldly as she sat down. "I may look a fool, but I assure you I'm not! Neither do I think I am addressing one. You know perfectly well why I would want such a guarantee. I could be—I could be—" Desperately she searched for a word that was less graphic than the one that sprang to mind.

"Molested in some way?" he suggested politely, a small smile playing about his strong mouth.

"Yes!" she said in angry embarrassment. "That, or—or beaten and starved—"

"My dear Miss Martin!" Jeth could not suppress his laughter. It had a nice, hearty ring to it, and had he not been laughing at her, she might have enjoyed it. She seethed while, still amused, he blew a final stream of smoke and tamped out the cigar in the ashtray. "You've been seeing too many Italian Westerns," he chuckled.

"I see no Italian Westerns, Mr. Langston. I do not care for them. I am merely stating the obvious vindictive approach you and the people who work for you might take toward me for what you suppose I did to Ryan—"

"Suppose? Did you say *suppose*, Miss Martin?" He was out of his chair before she could blink, all humor vanished, the arctic coldness back in his eyes. "Let's get a few facts straight," he said very clearly, bending down to imprison her in the chair by clasping each of its arms. "I don't like dealing in suppositions."

Cara shrank back from him, the closeness of the granite features and the unaccustomed male scents of cologne and leather and tobacco sending her senses spinning. "Now these are the facts as I see them. I am sure you will correct me if I'm wrong."

"Given the opportunity," Cara managed, pressing back against the chair.

"You prevented my brother from coming home to die. Oh, he came back for a last token visit, but he never mentioned he was dying. If I had known his illness was terminal, I would have kept him there, and that would have meant curtains for you. I would have found out about the altered will."

"That's not true!"

"Isn't it, Miss Martin? Then why didn't he tell me about you, the woman he loved? Why didn't he tell me about the change in the will? Ryan would have known that I would have accepted any decision he made concerning his half of La Tierra. It was his to do with as he chose."

"Mr. Langston, I honestly don't know the answers to those questions—" He was so close. If she moved, they would touch.

"Then try this one. Why didn't *you* tell me he was dying? You had to have known that I didn't know. You were the woman who answered the phone a few weeks ago when I called, weren't you? Why didn't you tell me?"

Cara could not answer. Helplessly, she stared into the suddenly bleak eyes. No wonder Jeth Langston despised her. It was not the loss of the land that sharpened the edge of his hate against her, but the belief that she had denied him the last days of his brother's life.

"What power you had over him, Cara!" Jeth said in soft anguish. "A man doesn't need much imagination to know how you made sure he returned to Boston. I'm sure you had your ways of convincing him that your arms were better for holding him in his final days than mine would have been."

A stab of pity for him brought the shine of tears to her eyes.

She would not, could not, add to this man's grief by telling him that Ryan himself had refused to return home to die. Without meaning to, she looked longingly at the broad set of shoulders encased in the buttery soft leather. She was so desperately tired. How pleasant it would be to slip her arms around that strong neck and rest her cheek against the leather's yielding softness. Instead, she closed her eyes and lowered her head wearily, feeling a strand of hair brush Jeth's chin.

"I—I can well understand how all this must look to you, but—but—"

"But I'm wrong, is that it?" Jeth finished for her, his tone almost gentle.

She shook her head.

"Oh, Miss Martin—" He straightened up, an impotent rage filling his soul. Long ago he had dispensed with dreams, especially those about women. But occasionally, when he felt especially lonely and the long evening hours in the study stretched out before him, he wondered what it would be like to know, like his father, the love of a devoted woman. Sometimes his thoughts wandered further, and he envisioned what she would look like, this woman of his dreams. A small, shapely figure, eyes that could melt the needles from a cactus, honey-gold hair, and a mouth so sweet and passionate that it was like drinking ambrosia to kiss her—that was the description of the woman he yearned to give his heart and soul. A woman who looked like Cara Martin.

"Let's see if I'm wrong about this, too, Miss Martin," Jeth said, his voice dangerously soft. He reached down and slipped an arm around her waist. Cara was in the leather enclosure of his embrace before she could close her astonished mouth.

"Let me go!" she demanded, aware of the sudden intimate pressure of his chest against hers. His move had been so sudden,

.he was pressing her so close that her arms dangled uselessly. They had nowhere to go but to his shoulders, and she must not put them there.

"This is your chance to prove me wrong about you, Miss Martin, that you are not what I think you are, that you were never Ryan's—"

"Don't say it!" Cara said desperately. "I can't bear to hear you say it."

"Then prove to me how wrong I am."

"Don't—" The word was just forming when Jeth's lips closed over her mouth.

Cara stiffened against him, tightened her lips in rigid protest against such a violation of her privacy. Small fists pummeled his shoulders with powerless blows that drained her remaining strength. Jeth, his hand a gentle vise under the silken fall of her hair, felt the tension suddenly leave and released her mouth. Cara's lids fluttered open, the depths of her eyes starry and deeply violet. Jeth stared down into them, and she was conscious of a strange, frightening desire asserting itself deep within her. "Please let me go," she pleaded, her mouth so close to him that her lips stroked his when she spoke.

"No," he murmured and kissed her eyes. She whimpered—to Jeth's ears like a kitten lost in a storm—but he could not afford to be merciful. He pressed her closer and she gasped and tensed as his lips closed over hers again. He might have let her go then, but she did not pull away. Against her mouth Jeth groaned in gratitude, for he could not have borne the sudden release of her from his arms, the denial of her lips, the feel of her body. The fragrance of her filled his nostrils and drifted down into the hollow of his heart where he had conceived the image of her likeness. Exultantly, hungrily, tasting and devouring her, he led her deeper into a world of sexuality where he could not have known that she had never been before.

And Cara, the sudden, unexpected need of him destroying her defenses, could not prevent the ardor with which her flesh responded.

Long after her body had helped Jeth to prove his point, she stayed within his embrace. Finally, he pushed her from him. Shame would not let her meet his eyes. To finish her humiliation, tears began to run down her cheeks.

"Believe it or not," he said quietly, "I wish I'd been wrong. It would be comforting to know that Ryan had loved a woman who could have remained faithful until his body was cold."

Jeth brought out a folded white lawn handkerchief and tossed it to her. "Now let's do a little reconsidering, shall we? I'm sure that you realize that it's out of the question for you to live on the ranch."

Cara dabbed at her eyes. "I have to come, Jeth," she said. "I have to. I don't expect you to understand, but be assured I won't ask a thing from you. I won't be in your way. What happened just now will not happen again—"

Jeth asked in astonishment, "You mean you *still* intend to go through with this? What the hell for? What can you possibly hope to gain? I'll pay you now for Ryan's share of the ranch!"

"It—it's not for sale until the estate is settled, which will take approximately a year, or so I'm told. I'd like to arrive March twentieth, two days from now. Probably by this time next year, the paperwork will have already been drawn up to restore Ryan's portion to you. You have my word that I will ask no more than a fair price for it. And you have to promise—"

"Yes, I know," Jeth grated. "My protection from physical abuse. Okay, lady, you have a deal, but I hope your psychological health is in good shape. You'll need it where you're going."

He turned to pick up the Stetson. "By the way," he asked, "just how do you expect to get to the ranch?"

"I intend flying to Midland Air Terminal. I'd like for you to have someone pick me up when I arrive. I'd rent a car, but I would have no way to return it."

"Suppose I say no."

Cara had to moisten dry lips, but she stood her ground. "Jeth, you have to cooperate with my inconsequential requests if you want that land back."

He came back to all but gape at her, his strong brown fingers curved around the brim of the Stetson. Cara found herself gazing at them in fascination. "I won't bore you with the results of the last attempt to coerce me, Miss Martin, but let it suffice to say that the individual regretted his impulse. You will hand over that land no later than next March twentieth with or without my cooperation to your *inconsequential* requests, do you understand? And another thing: you have lapsed twice and called me Jeth. Don't do so again."

Without another look at her, he strode from the room and closed the door behind him with the finality of an exclamation mark. Cara stood staring at it with a strange sense of loss, raising to her lips the monogrammed handkerchief he had forgotten.

Chapter Four

He wouldn't see me, you know," said Harold St. Clair after he and Cara had been seated in the dining room of the Dallas Hilton where he had reserved rooms for them.

"Mr. Langston considers you a traitor," Cara said regretfully, practicing the form of his name that she'd been ordered to use. "But even so, I'd think he would want to hear about his brother from one who had been his colleague and friend."

"Jeth Langston is a hard man, Cara. Apparently he feels that I am partly responsible for this unpleasantness since I knew about the will and didn't tell him in time for him to exert his influence. I plead innocent of knowing that Ryan's illness was terminal." He looked across at Cara with a despondent smile. She was ravishing in a red dinner dress that heightened the translucent glow of her skin. Under the flattering lights of the chandeliers, her eyes and hair were dazzling. Harold was aware that glances from other diners kept returning to their table. He only wished Cara's admirers could have the pleasure of seeing her smile. The lovely heirloom pearls encircling her throat were nothing to the pearl perfection of her smile.

Gently, Harold covered the small hand toying with the stem of a wineglass. "If he had agreed to see me, I could have told him that he is mistaken about you."

"How can you be sure of that, Harold?" The lawyer's first name sounded unfamiliar to her still. This afternoon he had asked her to use it. "You know no more about me than he does."

"I know that when I first read to you the contents of the will, your face lost all color, and you immediately wanted to give— not sell—the land back to Jeth. Your specific words were 'Ryan would never have done that to his brother.' Remember? You only changed your mind after I left you alone with Ryan's envelope. What was in it, Cara? What was in it that made you change your mind about the inheritance and decide to wait out the settlement of the estate at La Tierra?"

Cara drew her hand away and clutched the napkin in her lap. She was becoming adept at hiding her thoughts, and now a curtain seemed to descend over her features. If Harold probed any further, he might guess at the promise she had made to Ryan. Warmth remained in her eyes, however, and Harold was rewarded with a faint smile. "I'll have to tell you what I told Mr. Langston, Harold. My reasons are personal. A year will go fast and then I'll have to impose upon you again by asking that you arrange the sale agreement."

"Do you...know what you'll be asking?" Harold inquired blandly, studying her covertly over the rim of his martini glass.

"A reasonable price," was her evasive answer. "Now tell me, when are you going back to Boston?" The question made her heart move strangely. Harold was her last link with home, with what was familiar and safe. He had been a steady and comforting presence at her side throughout the strain of the last few weeks. To be suddenly without his counsel and support, his easy companionship, would be especially hard after the tragedy of Ryan's death and the fear of the ordeal ahead.

"Tomorrow morning," Harold told her reluctantly, reading her thoughts. "Cara. I want you to consider me your friend. You have my card. If for any reason you need me, you've only to call. I could not bear to think of your needing help and having no one to turn to. I'm only a return flight away." He looked at the girl as gravely as he dared. Heaven knew, she was frightened enough for all the composure she was trying to show. "And my dear—" He took her hand into his smooth, comforting one. "If I may offer some advice?"

"Please do," Cara invited quietly, but her heart fluttered sickeningly at his tone. Into her mind leaped the image of Jeth and the hatred and repugnance that had been in his eyes in the last few moments of their interview. She did not fear anything he could do to her if only he did not prey on the weakness he had discovered, the weakness she had not even known she possessed.

"Then it is this, Cara. Do not love anything while you are out there. No man, woman, or child. No horse or dog—not even an armadillo—" His attempt at humor failed. The beautiful eyes darkened with anxiety, but he pressed on. "Care for nothing or no one through which he can hurt you—" Harold broke off as a waiter appeared to present them with menus.

"You don't have to go, you know."

"Yes, I do."

Harold sighed. "I have transferred a sum of money to your account on orders from Ryan. No, don't protest, Cara, and don't be foolish, either. You're broke. I know it, and Ryan knew it. You will have no income while you're in Texas, so don't let that New England pride of yours prevent you from spending it for the things you need."

Cara opened the menu. Ryan had thought of everything. Everything but an explanation for why she was here. "I don't think I'll have anything but a salad. I seem to have lost my appetite," she said.

The next morning Cara saw Harold St. Clair off on his return trip to Boston from the huge, modern Metroplex airport that sprawled between Dallas and Fort Worth. As the aircraft lifted off, a bleak depression settled over her, and she clutched even tighter the small box she held. It contained a gold charm in the design of a seagull that Harold had given her just before boarding.

"For luck," he explained, looking down at the golden head bent in surprised pleasure over the trinket. "You can attach it to that thin gold chain you wear around your neck. If you have any bad moments, just reach up and touch it. I hope it reminds you that you have a friend."

"Harold—" Words failed her, and so she reached up and kissed his smooth-shaven cheek. Blinking at the tears that threatened, she stammered, "You've been so kind. I can never repay—"

"Shh." He stopped her gently by touching a finger to her lips. "Take care of yourself now, and let me hear from you."

Once he had gone, Cara found a secluded seat in a vacant passenger lounge and cried out the grief and despair that had needed release for weeks. She felt better afterward and resolutely drew a breath. That will have to do me, she thought. No way can I afford to do that once I'm on The Conquered Land!

The next morning she was wide awake long before the desk called to awaken her. She lay in bed staring at the ceiling and tried to calm herself by mentally lining up the defenses she could call on to protect herself from Jeth Langston's expected vengeance. There was the matter of the land, which would be hers by law within the year. She must not be squeamish when it came to holding that over his arrogant head in case he decided to get rough with her. Also, she would watch her decorum carefully and in no way give anyone reason to call her—she could hardly bear to think of it—Ryan's whore! She would stay out of everyone's way, but if allowed, she would certainly pitch in and help with whatever needed doing.

But for all the practical advice she gave herself, the knot remained tied in her stomach. Not even the elegant suit she chose for her flight helped to soothe her anxieties. She had come to take pleasure and comfort in the large assortment of beautiful clothes that soon would be hanging in her closet on La Tierra. They reminded her of Ryan and brought him close to her in memory. She wore them proudly, knowing that he would have wanted her to.

Cara preferred time to drag, but it did not. By the time she had finished packing and forced herself to eat several bites of melon for breakfast, she had to leave for the airport. She dressed warmly in the sable-lined raincoat, for spring was late arriving in Texas, and in no time at all she was deposited before the flight desk and her bags were being checked.

A flurry of worrisome questions besieged her as the airliner winged its way over the vast reaches of Texas. Were the two big boxes containing her clothes and the belongings she had sent by air freight waiting for her in the small airport where she'd be landing? Would there be someone there to meet her? Cara cringed at the thought that it might be Jeth Langston. She shrugged off that worry immediately, thinking it unlikely that the owner of La Tierra Conquistada performed such menial chores. How would she get to the ranch if no one was there? She could rent a car, but how could she return it? Finally, already exhausted from the burden of her anxieties and a sleepless night, she laid her head back, closed heavy lids over troubled eyes, and slept.

The steward woke her, it seemed to Cara, just a few minutes later, and yet she felt a surge of fresh strength and well-being.

The young man smiled down at her, enjoying her beauty. "I thought you'd like to be awake before we land," he said, "especially if this is your first trip to West Texas."

Cara thanked him, and the steward remained at her seat to get her reaction when she looked out of her window. The sight below made her gasp. The handsome young steward smiled. "That's something, isn't it? Everybody has that reaction the first time they see West Texas from the air. Someone once said this part of the state can best be described as 'miles and miles of miles and miles.' "

An accurate statement, Cara agreed, as she gaped down at the vast, seemingly endless desert that surrounded two oasis-looking patches of green. Cara assumed they were the only towns of any size in the area. In between them was the airport, but beyond and around them was nothing—no trees, lakes, or highways—to break the sweeping brown panorama of the West Texas plains. A tough, rugged land, she decided—like the man who had conquered it.

The thought of Jeth Langston brought shadows to her eyes, and the steward, who had already summed her up as some rich man's toy, ventured curiously, "Somehow you don't look like you belong out here. Are you just visiting?"

"Yes," Cara replied, giving him a brief smile before turning back to her window. The steward took the hint and moved off down the aisle, wondering about the man rich enough to afford something like that.

A dry, stiff wind lifted Cara's blond hair when she stepped off the departure ramp at Midland Air Terminal. There was no amenity of a covered ramp from plane to terminal, and she pulled the warm fur at her neck closer. Quickly she scanned the assembled group of relatives and friends for anyone who might be from La Tierra Conquistada. Subconsciously, Cara realized, she was looking for Jeth. No one nearly that tall or dominating was among the group who waited inside the terminal building. She looked searchingly around, but her gaze was met only by those arrested by her striking appearance.

He hasn't sent anyone! she thought in dismay. So this was to be her first taste of what she could expect as Ryan's whore.

She went into the small restaurant for a cup of coffee and to plan her next move. There was a car rental service here. Perhaps she would have to rent a car and simply hope that she could prevail upon someone from the ranch to return it. Oh, for her trusty old Volkswagen, she was thinking, just as someone tapped her on the shoulder.

Cara looked up in surprise. A tall, rangy young man about her age, wearing low-slung jeans, scuffed boots, a sleeveless fleece-lined jacket, and a frowning expression, was regarding her uncertainly. He had a dusty cowboy hat pushed back on his curly blond head. "Yes?" she inquired.

"You Miss Martin?"

"Yes, I am. Are you from La Tierra?"

"Yeah. The boss sent me to pick ya up."

"Well, that's wonderful!" Cara exclaimed, a brilliant smile of relief lighting her eyes.

The young man looked away, momentarily disconcerted. Cara suspected that the tough-guy pose did not come naturally and was being worn for her benefit. Orders from headquarters, she surmised with a flash of temper.

"Let's go, then," he said gruffly.

"There are a couple of things that I must do first—"

The young man dug his heels into the carpet, thrust fingertips into tight jean pockets, and surveyed her with disapproval. "Like whut?"

"Paying my check for one thing," she said pleasantly. "And

then I have to pick up my luggage. After that, I have to go to the air freight office to collect the boxes that I sent from Boston."

"That take long?"

"No-o-o." Cara's eyes rounded innocently. "Not nearly as long as it would take to make a return trip here and back."

"Well…" The young cowboy thought this over. "I guess it's all right. But I have strict orders from the boss to pick ya up and head right on back to the ranch. This is roundup time, ya know."

"No, I didn't know," Cara said congenially, fishing in her bag for money. She indicated her bags. "Would you mind getting those while I pay the check?"

The young man picked up Cara's weekender and cosmetic case. "My name is Cara," she said, taking the cosmetic case from him as they were heading for the luggage pickup.

"Mine's Bill, but I don't think we oughta get too friendly, miss. Let's just get what ya got to get and quit the jawin'."

Stung, Cara remained silent while the luggage was collected. Bill's only words were, "The jeep is out here."

"Jeep?" she cried, following him out to an immaculately painted light-gray jeep with the name of the ranch in small yellow letters on its side. The wind was beginning to pick up. Cara's ears already felt cold, and she did not relish a ride in an open vehicle. She was glad that she'd remembered to tuck a light wool scarf into her handbag.

All his attention on the road, Bill drove the jeep to the freight office where to her relief the two big boxes from Boston were awaiting her. Without a word, Bill loaded them into the back of the jeep with her other luggage, then looked impatiently at her standing beside the vehicle tying on her head scarf. "Let's go, miss. We're late enough already."

With Cara clutching the side of the jeep with one hand and

her scarf with the other, they tore off down the road leading out of the airport. They headed west on a wide modern interstate for a few miles until Bill turned left onto a two-lane highway. The wind tore at Cara's scarf, stung her eyes and cheeks, and carried away all attempts at conversation. Finally, receiving no response, she fell silent, trying to make as much as possible of the terrain they were passing through. Still in its wintry pall, it was indeed a bleak-looking landscape. Little vegetation grew from the hard, sandy ground, and what there was appeared stunted and sparse. She recognized the gnarled mesquite trees that Ryan had described to her. "They won't bud until the last freeze is over," she remembered his telling her. "Everything else out there can be fooled by Mother Nature, but not the mesquite." Cara had no idea what mesquite looked like when in bloom, but since there was not a single speck of color on the barren landscape, she deduced that winter was not yet over.

She was managing to hang onto her seat and the scarf until Bill turned off the highway across the open plains. "Shortcut!" he yelled, driving the jeep at full speed. Cara glanced back in alarm at the boxes jostling around on the backseat. If Bill hit a bump, they could easily be bounced over the side of the jeep onto the hard ground, and already they seemed to have had all the abuse they could stand. One look at the grim satisfaction on the young cowboy's face, the malicious delight he was taking in her discomfort, and the whole picture became clear.

"Stop this jeep this instant!" she shouted, and when he ignored her, she simply reached for the keys and jerked them out of the ignition. The jeep ground to a halt, and Bill turned to her in stupefaction. "Now you listen to me, you ill-mannered smart aleck!" Cara exploded. "You need reminding of a fact you seem to have forgotten. I own half of La Tierra Conquistada, and you will drive this jeep at a sane speed and get us to wherever we're going in one piece, or I may have to exercise a prerogative of my position that I'd just as soon not. Do I make myself clear?"

Bill looked across at her uncertainly, trying to decide if she was bluffing. The furious brilliance of the violet-blue eyes convinced him she was not. "Yes, ma'am," he conceded gruffly, and held out his hands for the keys.

Ultimately, out of the vast ocean of nothingness, there appeared in the far distance a white sprawling structure that momentarily gave the young Bostonian an impression of the Taj Mahal planted in the middle of the Sahara. The suddenness of its appearance was relieved by the beginning of a fence, made not of wood but of white steel pipe, which suggested that civilization was not far off. The white fence contrasted peaceably with the green winter pastures it bordered. In them here and there, groups of healthy-looking russet-colored cattle grazed placidly.

As all of this came into Cara's awed view, the jeep reached a well-paved road that ran beside the fence, and Bill turned left, heading, Cara supposed, to a drive that had access to the shining edifice sitting in the middle of the plains.

"Is this where the ranch begins?" she asked.

The young cowboy shot her a disgusted glance. "You been on La Tierra since we left the airport," he stated scornfully, but he could not conceal the note of pride Cara heard in his voice. She recalled that Ryan had spoken of the loyalty and devotion of the cowhands to the ranch. Many of them, she remembered, represented the fourth generation to work at La Tierra. Cara wondered if Bill was one. If so, she could understand the contempt that he was trying hard to show her.

They drove for several more miles before they reached the massive wrought-iron gate flanked by equally imposing limestone posts. The gate was heavily scrolled, but the intricate metalwork did not interfere with the brand of La Tierra, which had been worked into the two joining centers of the gate. When the gate opened, the brand was divided. Bill pointed this out to her, adding meaningfully, "The boss had it designed that way on purpose. He wanted everybody to understand that half was his and half was his brother's."

His words brought home to her what for a short while she had forgotten in the curiosity of her new surroundings: Jeth Langston. Sometime this day she would see him, and the thought chilled her blood. She wished that she could appreciate the beauty of the wide paved drive that was leading her closer to a man who detested her, who already had begun his vengeance upon her. Nonetheless, she noted that the drive had been lined with tree after tree of fuschia oleanders just beginning to bloom. Apparently they did not take their cue from the mesquite. She imagined, once they were in bloom, the profusion of blossoms that would greet the visitor through that exalted gate, bowing and swaying in the wind like a receiving line of plumed courtiers welcoming guests to the throne of a king.

The drive led uncompromisingly to the broad, wide-porticoed entrance of the house. The impeccable white stucco finish and sloping red tile roof did not surprise her. She was somewhat knowledgeable about Spanish architecture and recognized the style as that of the Spanish grandees who had settled in this area. This one, however, rather than having the usual low, long lines with thick walls to preserve the maximum temperature comfort, was two-storied. A scrolled, black wrought-iron terrace ran the circumference of the top floor with French doors opening to it. Interesting, thought Cara, and very impressive, but somehow un-seasoned. She recalled that Ryan's parents had died before they had occupied the house.

"Where is everyone?" she asked Bill, for there was no sign

or sound of any human activity. The young man was struggling with her big boxes impatiently. He set them down on the limestone porch and rang the doorbell. "At the roundup of the remuda in the high country," he told her, his tone implying that that was where he should be.

Cara shaded her eyes to better see the low range of mountains toward the north, far beyond the oasis of the ranch.

"By high country, I suppose you mean over there?" She pointed. Bill followed her finger with derisive amusement.

"Yes, ma'am. You're sure a greenhorn, ain't ya?"

"I'm afraid so." She smiled, determined not to be nettled.

Before she could inquire about the whereabouts of Bill's employer, the wide double doors opened. A weathered, stern-faced Mexican woman of indeterminate age, smaller in stature even than Cara, stood surveying her with cold dispassion.

"She's here, Fiona!" Bill announced grimly, as if she were some dreaded tornado they had been watching for on the horizon. Cara stared at the little woman. So this was Fiona, the housekeeper that Ryan had spoken of with such affection.

"So I see," the woman said abruptly, turning her glance from Cara. "Bring her things in, Señor Bill, and take them up to the first bedroom on the left. Then you better go on up to Diablo Canyon where the trap is. He caught Devil's Own, but that son of Satan slipped his noose and got away again. He is not in a good mood."

Which did not bode well for her, Cara thought, whatever it was that they were talking about. "He" must be Jeth Langston. She did not know whether to be happy or dismayed that she had been reprieved from an immediate meeting with the ruler of this isolated empire. Maybe the initial confrontation was better over as soon as possible so they could go their separate ways. The house looked big enough to allow that arrangement.

The woman called Fiona returned her inhospitable gaze to Cara as Bill brushed by carrying her things. "You can come in," she said.

"Thank you," Cara responded pleasantly, and walked into the manor house of La Tierra Conquistada.

She was shocked immediately by its monastic severity. A tomb, Ryan had called it, and Cara felt obliged to agree with him. Immense and silent, the house had an almost menacing sterility about it, like a sanitarium. Furniture was sparse and utilitarian. No paintings or portraits enlivened the stark white walls. And everywhere, in all the rooms open to her view from the spacious entrance hall, she could see the gleaming gray terrazzo, creating an impression of cold, obsessive cleanliness.

"Come," said Fiona, waiting for her at the foot of the wide staircase.

The bedroom the housekeeper led her to, however, surprised her in another way, for it was obvious that feminine consider-ations had gone into its decor. Gray and yellow had been used, which Cara now assumed must be the colors of La Tierra. The inevitable gray tile was on the floor, but it had been covered with a large yellow area rug. Draperies and a bedspread in a sprigged print of the ranch's colors matched the window seats of the two small deep-set windows that flanked a slender French door. The big four-poster bed and other furniture—a dressing table, writing desk, chairs for both, armoire, and chest of drawers—were of mellow oak. Two upholstered yellow wing-back chairs sat on either side of the fireplace, which had already been laid with a supply of wood—scrub oak, Cara supposed, and remembered her comment on the day she had met Ryan at the airport.

He had known then that she would be in Texas now.

The memory sobered her surprised pleasure in the room and

made her eyes reflective. Fiona had nearly slipped away before Cara realized she was leaving. "Oh—I—thank you," she said quickly to the unsmiling woman. "The room is quite lovely, very cozy and feminine. Is it someone's special room?"

Fiona's hand was on the doorknob. "You've missed lunch," she said with undisguised hostility, and was gone before Cara could reply.

The young woman was left facing the closed door, and in the silence, like bugs scampering out in a house when the occupants leave, all of her fears crawled out from the woodwork to assail her. She looked about her at the luggage and boxes that needed unpacking but was reluctant to begin the task. Reaching inside the neck of her sweater, she fingered the small seagull. A whole year in the remote silence of this monastery? Would there be no one who would talk with her, nowhere to go for relief from loneliness, from the animosity of the man in whose cold eyes she was condemned beyond any reclamation of her innocence?

Determinedly putting those questions from her mind, she shed her coat and took a penknife from her purse. Cutting the tape of one of the boxes, she began to search for the three items her mood dictated she unpack first.

When Cara found the bag of sea glass, she held it up to the gentle March sunlight, which had come into her room to play. The pieces of glass glowed softly like a cache of dull gems recovered from the sea. She found another bag, this one filled with the broken pieces of the lobster traps that she and Ryan had collected on their last visit to Devereux Beach. Glancing at the fireplace, she thought how comforting the fire would be with these reminders from home added to the flames. Lastly, she found the enlarged snapshot that had belonged to Ryan. She gently touched the glass that covered his face, swallowing at the ache that filled her throat. How hard to believe that he was gone, that she would never see that boyish smile again or hear his laughter or feel his friendly arm around her shoulder. "Do you trust me, Cara?" he had asked. "Remember always that I had only at heart the interests of those I loved."

That's you and me, Jeth, she said silently to the other man in the picture. I intend to carry out your brother's wish no matter how hard you make it for me to do so.

A strange rumble that gave her the sensation the earth was shaking brought Cara's head up, and she held still a moment, listening. Placing the picture on the mantel, she went out on the terrace that faced the mountains, and an awesome and unforgettable sight met her eyes.

A great herd of horses, their manes and tails flowing behind them, had come from the mountains to begin a thundering, dusty trek across the plains toward the ranch. Dozens of whooping, hollering cowboys on their own galloping mounts rode at their sides, keeping them maneuvered into a V-shaped formation by waving hats and coiled ropes. Cara looked for the objective toward which horses and men seemed to be headed, but her vantage point told her nothing. Compelled by the rough, masculine drama she was witnessing, she followed the terrace past other French doors until she had a view of the maze of corrals that had been erected beyond the grounds of the house.

So that's their destination, she thought, feeling suddenly sorry for the animals, whose life of freedom in the mountains would soon be at an end. As the horses drew abreast of the series of lanes that would feed them into the corrals, sounds that she had never imagined filled the air along with the dust. Leather saddles and chaps popped, ropes slapped, men cursed and yelled orders, horses whinnied and screamed.

Cara was so fascinated with the unusual scene that she was unaware of having been spotted on the terrace. First one man and then another jerked a head in her direction, but several minutes went by before she realized she was the cause of the gradual decline in activity. None of the men looking at her nodded or tipped his hat. They merely stared, and even from that distance Cara could read the stony unfriendliness on their weathered faces.

A rider on a huge bay, whose back had been to her, turned his mount swiftly to see what had distracted the men, and Cara saw with a sharp intake of breath that the man was Jeth Langston. He sat immobile for a few seconds, staring straight at her from beneath the brim of his black hat, and Cara cursed herself for not having recognized that imperious back. Suddenly one of the horses, sensing an opportunity for freedom, reared and bolted from the orderly line. Other horses quickly followed suit, sending the men scrambling after them. Shouting an order, Jeth wheeled his horse sharply, at the same time uncoiling a rope from the saddle horn. With held breath she watched him streak after the escaping ringleader, his rope twirling above his head until he was close enough to the animal to throw a noose cleanly over its head. Jeth led the horse back to the line without looking in her direction again, and Cara saw that the men had resumed their work with even more fervor than before.

She turned quickly and sought the sanctuary of her room, wondering if there was to be no end to the trouble she caused Jeth Langston. A strange sensation had begun to play in the pit of her stomach, one that had nothing to do with the fear that she would be blamed for the mishap. The sunlight was chilly, but she was suffused with warmth, and her cheeks felt hot. She began to unpack with furious energy, trying to keep from her mind the sight of that dominant figure on horseback whose hatred she had felt even across the distance that lay between them.

Chapter Five

The sun was gone, the rough voices of the cowboys were silent, and her clothes hung neatly in her closet when a sharp rap came at her door. "Yes?" Cara called.

The door opened and Fiona stood in the doorway. She had changed from her faded jeans and flannel shirt into a neat cotton dress worn under a starched yellow apron. The unsmiling face, however, was the same. She announced with cold disdain, "El Patrón will see you now."

"I'll only be a few minutes," Cara said evenly, hoping the woman could not hear the rapid beating of her heart. El Patrón? *El Patrón?*

The woman said warningly, "It would not be wise to keep him waiting, señorita," and closed the door with a sharp click.

He can wait long enough for me to freshen up, declared Cara to herself. She was not going to face him from the disadvantage of a pale face. In the adjoining bathroom, she brushed her teeth and applied fresh makeup. She was still wearing the suit skirt and cowl-neck sweater from her flight and saw no need to change. She brushed her hair, letting it fall into the easy, natural style that she had come to enjoy. "There," she said aloud in satisfaction to her reflection in the mirror when she was ready, then added tremulously, "Go with me, Ryan."

Fiona was waiting for her at the foot of the gray-tiled stairs. The housekeeper's face registered nothing as she watched Cara descend. "He's in there," she said, indicating with a stern jerk of her silver-threaded head two double doors off the living room.

Cara pondered Fiona uncertainly. Was Fiona to announce her? When the housekeeper moved off to other regions, with only a last disapproving glance over her shoulder, Cara decided she was on her own. Approaching the heavy, forbidding doors, she knocked decisively on one of them.

"Come in," came the deep voice that Cara remembered, and the young woman took one last steadying breath before entering Jeth Langston's inner sanctum.

She did not see him at first in the darkly paneled room. Besides the light cast from the fireplace, the only other illumination in the large room came from a lamp on a massive desk to the right of the door. The leather chair behind it was empty.

Jeth was standing at the fireplace, in the process of lighting a cigar with a glowing piece of kindling. He drew on it, and the smoke wafted across to her, its aroma recalling to Cara the memory of his arms around her and the demands of his lips. "Good evening," she said.

Jeth turned to her, the gray eyes beneath the dark brows steady and assessing as she stood in the center of the room with her arms calmly at her sides. He looked as formidable as she had feared. The light from the fireplace cast its shadows over the granite face, throwing in relief the high cheekbones and the cold, metallic brilliance of his eyes. He had changed from the black range wear of the afternoon to casual slacks and shirt in a deep blue. Black boots of superb leather caught the flames in their sheen and added inches to his already intimidating height.

The rancher removed the cigar from his mouth and reached on the mantel for a glass of heavy cut crystal. "Welcome to La

Tierra Conquistada," he said, without meaning it, and lifted his glass in a mock toast. The amber liquor glowed like liquid fire.

"Thank you," Cara returned in a neutral tone.

Jeth's lip curled mirthlessly. "I see you survived Bill's jeep ride."

"Yes. It was...typical of the welcome I expected."

"Then I'm glad we didn't disappoint you, Miss Martin."

"I doubt that you could do that, Mr. Langston."

Their gazes struck and sparked, like the opening parry of swords in battle. Finally Jeth walked to his desk and said amiably, "Sit down, Miss Martin, sit down. This is likely to be a long conversation."

"I hope not," Cara rejoined briskly. "I'm very tired."

"In that case a glass of wine would be in order. I'm aware that you do not drink hard liquor." Ignoring her faint look of surprise, he pressed a button on his desk and indicated with a motion of his cigar that she was to take a leather chair opposite his desk. Cara sat down on the edge of it. Her nerve endings were beginning to quiver. The subtly patronizing tone of his voice sent unpleasant tingles down her spine. Perhaps the wine would ease the tension gripping her neck and shoulders.

Jeth sat down and leaned indolently back in his sumptuous chair, the cigar in one hand, the fingers of his other toying with the glass on his desk. The diamonds in the black-faced ring winked derisively at her.

"Well, Miss Martin, how do you like your room? Adequate in size, I hope?"

"Yes, indeed. It's a lovely room, very feminine. I—it seems to have been decorated for someone special. Was it?"

"No one in particular, Miss Martin. It's for female guests."

In any other household, the statement would have been innocuous, but Jeth's meaning did not escape her, and he had not meant it to. He took a draw on the cigar, hooding his eyes against the smoke and observing with cold amusement the two bright spots Cara felt flare to her cheeks. *Devil!* she thought, acknowledging in spite of herself that many women would find his type of rugged virility and wolfish lean looks irresistible. No doubt the guest room she occupied was seldom vacant. "How kind of you to let me have it, Mr. Langston," she returned with equanimity. "I hope I won't be inconveniencing any of your women guests."

"You won't be, Miss Martin. I'll have no trouble finding a room to their liking when they visit."

Her cheeks glowed brighter at this rejoinder, and she was relieved that Fiona entered just then with a tray bearing her glass of wine. "*Gracias*, Fiona," said Jeth as the housekeeper bent down to let Cara take it from the tray.

"*De nada*, Patrón," murmured Fiona and she left the room on silent feet.

Jeth sipped his drink while he waited for Cara to try the wine. She knew vintages, and this one was excellent. The bouquet tingled her nostrils pleasurably, and she said, "How very nice," in honest appreciation after she had taken a generous sip.

"I'm glad you like it, Miss Martin. I've ordered a case for your enjoyment while you are here, knowing you to be quite a connoisseur of wines."

Cara showed her surprise. That was thoughtful of him, she granted. "But how could you possibly know that if, as you say, Ryan never mentioned me to you?"

"Well, now, Miss Martin," drawled Jeth, reaching for a brown folder that had been in evidence all the while on his desk, "one of the advantages of wealth is that it provides the means to find out about one's enemies."

A detective! He had hired a detective!

Cara placed the wineglass carefully on the slate portion of the desk's gleaming surface before standing up. The fury mounting within her did not affect the crystal clarity of her next words. "How dare you, Mr. Langston! How dare you pry into my private life!"

"I will dare anything I choose when it comes to you, Miss Martin. When I say anything, you'd better believe it, so sit down like a good girl before I prove that, too, is an open book for my enjoyment and...perusal."

Cara sat down, violet eyes flooded with anger and dismay. They shot daggers at him while, unperturbed, Jeth opened the folder and glanced at several pages before enlightening her of their contents. "I understand that your parents died within the same year when you were still in college, Miss Martin. Is that right?"

Cara did not reply. She picked up the wineglass and defiantly pushed herself back into the supple comfort of the leather chair. Why should she care what he knew about her background? There was nothing in it to incriminate her further.

"I don't blame you for not responding, Miss Martin," Jeth said understandingly. "I can appreciate their loss must be painful to you. Let's push on to other areas. Your family incurred a large number of debts, which were left to you upon their deaths. Your father, it would appear, thought working for a living far too common a responsibility for the blue-blooded aesthete that he was. He preferred to live off the fortune made by his forebears, and when that ran out, to live on credit." Here Jeth paused but did not lift his eyes from the file. Cara interpreted the lull as an opportunity to defend her family and refute what he was reading. She had been right guessing that he would hold her parents in contempt. She chose to remain silent.

"Since your father did not take the precaution of providing life insurance, you were left virtually penniless. You took it upon yourself," Jeth went on, "to clear your family's financial name rather than declare bankruptcy—very noble of you—and you worked very hard for several years as a librarian, which I understand is your second choice of vocations. Gradually the mountain of debts began to be whittled down. In that time you lived frugally, allowing yourself few luxuries—" Here Jeth glanced up at Cara and let his gaze linger pointedly on her expensive attire. "And then," he continued smoothly, "you met my brother..." He contemplated her again, the affable manner gone, the pupils contracting into two deadly omens of danger.

Cara stiffened in her chair. "What are you implying?"

"I'm not implying anything, Miss Martin. I'm *stating* that you saw my brother as a way to pay off your debts. You were suddenly tired of living in a one-room apartment. You were tired of your old clothes and your old car and of trying to stretch each paycheck to make ends meet. You knew Ryan was dying when you met him. You learned how much he respected integrity. God knows he'd seen little of it in his lifetime, especially from women. How cunning of you to make him think that you were too highly principled to let him pay your debts while he lived, but you sure as hell made sure he would pay them after his death, didn't you?"

"No!" Cara denied, jumping up from the chair. "Those are terrible, unjust accusations! I didn't know Ryan was dying! I had no—" She had begun to say that she had no knowledge about the will, but she could not defend herself too strongly. She had to be careful in the heat of these confrontations not to blurt out why she was here. Cara moistened her lips. "Mr. Langston, I know it looks like that, but—"

"Where did you get that outfit you're wearing, Miss Martin?"

Cara looked askance at him. What did that have to do with anything? "I beg your pardon?"

"Ryan bought it for you, didn't he, as well as a"—he consulted a sheet in the dossier—"sable-lined raincoat that I believe you wore upon your arrival here. Isn't that correct?"

Cara stared at him, stricken speechless. How cleanly the noose slipped over her head, just like the one thrown over the head of the hapless horse this afternoon.

"I have nothing to say to you," she declared at last. "You may believe what you like." How could she convince him that Ryan had insisted on buying her the clothes? That she alone would continue to pay her family's debts with money she earned with her own hands? That she had no more intention of using La Tierra Conquistada to pay off what was her obligation than she could fly to the moon without a rocket. She would not waste her breath trying to tell this galling, overbearing, full-of-himself land baron *that*!

The wine on her empty stomach had made her tipsy, she realized, as she set the wineglass down. "Good night, Mr. Langston. This interview is over."

"No, it isn't, Miss Martin, and if you don't sit down, I will come around this desk and make you sit down."

"You do, and I will scream bloody murder, you rude, arrogant...jerk! How somebody like you could be related to Ryan Langston should be documented as another wonder of the world. Not that anyone would be in the least interested outside Texas, which, in case you do not know, is not the end-all, be-all universe!"

Was she reeling? She rather thought so, because the desk and the dreadful man behind it had begun to weave before her blurred vision. The big leather chair, even as she looked at it, was all at once empty, and she wondered where the awful man could have gone when suddenly there he was beside her, taking her arm rather gently and lowering her into the chair. "When did you eat last?" he demanded gruffly.

"Last night, I think." She pursed her soft lips in complex thought. "No, I had a bite of melon this morning. Why do you ask?" She looked up in sudden suspicion at the tall form.

Was it her imagination, or were the gray eyes actually glinting with something related to humor? "Because you are drunk on a partial glass of wine. Finish it, Miss Martin, while we talk some more. Then you may go have your dinner. Fiona will bring a tray to your room."

An urgent question occurred to her. "I won't be expected to stay in my room, will I? I will be allowed to come and go about the house?" Not to do so was a prospect even bleaker than any she had imagined about living at La Tierra.

Jeth sat down on the edge of his desk near her. His eyes roamed over her at will, taking in the clean-lined beauty of her features, the glowing hair, the round fullness of her breasts softly outlined by the cashmere sweater. Cara was concentrating on her wine. He had said to drink it. What was there about him that commanded and others did?

"You may come and go as you like, Miss Martin, but stay away from the working compound. That little exercise this afternoon should be proof to you that you invite disaster wherever you are."

"I—I'm sorry about this afternoon." Cara bit her lip, keeping her eyes on her glass. "I had no idea that I would be the cause of those horses bolting. I was so far away."

"Not so far that you couldn't take the men's minds off their work, Miss Martin, something that I don't intend to allow while you're here. Cowboys suffer accidents when they're distracted; so do animals. I don't want you anywhere near the breaking corrals in the next few days, not even watching from the terrace."

"Is that what you're going to do to those horses you brought in this afternoon—break them for riding?"

"Yes. We need them for the roundup that will be taking place in the next few days."

Cara couldn't imagine why she said aloud the thought that next popped into her head. She did not think it was the wine that provoked her impudence but rather the way Jeth Langston sat on the desk, handing out orders to her like some feudal lord. "How unfortunate for you," she said innocently, "that you lost that horse you so had your heart set on capturing. His name says a lot about him. Devil's Own, isn't it?"

The sudden stillness in him communicated itself to her, a coiling tension that had the potential to unleash like a whip. "Watch it, Miss Martin," Jeth cautioned, his voice soft as a feather along her spine, raising goose bumps.

"Oh, I intend to," she assured him, deliberately ignoring his meaning. "Next time I'll be prepared for the punch behind this marvelous wine."

Jeth observed the bewitchingly beautiful face she turned up to him. A muscle along his jaw twitched. With great control, he reached down and took the glass from her hand. "You'd better leave now," he advised. "Go on up to your room. I'll have Fiona bring your dinner up immediately."

"How kind of you," said Cara demurely, giving him a smile prompted more by the alcohol than by any sincerity. He followed her to the door, but at it she thought of something and turned unexpectedly. "Mr. Langston—oh!"

She found herself caught in his arms. He held her steady against an immense, well-remembered chest and looked down at her almost indulgently. "Yes, Miss Martin, what is it?"

"Mr. Langston, where is Ryan buried?"

The arms fell from her immediately, and she nearly fell against the heavy doors. "At La Tierra," he informed her coldly, "where he should have died."

That night Cara slept deeply but fitfully. Her dreams see-sawed between two fuzzy realms in which she heard the whinnying lament of horses mixed with the cry of seagulls. Ryan appeared often. Each time he did, she cried his name in delight and ran excitedly after him down a long sandy shore only to have him disappear in the waves that washed his footprints from the sand. "Ryan! Ryan!" she called time and time again, flailing her arms in disappointment and bereavement. Once when she cried, someone else came to her, someone whose shadowy form hovered over her and spoke her name softly. The form bent and released her from the tentacles pulling her down into deep warm water where she wept for a nameless fulfillment eluding her heart.

The next morning Cara woke to a room bathed in sunlight. She had forgotten to pull the draperies the night before, which wasn't surprising when she remembered how exhaustedly she had climbed into bed. She lay in the warm nest of covers trying to remember where she was, and the events that had brought her here. The last vestiges of her dreams faded away and left her with the feeling that she had wrestled with them more than she had actually slept. Her neck and face felt sticky, as if she had cried sometime in the night.

Almost immediately after swinging her feet to the yellow rug she heard the sounds of horses and men. "They're breaking the horses today," she remembered, and recalled that Jeth Langston had forbidden her to go anywhere near the breaking pens.

"Fine," she said aloud to Ryan's photograph on the bedside table. "That leaves me free to explore the rest of the ranch without running into your brother!"

After she had dressed in slacks and tailored shirt, she wondered what to do about breakfast. Her dinner the night before had been excellent, but she had been too tired and woozy, she remembered ruefully, to eat much, so she was hungry this morning. Will I be allowed to eat outside my room? she wondered. Then a chilling discovery presented itself. She remembered with certainty leaving the photograph on the mantel just before going out to investigate the origin of that strange rumble. She had not moved it since, of that she was positive. Fiona had not even glanced at it when she came for her last night.

Then what was it doing on her bedside table?

Puzzled, Cara pulled on a sweater matching her blue slacks, then went out into the wide hall. Now that she did not have the disapproving Fiona at her shoulder, she could inspect her surroundings leisurely. Light streamed in through the series of arched windows in the white stucco wall facing her room, and she went to one and peered out. The layout below was as she should have expected. Indeed, La Tierra's big house had been built in the tradition of a Spanish grandee's hacienda, for its inner wall surrounded a tiled, verdant courtyard, enormous in size.

An Olympic-sized swimming pool, its clear blue water and deck of colorful tiles twinkling in the fresh morning sunlight, commanded the largest area. Set back from it was a cabana with a red Spanish-tiled roof like that of the house, and nearby was an entertainment area with a stage. Across on the far side was a commodious brick pit for barbecuing, its gleaming enamel hood the same bright yellow as that of the table umbrellas dotting the deck. Other matching patio furniture and an abundance of tropical plants providing greenery and shade completed what in Cara's mind was an opulent picture of Southwestern relaxation.

The pool reminded Cara that Jeth had once aspired to become an Olympic champion, a dream that had forever been deferred when he'd had to assume responsibility for La Tierra and a little brother named Ryan. Ryan had told her that Jeth still swam religiously every day, no matter what the weather, which accounted for the corded, well-toned body of the man and the lack of a pale forehead due to the constant wearing of a hat in the sun.

She followed the horseshoe corridor to the other wing, then came back to stand before heavy double doors leading to a room the width of the top floor. This has to be *his* room, she thought, wishing that her room was in the other wing so that she would not have to hear him pass by her door each night. She had not heard him last night, apparently having fallen asleep before he came to bed.

Going down the stairs, Cara encountered a fresh-faced young Mexican woman who actually smiled at her. She was carrying an armload of fresh sheets and towels. "*Buenos dias,* señorita," the young woman greeted her, and Cara's face showed her pleasure at the first friendliness she had been shown.

"Good morning to you," she responded cheerfully, but when she would have introduced herself, the young woman hurried away up the stairs as if she had been warned about speaking to the yellow-haired intruder.

Ignoring the sharp little pain from the rebuff, Cara went on down the stairs in the direction she guessed the kitchen to be.

She found Fiona at the gleaming kitchen counter busily chopping peppers and onions. The tantalizing smell of coffee came to her. "Good morning, Fiona," she offered politely. "May I help myself to coffee?"

For answer, Fiona pointed with her knife to a large stainless pot on the stove. "Thank you," Cara said, and then, "Fiona, could you tell me what's expected of me concerning my meals? Do I have to eat in my room or may I eat here in the kitchen?

I'm quite sure—er—El Patrón would not care for my company at mealtimes."

When Fiona did not answer, Cara persisted. "It would be silly for you to have to climb those stairs bringing my meals to me. As a matter of fact, I can even prepare my own—"

That statement got the attention of the impassive-faced Fiona. The eyes she turned on Cara had fire in them. "*My* kitchen!" she declared, pointing the sharp knife at herself for emphasis. "Nobody cooks here but me. You may eat here, but you—you don't cook here!"

Cara smiled at the feisty little woman and tried what little Spanish she knew. "*Gracias. Yo comprendo.*"

Without asking her, the housekeeper prepared for Cara a fluffy omelet containing a sharp Mexican cheese and topped with a spicy sauce made from onions and fresh tomatoes and peppers. With it were a small breakfast steak, so tender that Cara could cut it with a fork, and steaming, freshly made flour tortillas.

"Oh my," sighed Cara appreciatively when she had finished, "you cook as superbly as you keep this house, Fiona."

Fiona did not respond to Cara's compliment. She had kept her back to the Bostonian all the while she had been eating, but Cara sensed the woman was aware of every bite she took.

The housekeeper was obviously in charge of all matters pertaining to household personnel and maintenance, with the kitchen the office from which she dispensed her orders. Several Mexican workmen came into the kitchen by the back door while Cara was eating. They raised brows when they saw her, then nodded curtly and addressed Fiona in Spanish. The same was true of the maids who wandered in and out. Pointedly ignoring Cara, they discussed in their native tongue their duties for the day as well as, she was certain, their thoughts and opinions about the intruder who sat at the kitchen table.

With a sigh, Cara took her coffee through a swinging door into a large formal dining room. Again the icy atmosphere of the white walls and gray-tiled floors oppressed her. What a remote, cold, unfriendly house, she thought. No wonder Ryan had called his home a tomb.

The dining room let out through carved double doors into an alcove that probably had been meant for a sitting room. The furniture, though costly, appeared never used. Even the spring sun shining through a wide arched window could not dispel the pervasively Spartan atmosphere.

Cara strolled across the entrance hall to the living room she had passed through last night to Jeth's study. Her eyes were taking in the ample proportions of the austere room when an object in a far corner made her gasp with disbelief. A Steinway! A real, honest-to-goodness Steinway! She set her coffee down on a marble-topped table and flew to the majestic grand piano that sat augustly in a pool of sunlight.

"Oh…" she breathed, hardly daring to believe her eyes. Reverently, she pushed the cover from the keyboard. Her fingers gently touched the ivory keys without striking them, savoring the moment when she would summon forth the quality of tone for which this aristocrat of all pianos was renowned. Cara pulled out the bench and sat down. She flexed her hands—it had been a long time since she had played—then ran her fingers up and down the keyboard in a series of chromatic scales to limber both her fingers and the tone of the piano.

Borne away on the strains of a Chopin concerto, she had only been playing a short while when suddenly there appeared beside the bench an incensed and ferocious Fiona. Cara looked up quizzically, barely removing her hands before the housekeeper vehemently pulled the lid down over the keyboard. "What's the matter with you?" Cara cried, beginning to get angry, too.

"Señora Langston's!" the housekeeper explained explosively. "No touch! Señora Langston's! Not Ryan's whore!"

Cara was up from the bench instantly, her body shaking in rage at the presumption of this woman to call her such a name, but more importantly to deny her the exquisite release the piano would have provided from the horrors of her confinement.

Cara faced the housekeeper levelly. "Don't you ever do that to me again, Fiona," she said in a quiet voice that carried conviction. "And don't you ever refer to me by that name again—ever!" Leaving the housekeeper standing stonily at the piano, Cara marched from the room and up the stairs. Once in her room, trembling with fury, she searched in the closet for a warm jacket. She saw that her room had been tidied, the bed made. She could still hear sounds of loud activity coming from the corrals, but she had to get out of this house. Surely there was somewhere on this vast ranch where she could go without causing trouble.

Skirting away from the house, Cara walked in the direction of a tree-shaded rise of land some distance away. Hands in pockets, face up to welcome the sun and the dry, brisk wind that blew across the plains, she tried to deal with the aching disappointment that welled inside her. How could she live in a house with a Steinway and not play it? It was a crime to regard an instrument like that more as a monument to the dead than as a source of joy to the living.

Until now she had not realized how much she missed the piano that once graced her childhood home. On it she had learned to play the music that would later bring such solace to her life. The day the Steinway had been sold, she walked the beach for hours, mourning the loss of an old friend.

Cara was sickened, too, by the encounter with Fiona. She had hoped she could come to care for the irascible little woman whose industry and devotion to La Tierra impressed her. She doubted now whether the housekeeper could ever be induced to like the outsider from Boston, the woman she thought of contemptuously as Ryan's whore.

Cara reached the foot of the small hill and was intrigued by its number of trees and lush carpet of young grass when the surrounding land stretched bare and treeless. Staring up at its top, she glimpsed between the green, feathery branches of the mesquite trees something that looked like a wrought-iron fence, and her breath caught. Jeth's answer came back to her from the night before when she had asked where Ryan was buried: "At La Tierra—where he should have died."

Cara, certain of what she would find, climbed the hill to the black iron enclosure of a small, private cemetery. New spring grass grew tenderly between the stones to the dead, and Cara gave a sudden, startled cry when she saw the fresh earth that indicated a new grave. A monument, yet unbleached by wind and storms and time, rested at its head. Cara stumbled forward calling, "Ryan! I've come, Ryan, I've come."

Chapter Six

She did not know how long she had sat on the ground with knees drawn to her chest, forehead resting on folded arms, before she became aware of a pair of black boots and silver spurs planted apart on the other side of Ryan's grave.

"Oh!" Cara exclaimed, caught by surprise, and blinked up at the dark countenance of Jeth Langston. He frowned at her from beneath the firm set of his black Stetson, and for the first few seconds she did not know who or what he was. With the sun behind him, he looked menacing in black leather chaps and vest, and she thought at first that he was some angry god come to wreak his vengeance.

Cara got to her feet without his offering to help and braced herself for what was to come. When neither spoke after several seconds, she offered lightly, "You go first."

"Miss Martin, you cannot seem to stay out of trouble."

"Well, so it seems. I'm sure you're referring to my run-in with Fiona over the Steinway a while ago. She must have gone immediately to tell on me, although I will say that surprises me. I would have bet that she was one to fight her own battles."

"You would have won that bet, Miss Martin. Fiona did not *tattle* on you. I overheard the two of you when I came to see who was playing my mother's piano."

Cara brushed at the sand adhering to the seat of her slacks. "So which am I to be strung up for—playing your mother's piano or insulting Fiona's sense of propriety?"

"Neither, Miss Martin," Jeth answered in cold rebuke. "But for an intelligent girl, your willful ignorance of the shaky position you're in at La Tierra is astounding."

"I understand clearly the shaky position I'm in—I saw only that it was a Steinway," Cara defended soberly. "It didn't occur to me that it might have been your mother's."

"In that case, don't take liberties with the possessions of my house, Miss Martin, not unless I give you permission. Is that clear?"

"Quite," said Cara, finding it hard to look at him against the light. Her eyes stung miserably. She wanted to believe the sun or the dry, cold air responsible, but her honesty would not permit it. There was something about Jeth that transcended her growing fear of him, that forced her to admit that he was a man who stirred strange and bewildering emotions within her that she did not understand. "Is that all?" she asked him.

"No, Miss Martin, it is not." The words were exactly delivered. "Since this game is being played with a deck stacked in favor of the house—and since you can't seem to figure out the obvious for yourself—I am going to give you a little advice. You need Fiona. Don't antagonize her. You can avoid it if you understand that she reveres the Langstons, especially the memory of my mother. She is enraged that an outsider like you should try to usurp what belongs to the family. When you sat down at that piano this morning, when you began to play her patrona's most loved possession, you committed what to her amounted to a sacrilege—"

"I get the picture!" Cara broke in, unable to bear any more. She turned her head away so that he could not see the dejection sweeping through her. Hands in pockets, jacket billowing open, slight form buffeted by the wind, Cara presented a vulnerable picture to the tall, powerful man looking down at her. He saw how the sun played in the waves of her tossed hair, exposed the clear purity of her skin and the tender curve of her throat. He saw her blink at the sting of tears she was too proud to shed.

Jeth said in a less steely tone, "Miss Martin, sell Ryan's share to me and leave La Tierra. We'll call it a draw, and you will have heard the last of me. You would have no need to ever fear me again."

Cara shook her head obstinately. "No."

"Then you're asking to be broken, you know," he warned her gently, "just like all the other enemies of La Tierra have been."

"Rather like those poor creatures you brought down from the mountains will be, I suppose," Cara remarked with distaste, thinking of the proud, spirited horses who right now were feeling the grip of saddles, the dig of spurs.

"Not at all. Here at La Tierra we're rough with horses, but never punishing. With you, I would be both. Once our horses have earned their yearly keep during the roundup, they're set free to roam until the next one. But you, Miss Martin, I would never free to enjoy the spoils of your relationship to Ryan. I would make sure you carried the brand of La Tierra all of your life."

Cara, who had kept her head averted, faced him defiantly, her blood running cold. "You would never get the land back."

"Oh, yes, I would, Miss Martin. Have no delusions about that." He turned to go.

"There is one horse that got away from you, that doesn't wear your brand—one that you won't be breaking for the roundup!" The words were out before she could stop them.

Shocked at her outburst, she watched in dismay as the rancher paused, then turned slowly. His eyes gleamed with surprise and the thrill of challenge.

"You, Cara Martin, will not be so fortunate. Am I to take that as your final answer to my request that you leave La Tierra?"

"Yes," she said quickly. She would give anything to take back her taunt. What a fool she had been to ruffle his king-of-the-walk feathers. What could she gain from it?

"Then I'm looking forward to the pleasure of your company under my roof, Miss Martin. This evening you will have dinner with me. Wear something red, a most appropriate color for you in more ways than one. I'm sure that among all those dresses Ryan bought you there is something suitable."

"No," Cara said firmly.

"You will if you want to eat. Afterward you will play for me. Come to my study at seven and we'll have a drink. Now if you'll excuse me—" He touched his hat brim in mock respect. "I've wasted enough time for one day." Once again he turned to go.

"Mr. Langston?"

With a sigh of impatience the rancher paused, keeping the broad back to her. "Yes, Miss Martin?"

"Is...this place off-limits too?"

Without turning he answered, "No, Miss Martin, not unless I'm here."

Cara watched him descend the hill with supple ease to the untethered bay waiting patiently below. The man was so sure of himself, so sure of her. She was sure of neither.

Cara spent the rest of the day in her room. She wrote a letter to Harold St. Clair assuring him that she was still in one piece, infusing her comments with a humor she did not feel. Afterward she thumbed through a book she had brought with her on conversational Spanish, thinking that if nothing else was gained from the year, she could at least learn a new language. But her attention persisted in wandering, and after trying to read a few pages she put the book down and went outside to sit on the terrace in the sun. Her thoughts drifted to Ryan. "Do you trust me?" he had asked as he lay dying. Even now, with all of her heart, she did. But why had he left her his share of La Tierra? Why had he made her promise to come here, where he knew she would be at the mercy of his brother's vengeance? Had Ryan hoped to play matchmaker? But that was preposterous under the circumstances. He had known how she felt about men like his brother, and he would certainly have foreseen how his brother would regard and react toward her. The situation was impossible.

The lunch hour came and passed, and Cara's hunger pains reminded her of the evening ahead. Her pride rebelled that in order to eat she had to join Jeth Langston for dinner, but she knew that the rancher was perfectly capable of letting her go hungry. Cara flipped through the dresses hanging in her closet and found the red dinner dress she had worn in Dallas. Angry at her cowardice, she admitted she did not have the courage not to wear it.

Late in the afternoon when she was tired of her room, she took a stroll down the horseshoe hall to the other wing. A door was open to one of the bedrooms, and since she knew that no one occupied this floor but herself and Jeth, she peered in.

"Ryan's room!" she exclaimed to the lofty silence, for even though it was a cavernous room, it wasn't totally devoid of the warm, vital presence of the man who had once lived here. At one end was a small library she knew Jeth had ordered built for his brother when Ryan became interested in law. The shelves still contained some of his books.

The room echoed a loneliness that struck an unhealed

wound, and she left quickly, closing the door behind her. She felt closer to Ryan at the cemetery where the wind blew freely across the wide Texas plains.

A splash in the swimming pool brought her to one of the arched windows overlooking the courtyard. Looking down on the pool, she saw a long, tanned figure swimming underwater. A dark head surfaced, wet and sleek as a seal's. She watched him begin a routine of laps, cutting the water effortlessly with long, powerful arms, until suddenly she had to back away from the window, unable to bear watching him any longer. Her heart had begun a fierce beat. A strange longing throbbed in her stomach, forcing her to lean against the cool surface of the stucco wall to steady her breath. A sense of helpless anger flooded her. Was not even her own body to be an ally in this alien house against the enemy below? Would it, too, seek to destroy her?

At precisely one minute until seven, Cara descended the stairs. She had not heard Jeth come up to his room from the pool, but she did hear him go down. He had passed her door as she was finishing dressing, and her heartbeat stilled when she heard the firm tread of his boots striking the tiled corridor.

Not even the knowledge that she looked her best in the red dress that Harold had admired could inspire Cara with confidence. She drew in deeply as she knocked on one of the double doors, and pressed to her breast the framed photograph that she had brought with her from Boston.

Jeth himself opened the door. He was dressed in black tonight, the Western cut of his attire emphasizing the broad shoulders and trim waist and hips. With the lamplight behind him, he filled the doorway with a sinister presence. "Well, good evening, Miss Martin," he drawled mockingly, the cool gray eyes marking the red dress, then sliding down her from head to foot. "How nice of you to come."

"Did I have a choice?"

"No," he said dryly, "but let us observe the amenities as if you did." He moved aside just enough to allow her room to pass. "I suggest you sit by the fire. A norther is coming out of the Panhandle and will be here before we sit down to dinner."

Cara was happy to do so. She was chilled through and through, and her knees felt trembly. Taking a seat in one of the two tall-backed chairs flanking the fireplace, she asked, "When does spring actually arrive in Texas?"

Jeth had gone to the bar where a silver wine cooler waited with the exposed neck of what Cara assumed was a bottle of the wine she had been served the night before. She watched as he withdrew a crystal goblet from a bed of ice, then uncorked the napkin-wrapped bottle. "That depends on what part of Texas you're asking about," he informed her, pouring a clear, sparkling stream of wine into the glass. He refilled his own with bourbon and brought both to the fire.

"Thank you," she said, taking care not to touch his fingers when he handed her the glass. "You were saying?"

"Texas is a big state, Miss Martin. In our coastal areas, spring has already arrived. In the Panhandle it won't come until the last of May. Here we'll be lucky to see our last frost by Easter."

"Texas can be quite overwhelming." She smiled politely, hoping she didn't sound critical. The state had begun to fascinate her, and she wanted to know more about it.

"Like its people?" Jeth asked with a trace of mockery, settling in the chair opposite her.

"I never found Ryan overwhelming," she said. "That reminds me. I brought this for you. It meant a great deal to Ryan. He kept it on the mantel of his town house." She handed Jeth the photograph.

Jeth reached for it, the firelight flashing on the diamond

brand in his ring. "Yes," he mused, studying it. "I saw this last night."

Cara straightened in her chair. "You were the one who moved it! Then—then you were the shadow in my dream... You were the one who...rescued me."

"Did I?" Jeth raised a cynical eyebrow. "We fight such awesome demons in our dreams, don't we? You were crying out in your sleep. I was on my way to my room and heard you. You sounded desperate, so I went in. You were wound in the covers, so I loosened them. That's when I saw this picture."

Cara couldn't resist saying in surprise, "I'm amazed that you bothered."

Immersed in the study of the picture, Jeth said, "I might not have except that you were crying Ryan's name over and over. I've had a few of those nights lately myself."

"Of course you have," Cara said quietly, feeling sympathy for him. She knew how lonely it was to be facing a future with no family whatever. Ryan had been right about Jeth. This man needed a loving wife who would give him children to make this austere house a home.

Jeth placed the picture on the wide stone hearth, then stunned her by saying, "You have beautiful breasts. You are well-endowed for someone of your small frame, aren't you?"

Remembering the flimsy nightgown she had pulled on last night in her exhausted haste to get to bed, Cara choked on the wine, almost spilling some of it on the red dress. "How dare you!" she sputtered, holding the dripping glass over the hearth. Jeth produced another of the white lawn handkerchiefs like the one he had given her in Dallas, which she had not yet returned. Taking it, she said indignantly, "You had no right to—to look me over while I slept!"

"Why not?" he asked calmly. "And Miss Martin, don't use

the phrase 'how dare you' again. You are in my state, on my land, in my house, and I will dare anything I damn well please. Thank you for the picture. Tell me about Ryan. Were you with him when he died?"

Cara's head swam, and not from the wine. This man had the power to provoke the most quixotic feelings within her. In the space of a few moments, he had roused her fear, hatred, sympathy, anger, and now she found herself wanting desperately to comfort him, to tell him how much he had been loved by Ryan—that, like him, she did not understand why his brother had not told him about his illness, why he had left to her what rightfully belonged to him. But she could not share those thoughts with this skeptical man, and so she carefully took a sip of her wine and answered simply, "Yes, I was with him, Mr. Langston. He was in some pain, and had to be sedated the last few days of his life. But at the end he was very lucid. He spoke of you often, and I—I know he loved you very much."

Jeth tossed off his drink in one swallow. A smile, cold as an Atlantic swell, curved the well-shaped mouth. "He loved you more, Cara Martin, or he would never have stayed in Boston to die—or left half of La Tierra to you."

Cara had no reply to this. She sat in uneasy silence, fingering the small seagull charm on the gold chain she wore with her single strand of pearls. When she offered no response, Jeth asked abruptly, "Is that the red dress you wore with Harold St. Clair the other night?"

"Why—why, yes. How did you know?"

"There's little about you that I don't know, Miss Martin—or can't accurately guess. I'm sure he thought you looked ravishing in it."

"He liked it, yes," Cara replied evenly, becoming apprehensive about the direction of this conversation.

92

"And that seagull you keep reaching for—he gave that to you, too, didn't he?"

"It was a token of friendship, Mr. Langston—something to remind me of home."

"I'm sure. And the pearls? Did he give those to you or were they from Ryan?"

"Neither. These pearls came from the Orient on one of the first clipper ships over a century ago. They've been in my family ever since. They were given to me on my sixteenth birthday."

"Ah." Jeth sipped his drink. "You've come a long way since sweet sixteen, not in years perhaps, but for sure in kisses and... other skills. Did you sleep with Ryan?"

Now that was a hell of a question! he reproached himself. Why had he asked her that? Of course she had slept with Ryan. There was no way his brother wouldn't have had her in his bed. Yet part of him wanted to hear her deny it, while the other—the part of him that tolerated no threat to his empire—knew that such a denial would continue to seal her doom.

Cara began hesitantly, wondering how honestly to answer him without compromising her further in his eyes. "I—yes, we did sleep together, Mr. Langston, but not in the way you imagine. Ryan was very ill. We shared the same bed, but not to—to make love. It was just a matter of comforting each other, of being near each other through the long nights. We used to joke about how no one—certainly not you—would believe that we could do that and not—and not—"

Cara fell silent as she sensed the dangerous stillness that had possessed Jeth. In the richly black clothes, his eyes upon her steady and penetrating, the powerful body tensed in deep attention, he reminded her of a jungle cat watching his prey. "I'm telling you the truth!" she declared, the prolonged silence snapping at her nerve endings.

"You're trying to sell me a bunch of bull!" Jeth thundered, getting up to return to the bar. His back to her, Jeth in frustration sent his empty glass skimming along the polished surface until it came to rest in a padded leather corner. God. How could lips like those, eyes that guileless, concoct such a story and expect him to believe it? Since she was not a naive or stupid woman, she must be very sure of herself to take him on.

"Why can't you believe me?" she pleaded to his back, her voice very soft and small, projecting still the role of the innocent. He sighed.

"Because I knew my brother, Miss Martin. He would never have kept his hands off you. Why would he want to?" From the way she rose to meet him, clutching the handkerchief, he must present a terrible sight.

"He never touched me!" she cried as Jeth approached her. "You know, Mr. Langston, I was very hurt when you told me that Ryan had not mentioned me to you. I wondered why not. We were the best of friends, in the deepest, finest way. But now I can understand why he didn't discuss our relationship with you. A man like you isn't capable of understanding the way it was between us."

"You're frightened, Miss Martin. I wonder why. Is it because you think I might harm you? But I promised I wouldn't hurt you, remember? Do you think I'm not a man of my word?"

"I—oh, I believe you're a man of your word, but you are... misguided. You have the wrong impression about Ryan and me."

"Why should it matter to you that I think Ryan was your lover?"

"Well, because he wasn't!" Her eyes, he saw, had taken on the color of smoky lavender and widened in the alarm of an animal being circled by a predator. "I don't know why it's important to me that you believe that, but it is!"

"Don't you know why, Miss Martin?" Jeth's voice was as smooth as the sliding of a snake across her skin. Before she could register his next intention, he had reached out and pulled her into the inescapable confines of his arms.

Cara struggled like a wild thing caught in a trap, but it was too late. Jeth's embrace pinned her arms to her sides, and the boots protected his shins from the kick of her evening shoes.

"It would seem that it has become necessary one more time to make clear to you that I know what your game is, Miss Martin—why you are so hell-bent on staying here."

"You promised!" Cara choked, her heart beating like a maddened bird.

"I promised not to hurt you. Am I hurting you?"

"This is physical abuse."

"Nonsense. The denial of what you want is physical abuse. Come here."

His dark head was descending as he spoke, and Cara, held steady by the grip of his hand entwined in her hair, could not escape a kiss she knew was meant to punish and humiliate. She squeezed her eyes tightly and compressed her lips before he could reach them. Her hands gripped his back, intending to dig nails of protest into his flesh. She waited. The kiss did not come. A harsh chuckle reached her ears. "Miss Martin, you are the world's greatest actress."

The violet eyes flew open to find the kiss still hovering, the sensuous lips quirked in a slight grin.

"Is all of this necessary?" she whispered. "Can't we just have a nice dinner?"

"Are you hungry?" he asked softly, kissing each side of her mouth.

"Very," she answered, trying to ignore the traitorous flutter beginning in the pit of her stomach. Her heavy lashes lowered, and Jeth drew her deeper into the cradle of his shoulder. The contact of his breath on her earlobe sent a shock of awareness through her. Warm and sensuous, the fingers that he thrust through her hair moved to cushion her neck for the gentle play of his lips over her features. Slowly Cara began to yield to the soothing caress of his other hand moving down to her hips.

"Then let me feed you," Jeth suggested huskily, as his hand moved down her back. Expertly he clasped her to the waiting convexity of his body.

Cara yelped in dismay, but not before he had felt her response. "Cara—" Jeth said her name like a prayer, finding her mouth and drinking of it hungrily, cupping her tightly to him.

Enveloped in the sensual male warmth of him, conscious only of her need for him, Cara could not resist the desire that surged up from the most hidden depths of her being to meet the tide of Jeth's passion. Her fingers dug into his hard-muscled back, not to hurt but to press him closer, closer, with a terrible and urgent craving.

Then, unbelievably—just as she was poised on a crest of incredible longing—the hands that had caressed her with such finesse clamped a grip on her forearms and pushed her violently away.

Surprise exploded within her. Jeth's eyes bore into her with glittering anger. "Now will you deny that you and Ryan were lovers?" he raged. "You're too hot to stay out of many beds, Miss Martin—certainly not Ryan's, so don't ply me with any more Florence Nightingale stories. What really galls me is that you don't even have enough feeling for Ryan's memory to admit that you had an affair with him. You still hope to buy some kind of chance with me if I can be convinced that Ryan never touched you—though what kind of chance only that devious little mind of yours knows. Well you can forget it, Miss Martin. I don't take any man's leavings, not even Ryan's."

In a daze, Cara heard him. How could one human being have this kind of devastating power over another? What is happening to me? she wondered, recognizing the searing pain of grief.

"Cara?" Jeth spoke her name warningly and shook her for her attention. "Whatever role you're playing at now, cut it out, do you hear me?"

"Yes," she answered dully.

"Look at me!" he ordered. Cara lifted dazed eyes. "Tomorrow morning dress warmly in the oldest clothes you have. Come out to the breaking corrals. You are not getting a free ride this year, lady, no matter what you may have hoped. This is a working ranch and everybody works here, including you."

When she said nothing, he left her to open a closet door in the paneled wall, taking out a split-cowhide jacket lined with fleece. He buttoned into it while she watched, then returned to her carrying the fawn Stetson with the black band.

"I won't be joining you for dinner. I seem to have lost my appetite. I hope you haven't. You'll need your stamina tomorrow. Enjoy your meal and the piano, and be at the corrals by eight o'clock. Pleasant dreams."

Cara watched him stride from the room without looking back, much as he had left her the first day they met. At her feet was another of the white handkerchiefs, which, again, she picked up and held to her lips. This time, however, he had left her with the deepest pain and confusion she had ever known.

The next morning Cara threaded through the compound of ranch buildings to the maze of fences she assumed were the breaking corrals. Cowhands were assembled around one huge corral, unmindful of the rising dust and fresh manure that choked the brisk air. As she drew closer, she guessed that over fifty horses were in the enclosure, and standing in their midst, his back to her, was a tall, slim man with a clipboard. He happened to turn as she approached and surprised her with a nod.

She scanned the group of men apprehensively. Nearly all of them were eyeing her, some with boldly inquisitive eyes, others in embarrassment. Where in the world was Jeth? Even his contempt was better than standing awkwardly before the curious gazes of thirty or more strange men.

"Miss Martin?"

Cara turned in relief at the sound of the familiar voice. Jeth had come up behind her, apparently from a long, low building that bore the name "Feedtrough" over its entrance. "Mr. Langston, what am I doing here?" she demanded in a low voice.

"Right now, nothing. In a minute, you'll be working." The cold, clear eyes raked her up and down. "Those are certainly not the kind of clothes you'll be needing for the roundup, Miss Martin. We'll have to do something about that this afternoon, if there's time."

Some of the men were within hearing distance, and she felt their sharp surprise along with the jolt that hit her. "What do you mean?" she asked tensely, determined to keep her composure, but a tremor of foreboding rippled through her. Jeth's face wore the cynically hard expression that she had come to recognize as trouble for her.

"You're going on a roundup with us, Miss Martin—as Leon Sawyer's assistant. He's our cook. The man who usually helps him is in the hospital recovering from an emergency appendectomy. I can't spare a man to replace him, so I've decided that you will go in his place. When Toby gets well enough to ride out, he'll relieve you. But until he does, consider the next month to six weeks of your life reserved."

By now, Cara and Jeth had everyone's attention but the horses. They were cantering about the corral, stirring up dust around the tall man in the center. The men appeared to be busy with ropes and saddles, but Cara knew they were listening. "You can't be serious," she said between her teeth.

"Do I not look serious, Miss Martin?" Jeth took a step closer to her.

Cara restrained an impulse to draw back. "I thought you didn't want me to distract the men."

"You won't. That I can promise you. I've just been to tell Leon the good news. He wasn't any more excited about it than you are, which is too bad because I like to keep the cook happy."

"Mr. Langston, you surely don't mean what you're saying."

"I always mean what I say, Miss Martin, as you will discover to your grief if you decide to sit this one out. Your only alternative is to leave La Tierra—*after* you sign the papers releasing Ryan's half of the ranch."

Cara stared up at him. The sensuous mouth was an adamant line, the gray eyes the color of slate. There was no doubt in her mind that he would force her to go on the roundup. "So that's what this is all about," she said quietly.

"You got it, lady. I'm giving you one more minute of my very valuable time to make up your mind which it's to be. I'll take as your answer either your heading back to the house or going into the Feedtrough to find Leon."

It took Cara less than the minute Jeth gave her to make her decision. With a last defiant look at him, she did an about-face and marched into the Feedtrough.

Chapter Seven

The Feedtrough was the ranch kitchen where food was prepared and served family style to the men who worked for La Tierra. Leon Sawyer, the cook and chuckwagon master, ruled over his spotless domain with an absolute authority that even Jeth Langston took care not to breach. The appendectomy that had claimed Leon's helpmate and dishwasher the afternoon before had left the cook facing the coming roundup in a foul temper.

Cara walked into the Feedtrough to interrupt a profane berating the irascible cook was heaping onto the thin shoulders of a young Mexican cowboy picked as a temporary replacement.

"Now get outta here!" the small, wiry man finished, taking a booted swipe at the fast-retreating backside of the hapless young cowboy. "No-good worthless young pup!" he added, scowling at the swinging back doors through which the cowboy escaped.

Cara struggled not to grin. Leon was exactly as Ryan had described. He was indeed a caricature of the legendary chuckwagon boss of the late-night movies. Behind the ample white apron, the jutting, whiskery chin, the fighting-rooster stance, there had to beat the soft heart of a Gabby Hayes.

"Hello," she said, and Leon spun around on his boot heels

to discover Cara. With eyes as blue and round as robin eggs, he peered at her over the tops of his rimless glasses, dropping a jaw to reveal tobacco-stained teeth. "Who in the Sam Hill holy Moses are you?" he exclaimed.

"Mr. Langston's idea of an assistant for you, I'm afraid," Cara replied with a smile, and extended her hand. "Cara Martin, Mr. Sawyer. He said you were expecting me."

The bottom jaw snapped shut. "Oh, I see..." He gave her hand a swift shake. "You weren't what I was expectin' a'tall. However, young lady, ideas are for usin'. Especially the boss's."

By midmorning Cara found that for all his gruff manners, Leon was her kind of boss. He was an orderly man, accustomed to giving explicit, no-nonsense instructions that Cara's quick intelligence appreciated. She learned at once that the two of them had the double duties of getting the men fed for the next two days as well as preparing La Tierra's modern version of a chuckwagon for the roundup that was to take place the day after tomorrow. By lunchtime the shambles that had been breakfast had been cleared away, and an edge of Leon's temper soothed.

Cara was too busy to be nervous about serving the men or to be conscious of the stares she received when they trooped into the dining room. Each man seemed to have his designated place at one of the tables that surrounded a longer table in the center of the room. Every table was occupied when Jeth and the tall man she had seen in the corral entered with Bill and several others. They took their places at the central table. Jeth and Bill ignored her when she carried in their food, but the tall man again gave her a friendly nod. They were the last to be served, and afterward Cara had to pause for a tired sigh when she went back to the kitchen. Leon, standing at the huge stainless-steel counter, heard her. "I must say, for a li'l un, you got a lot of

work in ya," he said, and Cara flushed with unexpected pleasure. That was probably as close to a compliment as she'd ever
get from the wizened old fellow.

"What do you want me to do now?" she asked him.

"Rest yore feet awhile. Eat somethin'. Then we'll start
packin' the vans."

That afternoon, as she was packing the last pan into a box
for loading, Jeth Langston's big shadow fell across her. She had
pulled her hair back with a string, rolled up the sleeves of her
silk blouse, and was wearing an oversized pair of rubber gloves.
Cara looked up quizzically, aware that her heart had begun to
thump.

"I'm going up to the big house now," he said, "and I want
you to come with me. Leon can carry on from here. One of the
boys will help him serve supper."

Cara knew better than to argue. She pulled off the rubber
gloves and walked without comment into an adjacent pantry
where Leon was checking off supplies from a list he had
clamped to a clipboard.

"Mr. Langston tells me I'm to go now, Mr. Sawyer," said
Cara, watching the cook of La Tierra pause from his counting
to moisten the tip of his pencil with his tongue.

"That's reason enough to go, child," he informed her tranquilly. "He anywhere around?"

"I'm right here, Leon," Jeth said, coming up behind Cara to
lean against the doorway. She had stepped just inside the pantry,
and when she turned to leave, she found that Jeth had blocked
her exit. Their eyes met in an impasse—his challenging, hers
cold and still. Jeth did not budge. Over Cara's head, he said to
the cook, "Did you need me?"

"Looks like I could use one more case of coffee, if it's no
trouble."

"No trouble," Jeth said. "I'm going into town this evening. Is there anything else?"

"It can wait," said Leon, still counting his supplies, and Cara had the distinct impression that she was the matter that could wait.

"Good night, Mr. Sawyer," she said over her shoulder. "I'll see you in the morning." Pointedly she turned back to Jeth. The rancher eyed her with hard mockery for a few seconds before lowering his arm to let her pass. Cara walked outside into the cold dusk. The norther that had hit the night before still had its bite. She did not wait for Jeth but started toward the house.

Cara was halfway there before he caught up with her. "Wait up," Jeth ordered, clamping a hand on her upper arm.

Cara tried to pull away. "Let go of me!" she snapped.

Jeth looked down at her in feigned surprise. "Miss Martin, what do you think I'm going to do?"

"Mr. Langston, I could easily learn to loathe you."

"I'm sure you could, Miss Martin. You'll have plenty of reasons to." He steered her toward a large six-car garage that held an immaculate fleet of vehicles, all the same light gray. One was the jeep in which she had ridden from the airport and another was a gleaming Lincoln Continental, its Texas license plate bearing discreetly in one corner the brand of La Tierra Conquistada.

Jeth released her arm and strode around to the driver's side of the Continental. "Get in," he told her.

Cara looked puzzled. "Why?" she asked.

"Miss Martin—" Jeth drew a weary sigh. "Haven't you learned by now not to try my patience?"

Cara with sullen grace got into the passenger side of the luxurious car and felt immediately enveloped by a velour cloud.

Her tired, aching limbs all but sighed in appreciation of the sumptuous comfort of the contoured seat. "Where are you taking me?" she asked warily.

"Into town to get you some work clothes," Jeth informed her. "I doubt seriously that you have anything suitable for working around men on a roundup. What you'll need are jeans and flannel shirts—loosely fitting ones," he added grimly. "You need boots and socks, also a jacket that you can move around in. You didn't just happen to bring anything like that with you, did you?"

"Actually no. Roundups were not quite the in thing in Boston." She turned to him contrarily. "And this is a wasted trip. I don't have my checkbook with me."

"I will take care of the bill, Miss Martin."

"Oh no you won't! I don't want anything from you!"

"Really?" The dark brows rose satirically over a long, level look.

Enraged, Cara turned away from him to stare out across the flat plains. Dear God, let me hate him! she prayed. "I'll write you a check when we get home," she said, unaware of how she had referred to La Tierra.

Cara, her cheeks flaming and awash with loneliness, walked out of the old-fashioned dry-goods store of the small prairie town to wait for Jeth while he settled the bill with the gray-haired storekeeper he called "Miss Emma." Miss Emma had clearly not liked Cara. The woman's eyes had sparkled with pleasure at seeing Jeth, but they had turned hostile when lighting upon Cara. "So you're taking yourself off on a roundup, are you?" she had asked with a disapproving purse of her lips. "I must say, from what I've heard I'm surprised."

"We're in a hurry, Miss Emma. Let's get some things together for this tenderfoot here."

Without consulting Cara, Miss Emma and Jeth selected for her a wardrobe of Western work wear. The boots presented a problem because of Cara's small, narrow shoe size, but eventually a pair was found.

"Why is it so important for me to have boots?" Cara asked.

"Because you're going to be doing some riding, Miss Martin."

Cara closed her mouth without further comment. She would take this up with him later, away from Miss Emma's well-tuned ears.

The disapproval of the woman had hurt, and Cara felt cheap and soiled. When Jeth joined her, they walked in silence to the car where he chucked the packages to the backseat. Then they drove to a local grocery store to fill Leon's request for a case of coffee. Unwilling to face another Miss Emma, Cara remained in the car while Jeth made the purchase.

During the drive back to the ranch, Jeth broke the silence by reminding her, "You knew what kind of reception you would receive in these parts when you elected to come to La Tierra, Miss Martin. Surely you didn't expect to be greeted with open arms."

"Indeed I didn't, Mr. Langston," Cara said with crisp dignity, staring straight ahead with her chin raised an extra inch.

"I'll have Fiona wash the stiffness out of those jeans for you. Also I bought you a dozen pairs of rubber gloves that will protect your hands while you're washing dishes."

Cara's head turned in surprise. "That was very kind of you."

"Not at all. I don't want you crumping out on Leon because your hands can't take the soap and scalding water he uses."

Rebuffed, Cara gazed out the window at the star-filled night. Only an occasional pumping jack, outlined by the afterglow of the sunset, disturbed the endless prairie. To her, the strange-looking monsters that pumped oil from La Tierra's lucrative acres were a symbol of the land itself: proud, remote, relentless—like the man who sat beside her. She gave a silent sigh and withdrew into the folds of her coat.

Eventually the wrought-iron gates came into view and then presently the Continental was pulling to a stop before the porticoed entrance of the house. Cara's breath of relief was cut short when Jeth said, "You go on in, Miss Martin. I'll take care of the packages. You'll eat with me tonight. No need to change. We'll make an early night of it."

Cara could not face another evening with the rancher. Her eyes clouded with dismay as she spoke. "Mr. Langston, haven't we seen enough of each other for one day?"

Jeth's cool gray eyes held a hard gleam. "You'll be seeing a lot more of me, Miss Martin, so you'd better get used to the idea. As for me, I don't think I would ever tire of looking at you. It's your black heart I can do without."

Dispiritedly, Cara went upstairs to wash, thinking more about the ruin of a good silk blouse than those last words. When she came back down to the kitchen, she heard Jeth giving Fiona instructions about the jeans. They had been taken from their wrappings, and the bill had floated to the floor. Cara picked it up and tucked it into her pocket. "Good evening, Fiona," Cara said and was rewarded with a nod of the stern gray head. "I appreciate your washing the jeans for me."

Jeth turned from the counter to hand her a glass of wine. He had poured himself a bourbon. "Thank you," she murmured without meeting his eyes. She was acutely uncomfortable under his gaze and knew that he was aware of her discomfiture.

Fiona rescued her by saying, "Some mail came for you today, señorita. It is with El Patrón's in the hallway."

Cara followed Jeth to the entrance hall where a lone letter lay beside a bundle of correspondence neatly stacked on the refectory table. "Why, it's from Harold St. Clair!" Cara cried delightedly when she saw the return address on the envelope. Eagerly she opened it and drew out a letter, absently fingering the gold seagull at her throat while she read.

Jeth thumbed through his collection of mail. "Anything to do with the estate?" he asked casually.

"Oh, no," Cara assured him with a happy smile. "It's just a friendly letter, that's all—a breath of sea air from home."

"Is it now?" Jeth's voice had hardened. "Finish that later, if you don't mind. I'm hungry, and Fiona is waiting to serve us."

What a rude, bad-tempered man! Cara thought angrily, folding the letter and slipping it into her pocket next to the bill. She followed Jeth to the table, thinking how changeable his moods were and that the woman who married him was to be pitied.

They were served in a small dining alcove off the main one, and Cara hoped the food and wine would induce sleep. They ate in silence for the most part, Cara apprehensive of the even blacker mood that had come over Jeth since she told him about Harold St. Clair's letter. He probably thinks we're conspiring against him, she surmised to herself. Well, let him stew!

Waiting for coffee, Jeth pushed his chair back and remarked, "You know, of course, that there are no bathing or bathroom facilities at a roundup camp. When you pack, make sure you take that into account."

Cara gave him a dumbfounded stare, which Jeth met with an unruffled air of supreme indifference. "You've got to be kidding!" she exclaimed.

"It's not likely that I would ever kid you." He struck a match to his after-dinner cigar and drew on it. "Enjoy your bath tonight. It will be one of the last you'll have for a while." He smiled, quite pleased with himself.

She pushed back her chair and got up. "If you'll excuse me, it's been a long day. I'll have to deprive you of any further dubious pleasure you might get from my company this evening."

"Pity," said Jeth idly, tapping the ash from his cigar. "I had hoped you would play for me."

Cara paused in her escape from the room. Her expression when she turned back to him held its own irony. "You wouldn't enjoy my playing, Mr. Langston. The piano is one place where you cannot make a fool of me." She left him gazing after her, his eyes expressionless behind the smoke.

The next day passed too rapidly for Cara. Between serving meals, packing the vans, and watching what was going on outside the ranch kitchen with horses and men in preparation for departure to the campsite, Cara could hardly believe it when Leon said, "That's it for today, li'l lady. You go on up to the big house 'fore it gets too dark to see. I imagine you still have yore own packin' to do. Get plenty of rest tonight, now. Yore gonna need it."

Tiredly Cara removed the big white apron that Leon had let her use. "You won't have to tell me that twice," she said. "Good night, Leon. I'll see you in the morning." But as she stepped out of the swinging back doors, she collided with the tall man who had nodded pleasantly to her yesterday.

"Whoa there," he said in a friendly voice, steadying her. "You okay?"

"Of course." Cara smiled up at him. "How about you?"

"No harm done." He grinned. "This gives me a chance to introduce myself. I'm Jim Foster." With obvious reluctance he removed his arms from around her to hold out a hand.

"Cara Martin," she said, feeling her hand swallowed as he took it. "You're the foreman, aren't you?"

"That's right. I run things when Jeth's not around. You must be sure and let me know if there's anything I can do for you when we're out there."

Leon was at the sink still tidying up, his back to them, but Cara sensed he was taking great interest in the conversation. "I'll remember that, Mr. Foster. Thank you very much."

"Jim," he corrected with a smile, and Leon turned from the sink.

"Time you were goin', Miss Martin. Daylight be gone soon."

With a polite nod to the men, Cara left, buttoning her new jean jacket against the stiff night wind as she walked across the ranch yard. There had been some sort of unfriendly undercurrent back there between the foreman and Leon. She was sure of it. She must be careful not to become inadvertently drawn into ranch politics.

Cara had glimpsed Jeth only once during the busy day. He had not eaten either breakfast or lunch in the Feedtrough. Now she looked back at the saddling pens that skirted the big central corral. In the pens were all the horses, the remuda, that Jim had assigned to each man for the roundup. Leon had said that each ranch hand would need a change of five horses a day for the work he must do. All day the riders had been shoeing them as well as preparing their own range gear for a month's stay on the open plains. Tomorrow there would be a giant exodus of men and horses, trailers, and vans to the first roundup site fifty miles away. In spite of herself, Cara felt a thrill of excitement about the coming adventure.

When she entered her room, Cara found neatly folded on the bed the new jeans and shirts laundered to an old-clothes softness and fragrance. She picked up the flannel shirts and buried her nose in them, inhaling the freshness with appreciation after a day of smelling horses, sweat, and manure. There was no way of knowing how many times these clothes had been washed to acquire the comfortable texture they had now. She must find a way to express her thanks to Fiona.

A knock came on the door. "Come in," she called, but it was Jeth Langston, not Fiona, who entered her bedroom. The hard light in his eyes warned her that he was in an irritable mood, possibly because he was as bone-tired as she was. A deep brim crease around his head suggested that he had not taken his hat off until a few minutes ago, and dust caked his clothes. Without preamble he said abruptly, "Here is a list of things you'll need. Have everything packed and ready outside your door no later than six o'clock in the morning, earlier if you can manage it. Do you have any questions?"

"Why—I haven't had time to think of any—"

"Too late now," he said curtly, turning to leave.

"That's all right," Cara said to the broad-shouldered back. "Jim Foster can answer any questions I might have."

Slowly Jeth turned back around to face her, and Cara could have kicked herself for the remark. Why had she said such a thing? she scolded herself. The rancher's eyes glinted like sun off metal as he walked back to her. "What do you mean by that, Cara?" he asked softly.

"Why, nothing!" Cara said, wide-eyed. She pressed the clothes protectively against her. "What else could I have meant?"

"You tell me," Jeth said, so near to her now that she could see the stubble on his face, smell the rough male scents of him. "You wouldn't be thinking of playing your little games out there with any of my men, would you?"

"I don't know what you mean—" Jeth stopped her protest by grasping her jaw in a firm hold.

"Because if you are," he went on as if she had not spoken, "just remember that I would take a dim view of such a foolhardy idea. That should dampen your enthusiasm considerably." He gave her jaw a stern little shake. "Those men will be without women for over a month. They don't need you to remind them of what they're missing."

"Then why am I going?" Cara demanded angrily, clutching his wrist.

"I told you why." He released her and she retreated against the writing desk. Something fluttered to the floor, and he reached down and picked it up. "What's this?" he asked, frowning.

"It's my check to you for these clothes," Cara said, rubbing where his fingers had been. What a beast he was!

Jeth looked at it with contempt. "Written on money that Ryan transferred to your account?" His scorn was as cutting as a scalpel. So he knew about that, too, did he? thought Cara. As he pocketed the check, she said in a futile, childish attempt at some revenge, "You are such a dreadful man."

"That is an opinion shared by a number of my enemies. Fiona will bring your meal. I suggest you turn in early. Now no doubt you will excuse me. I'm going for a swim."

The next morning was a virtual beehive of activity in the ranch yard as men gathered with their equipment to be stowed in the caravan of vehicles leaving for the campsite. The remuda had been assembled, and Cara overheard Jeth giving instructions to Jim about which men were to ride in the trucks and which were to drive the remuda to a canyon close to where the cattle would be gathered.

The atmosphere crackled with excitement. Cara could feel the eagerness in horses and men to get started. "I should be frightened, I suppose," Cara told Leon, "but actually, this is all very thrilling."

"The novelty will wear off for you after a day or two," Leon told her, "but for most of those men out there, this 'n' the fall roundups are the best times on a ranch."

What, Cara wanted to know, was the purpose of a roundup?

"To gather up for brandin' and inoculation all the new calves born this spring," Leon answered. "On a ranch the size of this one, roundin' up the cattle is about the only way to count 'em. At the same time we do that, we drive 'em up to the high country for the summer where the grass is more plentiful. Jeth believes in modernization, but there ain't nothin' like men on horseback to gather cattle. Some ranches have gone to usin' helicopters for roundin' up their herds. It wouldn't work for us. We got too many cattle. Them helicopters 'ud just start a stampede."

By eight o'clock the kitchen had once again been cleaned after breakfast, and Leon told Cara to climb into the pickup truck that would lead the two customized, refrigerated vans that made up the chuckwagon. Leon tooted the horn and yelled out of his window, "We'll have the chow waitin'!" as the three-vehicle cavalcade pulled out of the ranch yard. The cowhands cheered and waved their hats and lariats. Cara laughed, caught up in the excitement of the new adventure, and searched among the group for Jeth. She caught instead the eye of Bill, who couldn't suppress a grin when she waved at him, and then the rather stern, speculative gaze of Jim Foster. The foreman nodded to her without smiling and touched the brim of his hat. Puzzled, Cara gave him a brief smile before settling back to experience her second ride across the open range of La Tierra Conquistada.

Fifty miles later, in a high clearing fringed by scrub oak and mesquite trees, Leon drew up beside a great blackened pit dug in the earth. Beside it was stacked an enormous supply of firewood, cut and piled, Leon explained, before the roundup began. "This is where the first campsite was last year," he told Cara as they climbed out of the truck. "We'll have to get the fire goin' so we can get the coffee on and the steak fried 'fore the men get here."

Cara took a minute to stretch and take stock of her surroundings. Her eyes swept acres of rolling, semiarid dun hills and mountain slopes, still under the last dull wash of winter. With a trick of the mind's eye, Cara thought, you could almost imagine you were looking at the Atlantic; the land had the same unbroken endlessness. She took a deep breath of the snappy morning air, letting some of the tense excitement ease out of her shoulders. If she could manage to keep from incurring Jeth Langston's wrath, maybe this wouldn't be such an unpleasant month after all.

By noon the chuckwagon was in operation. Tiered shelves had been unfolded from the back end of the covered pickup truck, and the earthen pit was crackling with red coals. A ten-by-ten-foot tarpaulin, in the gray and yellow colors of La Tierra, had been stretched over four metal posts anchored in the earth. Kettles of beans, chili, and stew hung from an iron bar over the campfire, simmering for the evening meal. Their spicy smells blended richly in the pure mountain air with those of coffee and fried steak. Lunch was a catch-as-catch-can kind of meal. As their work permitted, the men came in twos and threes to eat quickly the huge slabs of fried steak served between thick slices of bread. They washed the food down with scalding cups of coffee before mounting up to ride back to the draws and mountain passes to flush the cattle and lead them to a holding pen.

In midafternoon, when no kettle needed stirring or seasoning, Cara strolled over to an enclosure where three young calves were penned. They had healthy, russet-colored bodies and white faces, and the sun shone pinkly through their short, perky ears. One of the calves ambled up to Cara and let out a plaintive bawl. "What are you doing here, little fella?" she soothed. "Sounds like you need your mother." The calf seemed mollified by Cara's attention and let her continue to stroke it, batting tender brown eyes that she found endearing.

After a while she went in search of a place where she could wash and dress privately away from the hub of the campsite, and found an outcropping of brushy rocks that screened a shallow hollow. There were several flat boulders in the depression, perfect for holding a mirror and a pan of water. Cara returned to the pen and patted her new friend, then carried water and her clothes satchel to the depression to freshen up before she had to help with the final preparations for supper. She was able to manage a thorough wash, she'd like Jeth Langston to know, and after a change of clothes she felt as clean and refreshed as if she'd had a soaking bath. She applied fresh makeup and brushed her hair until it shone, securing it away from her face with a blue ribbon that matched the blue in her eyes.

Leon surveyed her over the top of his glasses when she rejoined him under the tarpaulin, but she could not tell from his permanent scowl if he approved her appearance or not. Busy ladling out flour into a huge bowl for sourdough biscuits, he remarked, "Put on that big white apron there and wrap it around ya two, three times, Miss Martin—that's a good girl." Cara did as he instructed, smiling to herself. In his own gruff way he was trying to protect her from the too-curious eyes of the men.

She was rolling out biscuits when the men began returning to camp. Her heart skipped a beat when she saw for the first time that day Jeth's tall figure astride the big bay. He dismounted without glancing toward the chuckwagon and strode quickly to a gray pickup that Cara knew contained a telephone for communicating with his office at the ranch.

Busy with her chores, Cara barely noticed Leon leave her to join a group of two Mexican cowboys, *vaqueros*, and a plump, merry-faced man who earlier in the day had arrived bumping over the plains in a white van. "Harry's Meat Market" was emblazoned in red on the door of the van, and Cara had thought the man had come to dicuss an order for beef. Leon had greeted him jovially, and the two had enjoyed a gossip session over steaming cups of coffee.

Now it was obvious they were discussing the calves in the pen, and Cara began to get uneasy. What could be of such interest about them? She watched one of the *vaqueros* walk cautiously toward the pen, twirling his rope. He threw the noose over the head of one of the calves—her calf—which immediately set up a bawling protest and tugged at the rope.

"What's he doing?" Cara demanded of Leon, but he didn't answer her. Intent on the calf, Leon pursed his lips to whistle. Cara saw the other *vaquero* raise a rifle to his shoulder. "No!" she screamed, just as Leon's whistle split the air. The calf turned its head inquiringly in their direction, and in that second a bullet slammed into its white forehead between the dark brown eyes.

In shock Cara whirled to avoid seeing what happened next and staggered into a pair of arms that held her comfortingly against a rough-vested chest. Jeth, she thought, but the voice she heard bent low to her was that of Jim Foster.

"Easy now, Miss Martin, no need to carry on so over a little old dogie like that. He's only good for eating. Come on, now. Let's walk a bit. Leon can do without you for a few minutes."

Trying to shut out of her mind the picture of the young calf crumpling into the dust, surprise still in its eyes as blood spread over its white face, Cara let herself be led away from the campsite. "This is no place for you," Jim said as they paused behind a small bluff that shielded them from the camp. "Jeth ought to have his head examined for making you come out here."

"I should have known why those calves were penned," Cara said numbly. "It was stupid of me not to realize—"

"You couldn't be expected to know they were for butchering," Jim cut her off. "You just content yourself here for a little while 'cause they're quartering that little fella right now. No use going back to camp until it's all over and done with." He took a package of cigarettes from a shirt pocket. "Want one?"

Cara shook her head. "No, thank you. I don't smoke." She was composed now and was worried about leaving Leon alone with the meal preparations. Besides, Jeth Langston might be wondering where she was. "I really must be getting back," she said.

"What you'll see won't be pretty, Miss Martin. Give it a few more minutes."

Cara shuddered, thinking of the merry-faced man in the white van. Now she understood his purpose in the camp.

"Here now, you're cold," Jim said, coming closer to her to put an arm about her shoulders before she could move away.

"Jim! Miss Martin!"

They both whirled guiltily at the sound of Jeth Langston's voice. Jim's arm dropped immediately and Cara felt the blood drain from her face. In the growing twilight, Jeth loomed down at them from the rise of land overlooking the ravine where they stood. His eyes, glinting like rapier points, impaled her as he addressed his words to the foreman.

"Jim, go down to the truck and phone in your cattle count to headquarters. I'd like a word in private with Miss Martin."

"Right, boss!" Jim said with alacrity and hurried past Cara without another word, not even to offer an explanation on her behalf to the rancher.

Chapter Eight

Cara tried to fight down the immobilizing terror that rooted her to the spot. Jeth was down the incline before she could move, his chaps making harsh leathery sounds as he spanned the distance between them. "Miss Martin, I warned you! I told you that you were to leave my men alone, that if you didn't—"

The rest of his reproof never had a chance for delivery. In fear of the fury that deepened the tan of his handsome face, Cara spun away from him, managing only a few steps before an ankle twisted. She heard the startled cry of her name before she went splaying, stomach side down, on the hard, stony ground. A sharp stone cut into the underside of her chin, but she lay oblivious to everything except the spinning carpet that offered to take her away from the demon towering above her. As he lifted her to her feet, she had a blurred glimpse of her blue hair ribbon lying on the ground.

Weakly, she flailed at him. "Leave me alone!" she sobbed. "Take your hands off me!"

"I will when you're calm," he said, pulling her into his arms and holding her steady against his chest. Spent and dizzy, Cara clung to him, wrapping her arms around his waist.

"What have you done to yourself?" Jeth asked sorrowfully above her head.

"No more than you would have done to me," she said into his chest.

"Oh, lady—" He sighed. "I was mad as hell, yes, but I wouldn't have hit you. A good shake was what I had in mind—to make you understand that while you're on La Tierra soil, you'll remain faithful to Ryan's memory. I will not tolerate your making a fool of him—"

She raised her head to look at him. "I wasn't making a play for Jim!"

His mouth hardened. "So you say."

"It's the truth!"

Suddenly the emotional and physical events of the past half hour overwhelmed her. Her chin and palms throbbed. She wanted desperately to sag against Jeth's chest again and rest there, but she could not afford such a balm. Her arms dropped from around him. "You are wrong about what you saw, Mr. Langston. I don't expect you to believe me. But surely you can believe that I would never do anything to hurt Ryan's memory."

Jeth's embrace loosened. Her small face was very pale, the smooth cheeks smudged with dust and the streak of tears. A thin line of blood had appeared beneath her chin. "Just your being here does that. Now go down and ask Leon to take a look at that chin."

Leon had already begun serving the evening meal. "Sorry," she muttered at his elbow. The cook turned around to find her gazing helplessly at her grazed palms. "I had an accident."

Leon took in the abrasions and the dusty apron, the disheveled hair that had been as smooth as polished gold a short while ago. "So I see," he commented without inflection. "Here's some clean water."

"I've not been much help, I'm afraid, Leon. I'm sorry."

"No need to be. You've been the best help I've ever had on

a roundup, and tomorrow is another day. Here's some salve for your hands. Now let me dab a little of this on that cut."

Leon was dabbing when Jeth came up under the canopy behind Cara. She felt the rancher's presence without turning around, and Leon looked from one to the other with a speculative tightening of his eyes. "How about some food, Jeth?" he asked, capping the medicine bottle.

"Pour me a glass of bourbon first, Leon. And open a bottle of Miss Martin's wine for her. I'm sure she can use it."

"Sure thing," Leon agreed, going to the van where his employer's private stock of bourbon was kept. Embarrassed, Cara kept her back to him. It was considerate of him to include her wine. What a fool she had been, running from him like that!

She finished washing her hands, discovering that the stinging cuts were only surface deep, and dried them on the clean towel that Leon had left her. She would wait until Jeth left before applying the ointment. She did not want him to know about her hands. Tomorrow she would wear makeup to hide the graze under her chin.

Cara felt Jeth's eyes follow her as she moved out from under the tarpaulin to clean up a spill on a portion of the long folding table where food was served. She took her time at it and presently Leon returned with the bourbon. With relief she saw Jeth stroll to the campfire around which the men were seated.

When she returned to her station, she found a cold glass of wine poured and beside it the blue ribbon that had fallen from her hair.

Cara ate her supper standing up and did not know what to do with herself when all the chores were completed. The men were sitting around the campfire exchanging jokes and yarns, and their rough, raucous laughter drifted to her in the night air. The stars had come out. Behind them were lingering traces of the sunset, which filled her heart with a strange melancholia that made her want to cry. She strolled a little way from the camp, afraid to go too much farther because she had overheard the men talking about rattlesnakes coming out of hibernation now. She remembered the pocket light in her gear, and thought that in the coming nights she would find a place to read to fill the time between the end of her chores and bedtime.

When Cara returned to the chuckwagon, Leon was waiting for her. "The men are beginnin' to bed down, Miss Martin," he said. "The boss give you any idea about where yore to sleep?"

"Why, no, he hasn't," Cara replied. With the busy activities of the day, that question had not occurred to her. "I don't seem to have a bedroll. Do you have any suggestions about what I should do?"

The cook studied the young woman's drawn face in the flickering light of the kerosene lamp. He had insisted she wear, at least for the night, ointment-soaked gauze pads taped to her palms. Now his jaw tightened. "Nobody said anythin' to you about a bedroll, Miss Martin? That don't seem quite right to me."

"Here's her sleeping bag, Leon," said Jeth Langston behind them. He had come up in the darkness, and now stepped into the glow of the light. "Don't worry so about Miss Martin. Believe me, she is very capable of looking after herself. Follow me, Miss Martin."

"Good night, Leon," Cara said gently to ease his worried frown, and followed Jeth's tall, striding form to a spot of ground just beyond where several men were already stretched out in their blankets. "You'll sleep here," he told her brusquely. "You should be warm enough this close to the fire."

"Thank you," she said stiffly, watching him unroll the long length of gray quilted wool trimmed in yellow. Jeth unzipped the bag and extracted a small pillow in a crisp white case. She had never been so tired in her life; everything inside and out of her ached.

Without another word to her, Jeth strode away to the truck that served as his office. He never seemed to rest from the duties of his ranch. Cara wondered where he was to sleep.

The sleeping bag was as warm as an embrace and imbued her with a sense of peace. Just before drifting off to sleep, she discovered a name sewn in yellow just inside the neck opening: Ryan Langston.

Sometime in the night she was dimly disturbed by something brushing her hands. Immediately afterward a welcome warmth spread through the chilled regions of her upper body, and she sighed gratefully in her sleep, the sound mingling with the cacophony of men's snores and the nocturnal noises of horses and prairie creatures.

The next morning before daybreak Cara was awakened by the aroma of coffee trailing beneath her nose. "Wake up, child; coffee's on," said Leon, setting a mug beside her head. "Mind you, don't knock that over." He was already dressed and in the long white apron he had worn yesterday, only this morning it was reversed. "There's time to wash 'fore you have to help me with breakfast."

Cara struggled out of her sleeping bag. She did not remember having zipped it all the way up under her chin the night before. Her chin! Gingerly she touched it, and winced. Something that sore had to show a bruise, and now all the men would think that their boss had worked her over. Despairing at the thought, she carefully picked up the hot mug in her padded hands and hurried away to her own nature-created dressing area. Bless Leon! He had left her a pan of hot water on one of the flat boulders. Better hope that Jeth Langston did not find out about this preferential treatment. She could not bear for Leon to get in trouble because of her.

Surreptitiously, Cara searched the campsite for Jeth as she ladled batter out on the hot grill for the pancakes the men would have for breakfast. The aroma was mouth-watering in the cold, bracing air, and she felt hungry for the first time in days. Jeth was nowhere to be seen, and she thought he had already left camp when suddenly the familiar voice ordered behind her, "Turn around, Miss Martin."

The tone was low, controlled. She picked up a drying towel to cover her hands before turning to find him very near her, conscious that Leon was deliberately leaving her alone with him on the pretense of going for more water at the windmill.

The rancher's gaze probed her chin, but when he made to touch it, Cara drew a sharp breath and stepped back from him. Jeth dropped his hand and eyed her grimly. "You must think the very worst of me."

It had been too dark to use a mirror for dressing. In the black hour before dawn, Cara had combed her hair and washed as well as she could, deciding not to worry about the scrape. Now she felt a flush of embarrassment. "Is it very noticeable?" she asked in a whisper.

"I'm afraid so. Not that it impairs your looks any, if that's what's bothering you."

"How like you to assume that's why I'm concerned," Cara spoke coldly. "Please excuse me. I'm busy." She turned her back on him, and after an interval of feeling his penetrating stare, she heard him leave.

In midmorning Jim Foster appeared unexpectedly at her side as she was returning from the windmill carrying a pail of water. No one but she and Leon were in camp, and she greeted the foreman in surprise.

"That cut under your chin—that come from Jeth?" he asked, taking the pail of water from her.

"Of course not!" Cara sounded horrified. "I turned my ankle yesterday after you left me and fell right on a sharp rock. Whatever gave you the idea that Mr. Langston hit me?"

"Because he was so hot at you yesterday when he found us together. I got the impression he suspected us of some hanky-panky and didn't like it. If I've ever seen a man in a jealous rage, he was one—although why, I wouldn't know. He makes no secret of the way he feels about you."

"Well, yes, that's true," Cara agreed, as a quick little pain darted between her ribs. "But Mr. Langston would never strike a woman, for whatever reason. Did you explain to him why you were with me?"

Jim averted his eyes. "It wouldn't have done any good, Miss Martin—believe me. Jeth believes what he wants to believe, and anything I said would have fallen on deaf ears."

You could have tried anyway, thought Cara, glancing at the foreman in a new, critical light. They had reached the long table, where Jim set the pail. "Thank you, Mr. Foster," she said, her tone cool. She faced him directly. "I believe, however, that we should avoid any kind of contact while we're out here. I wouldn't want to jeopardize your job, and I feel certain you wouldn't want Mr. Langston to suspect me of something that wasn't true."

The tanned, regular-cut features of the foreman slackened in disappointment. "But, Miss Martin—"

"What are you doin' back at camp?" Leon demanded, suddenly appearing from behind one of the vans parked close by. The wiry cook regarded the foreman with undisguised dislike. "I'll bet the boss don't know yore back here."

"So what?" Jim challenged. "Not that it's any of your business, but I brought a lame horse back to the corral." He touched his hat brim to Cara. "I'll say so long for now, Miss Martin. We'll talk again soon." He gave Leon a stony glance before stalking away to his horse tied to a corral post.

As they watched the lanky figure mount, Cara could feel the older man bristling at her side like a porcupine. "You don't like him, do you?" she stated quietly.

The cook's eyes narrowed on the diminishing horseman cantering across the plains. "Don't trust him," came the clipped reply. "That lame horse was an excuse to come back here and see you."

The cook and she were close in height, and, moved by affection for her bewhiskered new friend, Cara impulsively put an arm around his shoulders. "Leon, you mustn't get yourself involved in my battles. Like Mr. Langston says, I can take care of myself."

Leon spit a short burst of tobacco juice into the dust away from her, a gesture that Cara had come to recognize as a preamble to one of his terse to-the-point statements. "Yore about as capable of takin' care of yoreself as a lamb in a den of wolves, young lady. Not that you don't have plenty of grit, mind you. But you ain't got a smidgin of hardness in you, nothin' to protect you against either the likes of Jeth or Jim. Somethin' else I'm thinkin', too, child—" Another burst of tobacco juice and then Leon's words were tumbling over each other in embarrassment. "You ain't no tramp, neither, and yore not here to harm La Tierra. I ain't got it all figured out yet, but somehow I see young Ryan's hand in all of this. If that's so, knowin' him like I did, and knowin' Jeth like I do—and Miss Martin, there ain't no finer man in the whole world, even though he can be more ornery than a cooped-up bull in a barbed-wire pen—why, I intend to trust the hand that dealt this confusin' hand of cards."

He peered at Cara over his glasses, his eyes on the bluish tinge, which had begun to spread along her jawline. " 'Course it would rile me if I knew he'd mistreated you, child. Not to excuse him, but he'd be actin' out of ignorance, you understand, and 'cause he's hurtin' so inside."

"I know." Cara smiled in quiet appreciation of his loyalty to Jeth. "But Mr. Langston never laid a hand on me, Leon. It was my own doing." Cara related her shock about the calf and Jim's attempt to console her. "I confess I thought he was going to hit me. Mr. Langston was very angry, but he was concerned about Ryan's memory and how it would look for—for—"

"For you and Jim Foster to be seen keepin' company together," the cook said, concluding the narrative. "I can understand Jeth's thinkin'."

"Me, too," Cara said. Gently, Cara put a hand to the cook's whiskery cheek. "Thanks for your vote of confidence, Leon, and you are right about my not hurting La Tierra—or Mr. Langston. That I can promise you."

After that conversation with Leon, Cara saw the owner of La Tierra Conquistada only at meals, and often not then. At the end of the day when he rode into camp with the rest of the men, Jeth would frequently make for the truck that kept him in communication with the rest of his empire. On such evenings Leon would take a glass and a bottle of his employer's bourbon to the truck, then, after an interval, a plate of hot food.

The days began to grow longer and warmer and, for Cara, flowed into each other as tranquilly as sea swells bringing in the tide. She learned to ride again. True to either his promise or his threat, Jeth provided Cara with a gentle Appaloosa mare, which she liked immediately. "What's her name?" she asked Bill, who had apparently been tapped to take her out on her first rides to reacclimate her to the saddle.

"Lady," Bill answered, giving her a leg up to the saddle. He had softened considerably toward her in the weeks since the roundup began and had even haltingly apologized for the jeep ride across the plains. "That was my idea, and not the boss's," he admitted sheepishly, and Cara's heart had felt ridiculously lighter upon hearing the truth.

They began to ride every night after supper when her chores were done and while the twilight provided light enough to see. "The boss doesn't want us out after dark," Bill admonished her, giving yet another indication to Cara that Bill would rather do just about anything than disobey his boss. Even though the rancher was away from camp during many of their twilight rides, she knew that he must have approved them, or the young cowboy would never have accompanied her.

Twice the chuckwagon was moved higher into the mountains to be nearer the men who were driving a huge herd of cattle to its summer pastures. Now when Jeth left the camp, he did so by plane, a shining gray Beechcraft Bonanza with the brand of La Tierra painted in yellow on its fuselage.

One morning when she was out riding alone, she came across Jim Foster searching the brush-choked draws for strays. Thinking he had not seen her, she reined Lady in the opposite direction. "Hello there, Miss Martin!" he called to her, and with a sigh of reluctance, Cara waited for him to ride to her.

"Don't rush off," Jim said when he drew up beside her, his eyes roving in frank appreciation over the golden hair that flowed across her shoulders. It had grown since her last cut, and the sun had begun to streak it with platinum.

"I really must, I'm afraid," she said lightly. "It's nearly time to begin lunch."

"You own half of all this—" Impatiently, Jim's long arm swept the limitless, rolling rangeland. "Why don't you act like it instead of jumping every time Jeth or Leon pulls your string? You can do anything you damn well please."

"Why should you care if my string is pulled?" They had shared only a few words since their last conversation. Was it for her protection or his that the foreman exchanged only brief, impersonal pleasantries with her when she served his plate at mealtimes?

Shifting in the saddle, Jim answered candidly, "I care because I happen to think you are a gracious, beautiful lady who's getting pushed around. All I'm doing is reminding you that you don't have to take it. Use your power to keep Jeth Langston in his place."

"Mr. Langston's place has always been as owner of La Tierra, Jim. I am the usurper here. The problem is not so much what his place is, but mine. As for Leon, he has been the soul of propriety and courtesy toward me. I like him. And I'm enjoying the roundup. No one is abusing me or, as you put it, pulling my string." She dug her heels into Lady's sides and gave the foreman an impersonal smile. "Now I really must be off. Leon needs me."

As she cantered away, Cara felt a twinge of remorse. Maybe she was allowing Leon's judgment of the man to cloud hers. After all, Jim Foster had been the first to try to make her feel welcome. He had tried to comfort her the day the calf was shot. He didn't owe it to her to jeopardize his job by defending her to his boss. Maybe this backdoor friendship was all he could offer her in the light of the circumstances, all he had the courage for.

Another morning Cara had reined Lady high above where the men were working cattle and was able to watch without being observed how Jim and several other men maneuvered calves to be branded from among the herd in the holding pen. Fascinated, she watched as Jim rode unobtrusively into the milling cattle, then quietly pointed to the animal he wanted. The ears of his cutting horse perked up expectantly, for this was the work he had been trained for. In a few minutes' fast work, they had the calf edged to the outer rim of the herd, near the corral gate. A man lifted the corral bars, and another cowboy, ready on a roping horse, streaked after the bewildered calf to throw a noose around its neck. Instantly the horse reared against the rope, backing surefootedly until he was practically sitting on his own tail, holding the rope taut until his rider could dismount and finish tying up the animal.

A soft neigh from the brushy thicket to her left drew Cara's attention, and she felt Lady tense under the saddle. "Easy girl," she soothed, and patted the animal's neck. The nicker came again, this time accompanied by a considerable rustling of the thicket, and Lady backed away nervously as a great black stallion emerged to stand calmly eyeing them across a distance of a few yards. "Take it easy, Lady," Cara spoke gently. "It's all right. He just wants to say hello to us. Easy, girl."

The stallion was an awe-inspiring sight. Coal black with a full mane and tail, head held with the proud, graceful carriage of a Thoroughbred, he was the kind of horse that raised goose bumps just looking at him. Cara could easily understand how this equine king of the range had been able to outrun the fleetest of La Tierra's horses, and outwit the most cunning of her men, Jeth Langston. "So you are Devil's Own," she breathed softly. Beneath her, Lady's muscles twitched coquettishly. The mare's ears perked and her tail swished in outright flirtation.

"I can certainly see why Jeth Langston would like to get a rope around you," Cara said to the great horse. "But don't you ever let him. The likes of you were born to be free. Don't you ever let him put his brand on your flank. You'd never be the same."

Devil's Own gave a soft responding neigh and moved with a graceful rippling of muscles farther out from the thicket. "You'd better go now," warned Cara, realizing that the stallion had probably used this as a hiding place to observe the remuda corralled below on the canyon floor. She wondered if the horses were aware of their leader's presence, if in some kind of equine way he was able to communicate to them that he had not deserted them. "Go on, boy," Cara urged. "Go on, before the men find you here."

Devil's Own whinnied softly, then turned his beautiful body swiftly, catching the sun full on the sheen of his magnificent, unmarked flanks before he raced toward a mountain slope behind which he was soon out of sight.

Cara gave herself up to the routine of camp life and found that she loved it. She and Leon came to be a well-oiled machine working together in harmony and respect. Her bathroom anxieties were alleviated by the simple solution of using the time between the completion of her lunch chores and the beginning of the evening meal to bathe. It was then she washed her clothes and hung them to dry on a mesquite tree that had now budded out. No one but she and Leon were ever in camp at that time, and she could take her time washing and drying her hair. By the time the men returned to camp for the evening, she was decked out in a fresh set of clothes, hair brushed and shining, makeup—what little she used, for now her skin was lightly tanned—freshly donned. Sometimes a cowboy, his wit and tongue emboldened by an extra shot of bourbon before dinner, would sniff the air around her and announce, "It shore do smell better 'round here than when Toby was here, Leon!"

Gradually the roundup crew came to accept her presence in the camp without suspicion or hostility. They began to call her "Miss Cara" and made room for her at the campfire when Jeth was not in camp. They asked Cara to tell them about Boston and the sea, a topic that captivated them, and Cara with amazement learned that most of her audience had never seen a body of water larger than the famous Rio Grande.

When the roundup was five weeks along, she lay in her sleeping bag one night wide awake and gazed at the brilliant, low-hung stars that now seemed as familiar as old friends. She thought of Jeth, whom she had not seen for a week, and of Devil's Own, who must miss his favorite mare, now penned up in the remuda. Bill had told her that there had been evidence of the great stallion following the roundup.

"Really?" Cara had asked, round-eyed.

"Yep! And he'd better watch out, too! The boss'll get a rope around that jasper's neck yet. No horse gets free space and chow at La Tierra. They all have to earn their keep!"

"But what about Texas Star?" Cara asked. Bill had told her when she'd first inquired about Ryan's now thirteen-year-old stallion that the men had orders not to capture the palomino for the remuda.

"Oh, well...that's a different story. That was Ryan's horse, ya know. I figure the boss thinks that as long as Texas roams La Tierra, a part of Ryan does, too."

Now as she lay sleepless, watching the stars, she prayed silently, "Please, Lord. Do not let me come to love it here. Do not let me come to care too much for Leon and Fiona and Bill and...Jeth—for La Tierra—so that always, when I'm no longer here, my heart will be..."

The next evening after supper, Cara told Leon she was going for a ride by herself. "Bill hurt his leg and doesn't need any extra riding," she explained. All day she had felt strangely depressed and at loose ends with herself. She needed to be alone.

The leathery old cook gave her a worried frown. "I don't much like the idea of ya doin' that, child. My rheumatism is actin' up. A storm's brewin' and ya don't wanta be caught out on the high plains on horseback in lightnin'."

"I won't go far. If I see that it's going to rain, I'll come in."

"You do that, child. I wouldn't want anythin' to happen to ya out there. Yore comin' to mean a lot to me."

She smiled at him. "You too," she said, and went to the corral to saddle Lady.

Cara had been out less than an hour when dark clouds began to boil up over the mountains. Rain was such a rarity in this country that she couldn't take Leon's admonition seriously. But the cook's rheumatic warning had been correct. In another thirty minutes, lightning began to flash in zigzagged streaks buried deep in the gray clouds that obscured the remaining sunlight. Cara was too far from camp to return to it in the storm, so she looked around for a place where she might shelter until the clouds decided to formulate themselves into a full-fledged storm or simply dissipate into another disappointing promise of rain.

The elements made up their mind while she was still deciding what to do. The rain, bringing darkness with it, came down in buckets, drenching her and Lady, who protested mildly, having come to trust Cara as having the better sense of the two. This time, however, Cara was at a loss where to find shelter, and the mare was fast losing confidence in her mistress. She was nervous and high-strung, straining at the bit in her mouth, when a voice cut through the darkness, biting it in two. "Miss Martin, is that you?"

Oh, God, thought Cara, as Jeth Langston, glimmering in a

yellow rain slicker, emerged through the pouring rain into her vision. "Yes, I'm here," she called.

"Follow me" was the terse order, and Cara, aware that Lady knew a friend when she saw one, allowed the horse her head to follow after the owner of La Tierra Conquistada.

They found shelter in a cave whose mouth, covered with brush, she and Lady had passed dozens of times in their twilight sorties.

"Get down," Jeth ordered when they were in the safety of the cave. His own horse stood patiently, eyeing the duo with the faint suggestion that they were in trouble, while Cara, hair streaming with rain, dismounted to stand in the narrow space between Lady and Jeth Langston. Jeth did not move an inch to accommodate her, and Cara had to look nearly directly up at him from the disadvantage of her height, blinking rain-matted lashes.

"Of all the damnfool, irresponsible—" The rancher seemed at a loss for adjectives.

Taking advantage of the momentary lapse, Cara remarked, "I thought you were at the ranch."

"Which you interpreted as, while the cat's away, the mouse can play."

"I'm not a mouse."

"No. At the moment you look more like a drowned rat. Get out of those clothes."

"I will not!"

"Miss Martin, you have a choice of getting out of those wet clothes yourself, or *I* will relieve you of them. I'm not going to look. You can use my rain slicker to cover you." Jeth ignored the look she gave him and pushed her down on one of the large, weather-smoothed rocks that ringed a pit laid with fresh firewood that Cara supposed had been used countless times in just such situations as these. She snapped the slicker around her while Jeth went to work on the fire. Soon bright flames were crackling in the pit, and smoke was spiraling toward an overhead opening in the cave. The horses stood quietly, discerning perhaps, thought Cara huffily, that here was a man who knew how to take charge of things. Beneath the slicker she slipped out of her clothes, then spread them on another rock to dry while Jeth unsaddled the horses. She still had on her bra and panties, which felt cold and cloying beneath the rainwear. Jeth came back to the fire and sat down, shooting a glance at her spread-out clothes. "You don't have underwear?" he asked in surprise.

"Yes," she said through clenched teeth. "I happen to have some on at the moment. Do you mind?"

"*I* certainly don't, but you might. The important thing is for you not to get a chill."

"Why?" she asked. "That would put an end to your problem, wouldn't it—if I caught pneumonia and died?"

"That would certainly not be in my best interests," the rancher replied, kneeling down to stoke the fire. "You're worth more to me alive than dead. I need you alive to sign over Ryan's share of La Tierra."

Cara fell back into the folds of the slicker, abashed. Ryan's share of La Tierra was all he cared about. *She* had not been the reason he had braved the storm. *She* was not the concern of the moment. How could she be so in love with a man whose only interest in her was her signature?

With a muted cry, Cara stood up.

"What is it, Miss Martin?" Jeth glanced up at her in alarm. "You look as if you've been struck by lightning."

Chapter Nine

Tragically, Cara stared down at the dark head, the high cheek-boned face, the puzzled eyes caught in the flickering glow of the flames—and slowly sank to her seat again.

"What's wrong?" Jeth asked.

"Nothing," she whispered. "Nothing at all."

"Women always say that. They can be drowning in tears, or wringing their hands off, or staring into tomorrow—like you're doing right now—and still say 'nothing' when they're asked what's wrong. So what's wrong?"

Slowly she answered, "Ryan was on my mind—no, my heart—all day, or so I thought…"

Jeth turned back to the fire, his expression grave. He finished stoking it, then threw the stick he had used into the pit. Straightening up, he said, "You know how to ruin a good evening, don't you?" and went to the mouth of the cave to observe the storm.

Cara watched the tall figure gazing out into the lightning-illumined night, an ache within her so intense that she thought she would die from it. "I love you," she whispered. "I love you," the revelation so soft that it was lost in the sound of wind and brush lashing at the mouth of their shelter.

A bright crack of lightning struck near the cave. "Jeth!" She

was on her feet, shaking. "Come away from there! It's dangerous to stand so close to the opening!"

Startled, Jeth turned to her, his stature so great that it blocked
the light from the storm. His gaze held hers intently for a brief
moment before the horses nickered uneasily, and he went to
them, speaking low. Cara watched him run a hand along their
quivering flanks, heard his deep murmur, and sat down again,
consumed with envy.

"How did you know where to find me?" she asked, almost
sullenly, when he had joined her.

"I saw you from the plane when we were coming in to land.
If I hadn't, the entire roundup crew would have been out looking for you—led by Leon," Jeth added wryly. "You showed bad
judgment in going out on horseback with a storm coming."

"You cut it pretty close yourself. A plane is as susceptible to
lightning as someone on horseback. Doesn't that pilot of yours
know when it's safe to fly?"

Jeth gave her a long, measuring look. "No, Miss Martin.
That isn't going to work."

Perplexed, Cara asked, "What isn't going to work?"

"This sudden interest in my safety."

Cara sighed. "Can't you take anything I say at face value?"

"I'd be a fool to, wouldn't I? You're proving the most formidable enemy I've ever had to fight."

Taken aback, Cara exclaimed, "Me? What have I done now
to make you think such a thing?"

"You're trying to beat me at my own game, as if you didn't
know, and you've very nearly succeeded. I bring you up here,
expecting you to last maybe a week before you begged to sign
on the dotted line. I expected you to turn tail the first time a
scorpion crawled out of your boot, the first time you heard the
squeal of a rabbit being eaten alive by a coyote. But you turned

the tables on me. You made yourself an asset to the roundup rather than the liability I anticipated. You made yourself indispensable to Leon. You endured without complaint what has sent some cowboys packing their bags. You've been cheerful and agreeable when you could have been sullen and bitchy. Oh, Miss Martin"—Jeth shook his head in wonder—"the more I'm around you, the easier it is for me to see how you got to Ryan. The devil himself would have a hard time holding out against you."

Speechless, Cara thought sickly, He's twisted everything! "But why?" she demanded. "What would be the motive for my behavior except to survive the roundup?"

"To confuse the men's thinking about you, and in that way to drive a wedge into their loyalty to me—to La Tierra. You knew what they were expecting you to be, so you cleverly set out to present yourself as just the opposite—a dignified lady whose manners and conduct would be beyond reproach. Now the men don't know quite what to believe about the brave, lovely *Miss Cara*. They've become quite protective of her, as proved a while ago when they all wanted to come looking for the lost lady in the storm. They're beginning to think of her as the next patrona of La Tierra—of a La Tierra *divided*, Miss Martin, which I will never allow."

Chills had begun to sweep Cara from head to foot. She had to clench her teeth to keep them from chattering. Beneath the rain slicker, she hugged her body tightly to stanch the hurt spreading within her.

"But the cleverest move of all," Jeth continued, "is how I've been made to look like the heavy in this little drama."

Cara spoke through her clenched teeth. "What do you mean?"

"That bruise you wore for a while, your grazed hands—the men thought I was responsible for them."

"But I explained to Jim and Leon that I *fell*!"

"Leon believed you. Apparently Jim didn't. He must have intimated to the men otherwise."

"Oh, Mr. Langston, I am *sorry*! Truly I am. Jim thought—would you believe—that…you were *jealous* of us, and apparently that you had struck me out of—well, jealousy." Warmth flooded her face. She huddled miserably in the raincoat.

"I see. Well now—" He paused as if deciding whether to divulge his next thoughts. Then he resumed casually, "He was right, you know. I was jealous. I owe Ryan's memory an apology for using it as the reason for my reaction when I saw you and my foreman together. And while I'm on the subject of apologies, Leon told me why you were with Jim. If it makes you feel any better, I was doubly sorry that I had misjudged you when I saw your bandaged hands that first night when I zipped you in your sleeping bag."

Cara was stunned. Jeth Langston jealous? And it had been he who had zipped up her bag that first night? "Uh, Mr. Langston—" She wet her lips. "There's something here I don't understand—"

Jeth scoffed harshly. "Oh, come off it, *Miss Cara*. You know damn well Jim was right. I was jealous, and you knew it even before I did. I wouldn't put it past you to have set the whole thing up, just to get a show of feeling out of me. You're such an expert on men, you knew exactly how I would react."

"F-for your information"—her chattering teeth made it impossible not to stutter—"I w-would not be fool enough to risk y-your wrath by consorting with any man in y-your employ. F-furthermore, I don't know the foggiest thing about m-men. The only man I ever really knew w-was your brother, but not in the w-way you are determined to think!"

She was beginning to shake visibly from a gripping cold that had penetrated to her bone marrow. Giving her a stern glance, Jeth went to a dark recess in the wall of the cave where Cara could see an ancient wooden box. The lid creaked open as Jeth lifted out a blanket and something that resembled a towel. He brought them to her and explained, "That box is kept here with emergency supplies for La Tierra riders caught in a storm. Unsnap that slicker and wrap yourself in the blanket." He shook out the towel and inspected it. "This seems clean enough. Dry your hair with it. You've gotten a chill. And you can stop looking at me in such wide-eyed astonishment. I'm not deceived."

"Maybe you're not, but I certainly am!" Cara snapped, snatching the towel to her. "How could I possibly have known that you would be jealous of Jim and me? Why would you be?"

Only a small distance separated them, and Cara felt the volatile tension growing between them, heightened by the crackling, hissing flames. She countered his direct gaze as bravely as she dared. Then the tension seemed to drain from the broad shoulders.

"All right—" He turned his back to her with a sigh. "Suppose you wrap yourself in that blanket and dry your hair, then tell me about you and Ryan—and how a desirable twenty-four-year-old woman like yourself doesn't know anything about men."

Cara, warm at last, her hair and body securely wrapped in the towel and blanket, wondered where to begin. Jeth looked so disturbingly male in the way he sat with his elbows on his knees, long fingers locked. The fabric of his Western shirt gripped the breadth of his shoulders and arms, and the leather chaps emphasized the power of his long legs. "Well?" Jeth's dark brows rose. "Begin," he ordered.

Haltingly at first, Cara began to tell Jeth of her childhood, of how her first passion had been music. Her parents, she explained, had encouraged her to become a concert pianist. She had been educated, until Juilliard, in private girls' schools where, she realized now, her family's aspirations for her were not likely to encounter competition from the opposite sex. At Juilliard, she had just become aware that she was interesting to men when her world suddenly fell apart, went dark. The obligations she had assumed afterward precluded men. After several long years, there had been a light in the darkness. Ryan. He had offered her friendship, nothing else. His death had left her devastated and more alone than she had ever been. Jeth should know there had been no men in her life. They would have been named in that detective's report.

A silence, broken only by the crackling flames and an occasional whinny of the horses, stretched between them when Cara finished her narrative.

"So," reviewed Jeth, "you are telling me that you've never been with any man, not even Ryan."

Heat surged to her cheeks independent of the fever alternating with chills attacking her body. "Yes," she whispered. "You can make what you wish of that information."

"What I wish is to find out if you are telling me the truth."

Cara was snapped out of the musing introspection into which she had wandered. "What do you mean?"

"You know what I mean. No, maybe you don't, not if you're as innocent as you claim. I'm prepared to believe that you are— in that way. That doesn't change the fact that you schemed to get La Tierra. You didn't need experience with men to figure out that you'd be quite a prize to a man like Ryan. You held out on him until he was too sick, or too noble, to take what you promised. However, Miss Martin, I am neither." With lithe grace, Jeth rose to his full, awesome height.

Cara's heart began to race as she realized his meaning. She

stood up also, clutching the blanket tightly around her. She was wearing nothing beneath it. "No, Mr. Langston, you wouldn't."

"Not here, I wouldn't. This is neither the time nor the place. But I intend to find out just how innocent you are, Miss Martin, and then we'll go from there. I'll have at least one straight answer to this puzzle."

"If you didn't insist on twisting everything I say and do, you'd have all the answers!"

"I twist everything, do I? Do I twist the need I feel in you every time I've held you in my arms? Have I misread the message in those beautiful eyes, misunderstood those soft little moans—"

Her pride made her say it. "Yes, damn you!" Cara gritted, chilled from head to foot.

Jeth laughed down into her indignant eyes as he reached her. "You're such a liar, Miss Cara. I'll just take a moment to prove it to you."

His arms were wonderfully warm and strong. She could have basked, easily died, in them, but she had to resist. "You're taking advantage of me!" she wailed, gripping the blanket.

"Taking advantage of you? Never!" He trailed a series of warm kisses along her neck. "You'll come to me willingly and gladly. You know it and I know it."

"I'm inexperienced. You'll be disappointed—"

"You could not possibly disappoint me, that I can promise you." His lips had begun the return journey to the hollow of her throat.

"Mr. Langston?"

"Yes, Miss Martin?"

"I am going to sneeze."

Just in time he handed her another of the white folded handkerchiefs. While she sneezed into it, he took the slicker and snapped it around her. "That cold coming on is not going to get you off the hook. It just buys you some time. Sit down by the fire until I saddle the horses. The storm is over. You can wear that blanket beneath the slicker back to camp. Tomorrow you're going back to the ranch."

"But Leon can't possibly manage the chuckwagon by himself!"

"He won't have to. Toby came in the plane with me. He can take over now. I'd be taking you back with me in any event. I can't risk your splitting any more loyalties, now can I? No matter how innocently. And, Miss Cara, be convinced that I intend to find out just how innocent you are. If that prospect frightens you, you can always sign over Ryan's share to me and leave. The choice is up to you."

The next morning as they flew over the vast, pumping jack—studded acres that made up Jeth Langston's empire, Cara saw that in her absence spring had arrived at La Tierra Conquistada. The cactus, all varieties and shapes, were flowering, and the rangeland grass shone tender and green under the spring sun. She had forgotten how huge and sprawling the house and ranch compound were. From the air, the swimming pool sparkled blue and clear, and she wondered if Jeth had been able to get in his daily swims on his visits back to the ranch.

"Lucky for me your cold didn't materialize," Jeth said when he handed Cara down from the plane. The cool gray eyes held a mocking glitter. "You'll have dinner with me tonight. You still haven't played for me. Wear something pretty and join me in the study at seven."

Before she could reply, he was striding off toward the ranch headquarters. The pilot, a wizened, middle-aged man who served as a cowhand when he wasn't flying his employer's plane, taxied the Bonanza toward its hanger.

Left alone, Cara began the long walk to the house. It was true she did not have the usual symptoms of a cold, but her joints ached and she had a headache.

When Cara greeted her in the kitchen, the housekeeper instantly snapped, "What's the matter with you? Your eyes look bleary."

"I—I think I'm coming down with something, Fiona. I got caught in a rainstorm yesterday."

Fiona went to a cupboard and took down an aspirin bottle from which she shook two tablets into Cara's palm. "Take those with a big glass of orange juice and then go up and have a hot bath. Maybe you're just needing the comforts of civilization." A thin smile curved her lips. "I hear you managed fine."

"Who told you?"

"El Patrón. Off with you now."

Cara soaked in a hot tub, but the aches in her muscles did not loosen their grip. "I'll just crawl into bed for a little while," she said to herself. Her last thought was to wonder what she would wear that evening.

Cara sensed a dark presence looming over her and opened her eyes. At first she thought she was dreaming, for Jeth Langston often occupied the thoughts of her sleep, but then the dream materialized into reality and placed a tray from which steam rose on her bedside table. "You'll do anything to delay the inevitable, won't you?" Jeth said dryly. "Try to sit up. I've brought you some soup."

"What time is it?" Cara wanted to know. Her throat was sore and scratchy. The room spun dizzily when she tried to rise up.

"Eight o'clock. You've slept nearly twelve hours."

"Twelve hours!" As she spoke, Jeth thrust a thermometer into her mouth and indicated that she should move over so he could sit beside her on the bed. The mattress depressed under his weight, and Cara's hip rolled against his thigh. With a large hand that covered one side of her face, he felt her for fever, then slipped it inside her night shift to the supple curve of her neck and shoulder. When she tensed, he said, "Relax, I'm not going to take advantage of a girl in her sickbed."

Presently, he removed the thermometer and studied it with a frown. "You do have a fever, a respectable one. I want you to stay in bed for the next few days. A good rest and a diet of Fiona's soups should do the trick. They're worth getting sick for." After he had capped the thermometer, Jeth's eyes went back to her, moving over the clean, sun-streaked hair and flushed cheeks, the luminous eyes in the softly tanned oval of her face. "Did I say I wouldn't take advantage of a girl in her sickbed?" he mused, positioning both hands on either side of her hips and gazing deliberately into her eyes. "I would very much like to. Right now. You look deliciously enticing, cuddly as a kitten."

"And sick, too," Cara reminded him. "Probably with something highly contagious."

Jeth's lips twitched in amusement. "A good point. I'll just have to keep a tight rein on my ardor, won't I? Get well quick, little girl."

But though she rested and dutifully ate the delicious soups Fiona brought her, Cara was a full week in bed. After the second day, Jeth had gone back to the roundup, and Cara had felt a sharp disappointment. Lying in bed, she thought of him every waking moment and knew that she wanted him more than she'd ever wanted anything in her life. There was an aching void in her that only he could fill. She knew she would be incapable of preventing his making love to her. Indeed, she didn't want to. And perhaps when Jeth had positive proof that she had never been...Ryan's whore, he would then have to look at her in a different light. He would probably even intuitively perceive why she had come to La Tierra. She could not lead him to the truth, of course. Her promise to Ryan must be kept. But Jeth had known his brother better than anyone, and once he came to know her as well...then who knew where their mutual need of each other might lead once Jeth guessed the truth?

Finally Cara woke one morning and knew her illness was over. She threw the covers back and got out of bed. The early sun was streaming through the bay windows. She padded out to the terrace and followed it around to Jeth's bedroom, vacant now for nearly a week. She looked out toward the mountains, and her vision fell upon a caravan of horse trailers and pickups followed by a group of men on horseback. "The roundup is over!" she said aloud to the spring sky, eager to dress so that she could meet Jeth out of bed and on her feet.

In the kitchen, Fiona turned from her work to survey Cara with pursed lips. "You look better, but how do you feel?"

"Healthy," Cara answered, "and hungry."

"Good sign. El Patrón left word that you are to begin eating solid food."

"Left word?"

"He's gone to Dallas on business. Won't be back for a week or more. The roundup is over; so is the cold weather. The planting has already begun."

Cara barely heard her. She was suddenly not hungry anymore.

Leon greeted her with warmth and relief, and the members of the roundup crew with comradely good humor when she joined them for lunch in the Feedtrough. She ate with Bill and afterward he led her to the stable where the horses of the headquarters staff were stalled, including Jeth's. "The boss didn't want us to turn her loose like we did the rest of the remuda,"

Bill explained when Cara, spotting Lady, ran to the mare's stall with a joyous cry. "I figure he meant her to be yours to ride as long as you're here."

"That was kind of him," she said, her back to Bill. He didn't see the shadow cloud her eyes.

"Why is there no flower garden?" Cara asked Fiona that evening as they were eating their supper in the kitchen. Cara had gone exploring over the grounds of the house in the afternoon and found that, except for the oleanders bordering the formal approach to the entrance, no flowers of any kind had been included in the landscaping.

Thin shoulders shrugged. "Nothing at La Tierra is here for beauty's sake, señorita. Everything must have a function and be productive, be it man or horse, woman or child. The care of flowers takes up valuable time and soil and water. El Patrón has never ordered a flower garden be planted, only the vegetable fields and orchard."

There should be flowers at La Tierra, Cara decided, thinking of the barren graves at the cemetery. The house needed flowers to enliven its rooms with beauty and color.

The next day she found an ideal location for a flower garden. It was a bare, unused portion of land outside the ten-foot walls, facing the desert. "Do you think you could buy this list of flower seeds for me when you go into town tomorrow?" Cara asked Fiona.

The small brown eyes peered at the list. "You intend planting these? Without El Patrón's permission?"

"Yep!" Cara said emphatically, using the vernacular she had picked up from the roundup. The list contained the names of regional flowers she had read about in a book from Ryan's room.

The garden plot would be hard to clear. There were weeds

to pull, rocks to be moved, and rocky, sandy soil to be improved with manure and topsoil she'd have to persuade Bill to bring her from the vegetable fields. She had never seen them, but she knew they were the source of the vegetables she'd helped to prepare for the Feedtrough's tables. "Keep a cowboy's stomach happy," Leon was fond of saying, "and you keep him happy." Apparently that was one of the strategies that Jeth Langston employed to keep his men loyal and contented. Flowers were not a big seller.

That afternoon, Cara, wearing shorts and a halter top, began to clear the land for the planting of the flower seeds that Fiona promised to bring her. For several days she hauled out the larger rocks, which could serve, her mind ran ahead, for a natural limestone fence to protect the garden from the encroachment of grass. As she worked, the sun evened the light tan that she had already acquired on her forearms and at the V-neck openings of her shirts.

Bill, seeing her go into the barn to shovel manure into plastic bags, grabbed a shovel and helped her. "Boss know you're doin' this?"

"Nope! But what kind of guy would object to a flower garden?"

At the end of a warm day, she would look longingly at the pool. It would be just like him, she thought, to return unexpectedly and find me in it. "Miss Martin," she mimicked the rancher's deep voice, "didn't I tell you not to use the possessions of my house unless I give you permission to do so?"

May was nearly gone. The seeds of zinnias and portulaca, achillea and bachelor buttons had been planted and waited for the miracle of germination. Cara lay in bed in a thin, short nightgown, her limbs still warm and silky from her evening bath, her scalp still tingling from a vigorous brushing. But though she was bone-tired, sleep would not come. Pushing back the covers, she decided that Ryan's room might offer something to read until she grew sleepy.

Pattering in slippered feet back along the hall with an armful of books, Cara came to an abrupt halt. Jeth Langston, looking every inch the wealthy Texan in an impeccable light gray Western suit and Stetson, stood at his door, one hand on the doorknob, the other holding a leather briefcase. He registered her presence without expression for an interminable length of time, it seemed to Cara, long enough for her to wonder if he were having difficulty remembering who she was. "Oh, I—" she stammered, like a car starting up without the least idea of its destination. Her knees were weak from the sudden sight of him. "You've been gone for over two weeks" was all she could think of to say.

"You've been keeping count?" he asked dryly.

"Yes, I...have a calendar—" She had thrown it away only yesterday when she could no longer bear to keep track of the swiftly passing days of her tenure on The Conquered Land. Jeth's eyes had left hers and were roaming in cool calculation over her figure. Cara realized suddenly how scantily she was clad.

"Excuse me," she said, hurriedly moving past him. "I have forgotten my robe."

Jeth blocked her passage by simply stepping in front of her. "Not quite yet, Miss Martin. How are you? Over your bout with the flu, I see."

"Yes. I hardly remember it now."

"So it would seem from that glowing tan. Have you been riding Lady? If you have, it's been with nothing on."

"I have not been riding Lady with nothing on, Mr. Langston!" Cara was shocked. "I—I've been planting a garden."

Dark eyebrows rose. "A garden? What kind of garden?"

"A flower garden. I—I found a small area that wasn't being used for anything, and I planted some flower seeds."

"Why did you do that, Miss Martin?"

Cara hesitated. Why *had* she done that? "Why, I…thought your house should have cut flowers in the rooms. They're so… austere. And there are no flowers for the cemetery—"

Biting her lip, Cara bent her head in sudden embarrassment. Who was she to decide that his home and the graves of his family should be adorned with flowers? He had every right to think her presumptuous.

"You think my house austere, Miss Martin?"

"Well, I—it's a very imposing house, Mr. Langston, and… immaculately maintained—"

"But austere."

"Well, uh, yes, actually." Cara felt the light touch of two cool fingertips beneath her chin. They lifted her head to meet an inspection that showed a surprising trace of humor.

"Tomorrow morning you will show me this garden of yours."

"Yes, of course. Is it all right if I look these over?" In a fluster, she indicated the books. Anything to be rid of the disconcerting fingertips. "I wouldn't have taken them if they were yours, but since they were Ryan's—"

The humor vanished. "These belong to me now, Miss Martin. Everything that was once Ryan's belongs to me now— with one exception. However, take them along. Good night."

The rancher let her pass, and she hurried along to her room, conscious of his gaze following her. His last words lingered in her ears. She wondered which of Ryan's possessions was the exception to which he was referring: the land or her?

"He wants you to join him for dinner tonight," Fiona announced to her the next morning. "Seven o'clock in the study."

"I was to show him the garden plot this morning," Cara said.

"He's been gone since before daybreak," Fiona answered. "I don't know where."

Aimlessly, disappointment like a sharp knife inside her, Cara roamed around the kitchen. She was wearing a wraparound cover-up over a matching pair of shorts and halter top. The mornings were still cool, but even if they hadn't been, Cara would have worn the cover-up to show Jeth the garden.

"Where does Mr. Langston stay when he's in Dallas?" she asked Fiona. The housekeeper was sitting at the table drinking coffee and reading the Dallas *Morning News*.

"He has a town house there. Most often, though, he stays at the ranch of the Jeffers. They are longtime friends of the Langstons. El Patrón will be marrying Señorita Jeffers, the daughter, this year." Fiona folded the paper to a section she had been reading and handed it to Cara. "This is a picture of her. Very beautiful, no?"

Silently, her heart halted in midbeat, Cara took the newspaper. It was folded to the society page and showed a picture of Jeth with a stunning brunette who was looking up at him and smiling. They were in evening clothes, and the caption explained that they were at a charity ball. The accompanying article said wedding bells would be ringing for the handsome pair as soon as the estate of the famous La Tierra Conquistada was settled.

"Yes, she's very beautiful," said Cara tonelessly, returning the paper to Fiona. "I'll go on with my work since I don't think Mr. Langston will be coming."

Chapter Ten

The sun was shining in all its spring benevolence, but it could not penetrate the cloud of despair that descended upon Cara as she walked with bent head to the garden plot. So, she reasoned with sick bitterness, he wanted to make love to her for the sole purpose of divesting her of Ryan's share of the land. The sooner she signed, the earlier he could marry. No wonder he had looked less than happy to see her last night. Having just come from the warm arms of his fiancée, he could not relish having hers around him so soon. And to think that she had actually hoped that their lovemaking would resolve their conflicts and lead (Cara could hardly stomach the idea now) to Jeth loving her as—as she did him!

Jeth did not appear in the garden, and Cara worked strenuously in the sun, having long discarded the restricting wraparound. She was bursting with a bitter anguish that released itself in energy, and she pulled weeds and removed rocks on yet another section of land she now proposed planting. In her present state, she felt capable of clearing the entire desert. The garden and Lady, she had already concluded, would be her means of surviving the rest of the year.

He came in the late afternoon, just as Cara had decided to call it a day. Her skin tingled from the sun and shone with a thin film of perspiration. Knees, shorts, and halter top were smeared with dirt. Earlier she had wrapped the long swaths of her hair on top of her head, tucking the ends under in a way that secured them without pins. Brushing at the sand that clung to her golden legs, she did not see Jeth until he straightened up from the fence by which, she realized, he had been watching her for some time. The unexpected pleasure of seeing him momentarily arrested her, and Jeth's eyes glided over the golden swell of her full breasts to the long, shapely legs that gleamed richly in the sun.

Cara, clamping down hard on the absurd eruption of joy within her, stomped past him without speaking. "Whoa, little hoss—" Jeth gave an uncharacteristic chuckle and caught her upper arm, stopping her in her tracks. "Am I responsible for that long face? I apologize if I am. I couldn't come this morning. There was a problem in the Santa Cruz division."

Vaguely, the facts registered that El Patrón of La Tierra Conquistada had not only apologized to her but was also bestowing upon her what amounted to a smile. It affected his entire countenance, making it seem more youthful, less severe. "I wasn't really expecting you," she lied. "I know you're a busy man. However, I'm finished for the day. I'll show you some other time."

"Show me now," Jeth said. He looked at her in puzzlement. "Why so cranky? Maybe a good swim would cool you off. I came out here to ask you to join me for one."

Cara stared up at him, unsuccessfully willing herself to hate him. He was wearing summer range clothes: cords under chaps, of course, but in addition, a light cotton shirt, cut in the Western style so suited to his broad shoulders and tapering waist. Winter's black Stetson had been replaced with a soft gray one in lighter-weight felt. As her eyes traveled in longing over the beloved face, she realized she was memorizing its every detail to hold in her heart against the day when she was gone.

"What's wrong?" he asked softly, concern furrowing his brow. "Why are you staring at me like that?"

"May I take a rain check on the pool, Mr. Langston? As for the garden, here it is. Unless you know something about flowers, the names of what I've planted won't mean anything to you. In August, I'll plant cape daisies and calendulas in the area I cleared today. They're fall flowers and should bloom even past frost. There will be flowers blooming until Christmas if the winter isn't too severe."

"You plan to be here then?"

The query came mildly and could have meant anything. In Cara's frame of mind, she thought she heard a note of chagrin beneath the bland tone. "Yes!" she avowed belligerently. "No matter how hard you try to drive me away!"

He read her intention before she moved, so that when Cara made to march past him, Jeth's long arm shot out simultaneously to snare her waist and bring her back to him. She pushed at his chest and wriggled pugnaciously, toppling the topknot of hair about her shoulders. Cara heard Jeth's quick intake of breath, saw a fire ignite in the depths of his gray eyes. "You let me go, you monster!" she demanded indignantly, but Jeth's fingers interlaced in the platinum-streaked fall of her hair to hold her head still.

"Miss Martin, stop struggling or I will have to kiss you. I'm going to anyway, but first tell me about this burr under your saddle. What's got your dander up? You're generally pretty even-tempered."

Cara's heart fluttered like a covey of caged birds. In horror she felt her breasts hardening against Jeth's warm, male chest.

She could tell by the amused twist of his lips that he felt them, too. "Mr. Langston, let me go. I'm very tired. I'm also hot and sticky..."

"You feel cool and refreshing, Miss Martin, better than a swim on a hot afternoon."

Offended, Cara squirmed like a puppy held too tightly. "Take your hands off me! I'm not your afternoon diversion, Mr. Langston. I'm afraid you've been entertaining some wild illusions about me."

"Shh, be quiet, Cara." Jeth lowered his head and the shadow of the Stetson spilled over her face. His hand under her hair propelled her toward him. "You most certainly are a diversion. Morning, noon, and night, I find myself thinking about the uncommonly beautiful lady in the room only a few doors from me."

"Even when you're in Dallas?" she asked contemptuously. Immediately she could have bitten her tongue. She must not let him know that she was aware of his marriage plans. He would then see through her resistance and merely increase his attention. And she would rather die than let him know she cared.

"Especially when I'm in Dallas," he answered, his voice deep and husky. It stole around Cara's heart like a warm, fondling hand. "When I'm there, I find that I can't wait to get back to the ranch and you."

"To check up on me?" The derisive note she was reaching for failed. Her breathing grew shallow. The sound of her pounding heart filled her ears.

"No," Jeth said, "to do this..."

The kiss was like nothing Cara had ever thought to experience. Though she strained briefly against the iron embrace, her resistance capitulated to her need of him, and she let him take her lips any way he chose, first gently, then exploringly, then with a mounting urgency that sent her blood throbbing through her veins with an unleashed passion that cried for him to take her, take her. She pulled him down to her, her arms wrapped around his neck, the hat brim a shelter for the long, fiery intimacy of their kiss. She was standing on tiptoe to better reach him, yielding to the hands that now molded her tight against the hard muscular frame, exulting in the feel of his chest against her, the warmth of his chaps against her bare legs. When Jeth finally lifted his mouth, it was only for a fraction of space, of time, so that he might quiz her with his eyes. Cara's own fluttered open, very near the intent gaze, and she saw something in it that lust could not corrupt, something like a...shock of rapture. "God, Cara," Jeth groaned. "You are unbelievable. I must have you. I will have you. You're like a drug I need to live."

He brought his mouth down again, this time with a savage hunger that sought to consume and overpower her. But Jeth's fevered declaration had penetrated the sensual oblivion in which she was lost. Cara's pride, the legacy of her New England forebears, surged to the fore. She went down off her tiptoes and pushed at the arms engulfing her. What had she been thinking of, melting in his arms like that? She could not let Jeth use her like a common tramp to reunite his beloved La Tierra. He thought her nothing but a fortune hunter, his brother's whore. Once he got her into his bed, he would have the double satisfaction of kicking her out of it—as well as her signature on the papers in his desk drawer. Once he made love to her, she could not trust herself to deny him the land. And once she signed the release papers, she could not stay at La Tierra Conquistada. Her promise to Ryan would have failed.

There was only one thing to do—she must make him not want her. The idea came to her with the resurgence of her pride. As Jeth's lips withdrew questioningly from hers, she was already marshalling her tactics and praying for the courage and expertise to use them.

With a slow, triumphant smile, Cara forced herself to meet the stunned query in Jeth's eyes. Instantly the embrace tightened into a prison. "What the hell are you doing, Cara?" he asked darkly. "You didn't open that door just to slam it in my face, did you?"

For answer, Cara leaned languidly back in his arms. "That's one way of putting it," she purred, her eyes brilliant and gloating from beneath seductively lowered lashes. "I just wanted to get an idea of how much you wanted me." She sent the pink tip of her tongue on a teasing exploration of her lips, tasting Jeth's kiss. "Very much, I'd say. But I've decided that you'll just have to wait, cowboy. I never mix business with pleasure. With Ryan I had to, of course, and you are very tempting, and it *has* been so long...but I think I'll just stick to my old tried-and-true rule."

Jeth, his expression registering total shock, released her as if he'd been burned. "You mean that you and Ryan—? You're saying that story you gave me in the cave was all a lie?"

Cara gave a light, mocking laugh and slid her hands slowly up Jeth's shirt front, feeling the hard muscles tense, recoil. "Well, now, that's for me to know and you to find out, cowboy. But not until the estate is settled. Then if you're still interested, why, you'll find me more than willing—"

The name he called her resounded in the still afternoon. She stepped back from the explosion of his rage, even her ears burning from the insult of the expletive. "I'd rather snuggle up to a female coyote!" he thundered, wrath cording the muscles in his strong neck. "I wondered when the whore in you would finally surface. Dear God, to think Ryan loved the likes of you!" He took a step toward her, clenched fists held rigidly at his sides, repugnance so distorting the features of his handsome face that

Cara had to shut her eyes from the sight. "You just blew it," Miss Martin," Jeth said inches from her bowed head, his deadly soft voice flowing over her like a malediction. "I almost fell into the same trap that snared Ryan. Lucky me that your curiosity tripped you up. Unlucky you, lady, that it didn't."

Jeth stalked away from her back to the house, and Cara, dejection coursing through her, watched him go. A cool, consoling little breeze played in her hair and along her legs, but Cara was beyond solace. She felt cheapened and debased, but her plan had worked. She was repugnant to Jeth now. Not even the return of the land—his real mistress—was worth the price of seducing her.

But there had been that one, inexplicable moment—so brief that it had flashed like a vein of gold buried deep in a mountain, lost with the blink of an eye—that Jeth's soul had shone in his eyes. Bewildered, desolate, she began the walk to the house, steeling herself for what was bound to come.

The knock came on her bedroom door at nine o'clock, just as she had toweled herself dry from her bath and slipped on a floor-length robe. Hurriedly, Cara pulled on a pair of briefs as the door began to open. "Señorita!" came Fiona's harsh whisper, and Cara could have fainted from relief when she saw that it was the housekeeper's head that poked around the door.

"Oh, Fiona, you scared the liver out of me! I thought that you were—"

"He wants to see you immediately. He's in the study." The housekeeper drew into the room, her usually impassive countenance frightened and worried. "Please do not keep him waiting. I have never seen him like this. He is very angry, very dangerous."

"But I'm not dressed!"

"Señorita—" the brown eyes beseeched her. "I beg you to go to him at once. You would not wish him to come here."

Cara stared at the grim face of the housekeeper. She would never have expected to hear such words from Fiona. A cold terror began to grip her. "Very well," Cara said, following Fiona out. "Is he drinking?"

"The devil's blood from the looks of him, señorita." At the bottom of the stairs, she regarded Cara levelly. "I will be in the kitchen."

"*Gracias*, Fiona," Cara whispered in understanding.

The owner of La Tierra Conquistada was standing at the mantel of the cold fireplace when she entered his study. He held a glass of bourbon, and she could smell cigar smoke. His narrowed gaze traveled the length of the long terry cloth robe before he spoke. "Did I get you out of your bath?"

"Just nearly," she answered, her voice cool. "I was through, though. What did you wish to see me about?"

"I wish to see you about you, Miss Martin. No, don't sit down. I prefer that you stand. However, I will sit down. It's been a tiresome day."

Cara's scalp tingled. Fiona had been right: danger was here. The atmosphere was fraught with it. Jeth finished his drink in a long, deliberate swallow, then reached for his cigar burning nearby. When he turned to her, his eyes were like ice. "I have been lenient with you for my brother's sake, Miss Martin, because he cared so deeply for you. However, even he must by now be aware of what you are, so I see no further reason to show you consideration on his behalf."

"You have shown me consideration?" Cara queried, her brows raised faintly, but in the pockets of the robe her hands clenched.

Jeth's lips twisted in a cold, distorted smile. "I believe you will think so, Miss Martin, when you hear how you're to pay for your room and board the remainder of your stay here."

He drew on the cigar, watching her, reading her immediate thought. He laughed without mirth. "Relax, Miss Martin, you are safe from me. I've never been one for whores, not even Ryan's. No, I have better uses for that capable little body of yours. Tomorrow morning at seven, you will report to the tack room. The stable manager is Homer Pritchard. He will give you the equipment you will need to clean the stalls of the quarter horse stables daily. There will be other tasks involved, of course. Homer will explain. You're to work there until noon, and then you may have your lunch. Where, is up to you. At one o'clock, you will present yourself to Pepe Martinez, who is in charge of La Tierra's vegetable fields and orchard. He has an office of sorts about a mile from the stables. Homer will drive you out there tomorrow to show you where it is, but after that you'll have to get out there the best way you can. You will follow Pepe's orders concerning your chores. This will be your daily routine until something more…suitable turns up that I feel requires your time." The rancher studied her long and hard. "Miss Martin, you did hear what I just said?"

"Very clearly."

"Excellent. Of course"—he tapped a red coil of ash into the fireplace—"you can always exercise your option to leave, although I'm hoping you won't. I rather look forward to making your stay with us as memorable as possible."

"I'm sure you will, Mr. Langston, and be assured I've no intention of leaving. Is there anything else?"

"Yes. In regard to the piano. You have my permission to play it. It's an instrument that should be played. However"— his look was grazing—"as much as I am sure I would enjoy your artistry, I don't want you at that piano while I am in this house. My mother was a lady. I don't think I could stomach hearing her piano played by a woman who so obviously is not." He took a long draw on the cigar while Cara remained silent.

After exhaling a spiraling stream of smoke, Jeth went on. "And one other thing, Miss Martin. You have committed a piece of my land to a flower garden. Make sure it produces. I do not tolerate waste on La Tierra, certainly not the waste of water or time on dabbling efforts at an unproductive diversion. Is all of that very clear?"

"As crystal," Cara replied. "Will that be all? As you say, it's been a tiresome day."

Her composure proved her undoing. "No, by God, that will *not* be all!" Jeth threw the cigar into the yawning fireplace and reached Cara before she could take two steps toward escape, at the same time dexterously yanking at the belt that cinched her robe. "Now," he said grimly as the belt fell away, "I think I'll satisfy *my* curiosity and see what I'll be turning down when our business is finished—"

To her horror, Jeth wrenched the robe back from her shoulders, pinioning it in such a way that made her arms helpless to ward off his next intent. She tried to scream, but only a strangled whimper made it past the terror in her throat. Ruthlessly, his face a mask of scorn, Jeth commenced his slow, degrading inspection, unhurriedly traveling to explore, inch by inch, the lovely privacies of her body. Cold and numb, knowing better than to struggle, Cara closed her eyes in an agony of shame to wait for the long, painful seconds to crawl by.

At last she felt the robe jerked back over her shoulders. Jeth's voice, incisive, final, ordered, "Fix your robe, Miss Martin, and get out of here. But before you go, here's another collector's item for your vanity. You are every inch as desirable as I knew you would be. For that reason, I can forgive my brother for being besotted enough with you to divide our land. But you,

Miss Martin, I will never forgive. You are going to find that regrettable while you're on La Tierra."

After she had gone to bed, Cara lay a long time in the darkness waiting to hear the rancher go past her door. Long after midnight, she heard the firm tread of his boots on the tiled corridor, and her breath held in fear. She thought he paused at her door, and she strained to see if the door handle was turning. He had not. Her imagination and her sense of hearing were both playing tricks on her.

The next morning Cara went to the huge stable complex that housed the quarter horses used by the ranch hands between roundups. Jeth's big stallion and Lady were stalled in the smaller stable closer to the big house, and Cara was relieved that she would not have to see Jeth each day when he came to saddle Dancer, his bay. With a quick glance around as she entered the stable yard, Cara estimated there must be nearly one hundred stalls built around the well-kept compound. She wondered if she was to be responsible for cleaning them all.

Homer Pritchard was an unsmiling, tobacco-chewing stringbean of a man who let her know immediately that he disapproved of the presence of women in his domain. "But the boss's orders is the boss's orders," he grumbled, handing Cara a pitchfork and indicating that she follow him. He led her to a stall in which a quarter horse eyed her curiously. "Scared of horses?" Homer asked belligerently. Cara shook her head. "Well, that's a plus anyway. Ever clean a stall?" When Cara replied yes, Homer spit tobacco juice emphatically into one of the many brass receptacles for that purpose attached to the bridling posts. Cara shuddered inwardly. Surely her job would not entail cleaning *those*. "That's another plus," Homer said, his voice holding doubt. "These thirty stalls are yours. This is your wheelbarrow. The dumpsters are behind the stable. We try to be through with the stall cleaning by noon. That's when the truck comes by to unload the dumpsters and take the manure out to the fields. You'll probably need a few days to get the hang of it around here, miss, but after that, the boss wants you to pull your own weight."

Cara's lip curled. "You may tell Mr. Langston that he need have no fear of that!" she assured Homer curtly.

At noon Cara rode out to the vegetable fields in the cab of the dumpster truck with an untalkative driver who kept his eyes on the road. She had not had time to eat the sack lunch Fiona had thoughtfully prepared for her that morning, and now she discovered she had left it at the stable. Well, she thought with a sigh, I'm too tired to chew anyway and the day's only half over.

Pepe Martinez was a man of short stature, as plump and friendly as Homer was thin and hostile. The Mexican overseer of La Tierra's vegetable acreage looked her over sympathetically and gave an eloquent shrug when she introduced herself. "I am sorry, señorita, but I have my orders." He handed her a long instrument with two sharp prongs at one end. "For weeds," he explained, apologetically gesturing toward the countless rows of young beans among which she recognized blades of Johnson grass waving in the sun. His meaning was at once clear, and Cara swallowed.

"*All* of them?"

"*Si*, señorita."

As the days passed, it became apparent to Cara that in her new duties she was not to know the camaraderie that she had enjoyed on the roundup. Jeth Langston's orders concerning her were clearly expressed in the way both ranch hands and field-workers shunned and ignored her, leaving her to struggle with her chores on her own. Ranch vehicles, driven by men who had laughed with her on the roundup, passed her on the long trudges to and from her labors without stopping to offer a ride. She was not invited to join the coffee klatch of ranch hands who met each morning in the stable office, nor at lunch to eat her sandwich with the other workers gathered around the picnic tables beneath the yellow-trimmed gray canopy near Pepe Martinez's office trailer.

Cara learned that Bill, whom she missed, had been sent as foreman to run a subsidiary ranch in another county. Happy for the young cowboy, she could not help but wonder if the sudden promotion had not been designed to sever their friendly ties. Cara was confident that Bill would have remained friendly toward her in spite of his loyalty to Jeth. She rarely saw Leon, busy in the Feedtrough these days with the extra duties of butchering calves and preparing the daily bounty of fresh vegetables for La Tierra's freezers. Jim Foster alone remained accessible, but his commiserative manner made Cara uncomfortable. It suggested they shared a mutual alliance against Jeth Langston, an attitude that forced her to avoid the foreman whenever possible.

June passed into July and there were days when Cara did not hear the sound of her own voice. August came, and La Tierra baked under the hottest, driest sun that she had ever known. She worked steadily and hard, determined not to give Homer or Pepe reason to criticize her to their employer. She grew accustomed to her solitude and the loneliness of her days. The sun deepened her tan and lightened her hair to purest platinum. In her garden, the flowers broke through the caliche-stressed soil and bloomed, and in delight she cupped their colorful heads in her work-roughened hands, thrilling at their beauty and abundance. Great bouquets began to appear on gleaming tabletops in the house and before the headstones of the Langston graves.

Cara discovered that Jeth had not forgotten her garden. One

evening when she went to tend it, she found a man-sized pair of bootprints embedded in the moist sand where someone had stood to survey her handiwork. *Jeth!* she thought, and her heart had held in her throat.

Since the evening in the study, Cara had been able to avoid a face-to-face meeting with the owner of La Tierra. She knew his routine by now and was able to circumvent his comings and goings in the big house. At her request, Lady had been moved to one of the thirty stalls she had been assigned to maintain. When Cara's day was over, just as Jeth was finishing his end-of-the-day swim to change for dinner, she was saddling Lady for a ride in the long summer twilight. Afterward, while she was on the dusty trek to the house, Jeth, she knew, would have finished dinner and gone to his study for the evening. It was then, after a visit to her garden, that she would climb the stairs to her room and eat in solitude the dinner that Fiona had left her.

On the rare occasions when Jeth was away from the ranch, Cara spent her evenings before the Steinway, expressing her pain in selections written for the kind of deep despair she felt. Sometimes Fiona, who had come to have a grudging affection and sympathy for her, would come to lean in the doorway of the living room to hear her, her ever-busy hands motionless around the dish she meant to dry while she listened. One evening when Jeth was gone Cara sat down before the keyboard. Her fingers drifted into the haunting bars of "Full Moon and Empty Arms," from Rachmaninoff's Second Piano Concerto. The piece suited her mood somehow. That afternoon she had ridden Lady into the foothills and had come across Devil's Own again. In majestic splendor, the black horse had gazed down at them from the crest of a mountain, and Cara's flesh had prickled with a sudden portentous chill as she returned the stallion's stare. The message in the dark, equine eyes seemed quite plain: *You wear the brand of La Tierra Conquistada. You will never be the same again. You will never be free.*

So now she released into the music the sudden grief that had made her turn Lady sharply and knee the horse into a fast gallop back to the ranch. It was only as she was stroking off the last chords that Cara became aware of a familiar scent in the room—the aroma of Jeth Langston's cigar. Startled, she wheeled around on the piano bench to find the room empty. Afraid that her imagination was assuming dangerous proportions, Cara rose and walked slowly over to the large formal chair near the study door. Several coils of cigar ash smoldered in the ashtray. Jeth was home. He had been listening to her play the Second Piano Concerto.

In late August the knees of her jeans gave out. Cara trimmed the legs off above the knee, and while she was at it, decided to cut off the long sleeves of all her shirts. They had been fine when the weather was cool, but now they were confining and hot. She hemmed the edges as best she could, but her skill with sewing was limited, as the shirt hems testified.

"Fiona," she asked shortly thereafter, "will you cut my hair for me?"

Fiona's impassive face gave way to one of its rare moments of expression. "Cut your hair, señorita?" The housekeeper was dumbfounded. "But your hair is beautiful. It is like white gold!"

"It is unbearably hot, and I can't keep it out of my way. I can't wash it as often as I would like because it takes too long to dry."

"Very well, señorita," Fiona agreed reluctantly, "but it is a pity."

And so one hot Saturday afternoon after her chores in the stables were completed (like La Tierra's other employees, she was free until Monday morning), Cara sat in the kitchen on a stool, a towel draped around her, and submitted herself to

Fiona's scissors. Snip! snip! went the scissors. Down, down fell the hair.

"What the hell are you doing!" demanded a voice from the doorway, and the razor-sharp, pointed scissors arrested dangerously close to Cara's eyes as Fiona stammered, "I—I am cutting Señorita Martin's hair, Patrón. She asked me to."

"Stop it!" he ordered, but it was too late. A heap of hair lay on the floor, soft as silk, as shining as the most precious of metals.

Cara sat in total silence, staring straight ahead, as Jeth came to stand in front of her, his expression one of horrified surprise. "My God..." He let out a deep breath, and Cara wondered what in the world she must look like. Like a waif, she decided, feeling the blunt ends of her hair. Fiona had simply begun at one ear and cut around to the other. The towel did not cover the cutoff jeans, the flannel shirt with its amateurishly hemmed sleeves. "Your hair, your hair—" Jeth spoke almost in anguish.

It will grow again, she thought. It will darken by wintertime. A Texas sun will never again bleach it platinum. The thought made her heart close like a shamrock at dusk. Defiantly, her voice cold, Cara spoke for the first time. "My hair interfered with my work. It was hot and annoying."

"Yes," Jeth conceded. "I suppose so." With a swift movement he reached for one of her hands and inspected it critically. Cara flushed and snatched it away in embarrassment, hiding it under the towel. Her hands were rough and red, the nails broken and unkempt. She had once taken such care of her hands. "Don't you wear gloves anymore?" the rancher demanded. "What happened to the rubber gloves I bought you?"

"They were used up long ago. I don't need them now."

The look he gave her made Cara want to curl up and die. It

held a mixture of pity and disgust. She was sure that Sonya Jeffers's hands were as soft as kitten fur and that she would never have worn cutoff jeans and a tattered shirt.

Jeth left the kitchen, and the housekeeper and Cara stared at each other.

Chapter Eleven

There's a party this Saturday that I'd like to take you to," Jim Foster told Cara. He had followed her into a stall where she was filling a trough with hay. "Will you go with me?"

It was the end of September and in the mornings a crisp touch of fall was in the air. "Why—why, I don't know, Jim..." She was startled that things like parties still existed.

"Why not?" he demanded impatiently. "Are you forbidden to do anything but work?"

Good question, Cara thought, and looked up at him with a stirring of compassion. She had to admit that he had made every effort to be kind to her. He had even defied Jeth's orders by openly befriending her, a surprise move that had made her ashamed of her earlier suspicions. She wondered if Jeth was aware of their limited association. There was no reason for him to be jealous of Jim now. Impulsively, she said, "I'd love to come. What should I wear?"

She should wear, Jim told her without hesitation, a dress! She chose a dusky blue one with a scooped neckline and short sleeves and a full skirt that swirled just below her knees. To complement the dress she selected a pair of high-heeled suede sandals in the same shade of blue.

Cara spent all of Saturday afternoon readying herself for her date. She gave herself a beauty treatment from head to foot, rolling the short bob of platinum hair for the first time since Fiona had cut it and pedicuring her feet. The appearance of her hands, she was relieved to see, had greatly improved since the box of work gloves had mysteriously appeared in her room the day after her last conversation with Jeth. As the time neared to meet Jim at their prearranged spot outside the house, Cara found herself getting more excited about the evening ahead. She hummed to herself as she put the finishing touches to her makeup and slipped on her shoes. It had been so long since she'd dressed up, fussed with her hair—had fun! When she had finished dressing and stepped back from the mirror for her first full view of herself, Cara had to blink twice, she was so shocked at the woman staring back at her. Could that platinum-haired, golden-skinned, violet-eyed stranger possibly be her!

A knock came at the door, breaking into her bemusement. She drew away from the mirror, still enrapt, and opened the door, expecting to find Fiona on the threshold. Instead Jeth Langston stood there, taller and even more commanding than she remembered, dressed for dinner in a shirt and slacks of gray twill whose color was reflected in the hard clarity of his eyes. Cara stood stock-still. A faint fear that he had come to prevent her from going made her heartbeat quicken.

Jeth spoke first. "Jim Foster just called from the bunkhouse. Something has come up, and he won't be able to take you to the dance tonight. I told him I'd tell you. He sends his apologies."

Cara did not reply immediately. Disappointment cut sharply, and when at last she spoke, her voice was strained. "Is Jim still on the phone?"

"No."

"I see. Thank you." She moved back to shut the door, glad of the excuse to avert her face.

169

"Miss Martin…" Jeth put out a broad hand to prevent the door from closing.

Cara forced herself to meet his eyes with dignity, knowing she would find them alight with mockery, or worse—softened with pity. He was not the least deceived by her cool manner. The man knew exactly how she must be feeling. After all, she had been stood up, and now here she was, all dressed up with nowhere to go. But to her surprise, the gray eyes were sweeping over her in undisguised admiration.

"It would be a shame for all of that to go to waste," he said politely. "Fiona is visiting relatives tonight and has left me on my own to cook. I know it's not my company you'd hoped for tonight, but maybe you'd consider joining me for one of my steaks and a bottle of that wine you like?"

Cara's heart began to race at the temptation of the offer. The thought of spending the evening alone in her room, where she spent all of her nights and weekends, was abhorrent to her, especially since she had so looked forward to the evening.

"I'm surprised you don't have plans for the evening," she hedged, unsure of Jeth's motives. Was this invitation offered to give him another opportunity to hurt and humiliate her?

"Mine fell through, too."

"I hope you were not especially looking forward to them."

"I think I can rightly say that my disappointment is less than Jim's. How about it?"

"You are suggesting a truce for the evening?"

"Why not? It beats spending it alone in separate trenches."

Cara gave him a small consenting smile, her teeth as white and luminescent as pearls in contrast to the dark honey of her skin and the soft pink lipstick. Jeth took an audible breath.

"That's the first time I've seen that."

"What?"

"Your smile."

"Then as usual you're one up on me, Mr. Langston, for I've never seen one of yours."

Jeth lit the grill by the pool and prepared their drinks while Cara tossed a salad and put two potatoes into the oven to bake. There had been a tense moment in the kitchen when Jeth had returned to inquire about lighter fluid for igniting the mesquite. "Fiona keeps extra supplies of that sort up here," Cara told him, and made to get it, automatically pulling up the kitchen stool the two women used to reach items on high shelves.

Jeth saw her intention and said, "Don't bother with that; I'll get it," and came to stand behind her, reaching over her platinum head to rummage for the new can. His body touched hers. Her whole being tensed at his proximity, and for a few insane seconds she absurdly imagined that his lips had brushed the top of her hair. It seemed an age before he moved away. "I've got it," he said at last. "Come outside. I have your wine ready."

They sat sipping their drinks beside the pool and watched the last of the September sunsets hover near the horizon. Cara was convinced that nowhere in the world were there more dramatically beautiful sunsets than in West Texas: "To make up for the fact that we don't have much else in the way of nature to brag about," Leon had said to her on the roundup.

"This is such an ideal place for parties, Mr. Langston," she said, indicating the spacious deck and pool. "Do you ever use it for that?" There had been no guests in the house since her arrival.

She could tell from the way Jeth toyed with his drink and did not answer immediately that her question had touched sensitive ground. Without the slightest change in tone, he replied, "I find my Dallas town house more suitable for entertaining."

Cara stared at him. His meaning was unmistakable. "Because of me?"

"Yes," he replied, meeting her eyes steadily. "Because of you."

"But, Mr. Langston—!" She was genuinely distressed. "I don't mean to deprive you of the use of your home. Of course not! Why, it isn't as though I would *crash* your parties. Surely you don't think I would!" She was agitated and embarrassed. The wine had turned to vinegar on her tongue.

"Miss Martin, let's not ruin a salvaged evening by breaking our truce. It may surprise you, but I credit you with a great deal more propriety than that. I'm sure you'd be more than willing to stay out of sight while I'm entertaining, like some unsuitable relative confined to the attic while everyone else is having a good old time in the drawing room below. No, thanks. That's not my style. I go to Dallas often anyway. It's just as easy to fulfill my social obligations there."

He spoke with finality, and Cara's thoughts flew to the newspaper picture of Sonya Jeffers. No doubt his fiancée knew all of his friends and business associates; she probably made a splendid hostess. She was also probably very curious about the woman living in her future home. Cara would have been.

Jeth changed the subject by asking about Marblehead. She answered his specific questions about its history, then, without mentioning his name, found herself describing all the places that she had loved and shared with Ryan. She was oddly comforted by speaking of them to the brother who had loved him. She told Jeth about Marblehead Harbor and Devereux Beach and the waterfront with its never-ending variety of sights and sounds and smells. She had been talking for some time when she suddenly broke off, aware that she was monopolizing the conversation and that Jeth's thoughts seemed far away. *In Dallas!* Cara thought in stricken dismay.

"Forgive me," she said quietly. "I didn't realize I had become boring."

Jeth glanced at her quickly. "Nonsense. You know that you could never be boring. I was simply completely transported to Devereux Beach, that's all—with you and Ryan."

So he had known, of course, of whom she was speaking. A sudden remark trembled on her lips, unspoken. She had almost said, *I wish you could have been there with us.*

Jeth asked suddenly, "Do you miss Boston very much?"

"Not as much as I thought I would," Cara answered truthfully. In astonishment it occurred to her that she did not miss Boston at all.

"You must find West Texas vastly different."

"Not all that different, Mr. Langston," Cara replied. "Perhaps because I grew up on the edge of the Atlantic, I am accustomed to vastness and space and uncluttered horizons."

"Do...you like anything about this part of the country?"

Cara laughed. The wine had made her slightly reckless. "If I said that I like everything about it, you would probably interpret that as meaning that I intend to stay and claim Ryan's share of the land in order to live here the rest of my life!" When he looked startled, she said with gentle assurance, "I have promised to return it to you, Mr. Langston, and so I will. But to answer your question, yes, I like West Texas. I like the clear, clean air and dry, honest heat. I even like the wind, which blows endlessly like it's searching for a home. And I like the land itself because it's uncompromising and hard, like you, Mr. Langston. However, when I went to plant my garden, I found that, given attention to its needs, the land can be very giving, very loving..."

"Like me?" Jeth asked cryptically, the gray eyes intent upon her face.

"Oh, that I wouldn't know." Cara felt her cheeks grow hot. The wine had gone to her head and she had said too much. She should never drink. It was obvious that she couldn't handle alcohol. "Do you suppose we might put the steaks on? I'm getting a little tipsy."

Later, when the evening was over, Jeth did not offer to escort her up the stairs to her room, and she thought she should be grateful for this unexpected consideration. How awkward to be taken to her bedroom door when he knew full well that she felt the physical vibrations between them—sexual tensions that had increased as they began to play chess. Chess, she decided as the game wore on, was not a game to be played between a man and woman physically drawn to the other. Every move became fraught with a double meaning, and Cara grew more and more uncomfortable as Jeth's aggressive moves began to place her queen in hopeless jeopardy.

"Leaving before the game is through?" he asked with cool mockery when she remarked at the lateness of the hour and asked to be excused. He could not have known how close his remark came to the truth or how deeply it pierced. Her year at La Tierra was now half over. She had not needed the carefully marked calendar she had discarded long ago to remind her of the rapidly passing days. Yes, she would be leaving before the game was through.

"Perhaps another time," she said, giving him a polite smile and searching with her toes for the high-heeled sandals she had slipped off beneath the game table. The sumptuous fur rug had been too tempting for her stockinged feet to resist. Unhurriedly, Jeth placed his cigar in the ashtray and stood up, his fit, powerful body emanating a physical magnetism that stopped her heart. As she watched him wide-eyed, the rancher came around the table and gently drew her by the wrists to her stockinged feet. Conscious of the disparity in their heights, Cara tried not to tense as she felt Jeth's smooth, dry fingertips, his thumbs still in control of her wrists, slide sensuously to nestle in her palms. She was too inexperienced to know if the action was deliberately provocative. All she knew was that his touch sent fire through her and that she could hardly breathe as he lifted her hands for his examination.

"I am glad to see that you managed to salvage these. Now they look as they always should."

"Well—yes—" Cara was flustered and could not meet his eyes. She wondered if she should mention the box of gloves—she had sent a brusque thank-you by way of Fiona—but her pride and the shallow capacity of her lungs kept her silent.

"Do you think these hands can learn to hold and shoot a rifle?"

The question was so unexpected that Cara's glance shot up, and her lips parted in surprise. Jeth's eyes dropped to their moist softness, and Cara instinctively pulled at her hands. The rancher's thumbs pressed deeper, and she allowed them to remain in his. "Tomorrow morning after breakfast I'm taking you out on the range for some target practice. If you're going to ride Lady the far distances you do, you should take a rifle along and know how to use it. It's a practice of the ranch that I rigidly enforce so don't argue about it. You never know what you can run into out there, especially with winter coming and the coyotes hungry." He released her hands and with easy grace reached down the other side of the chair where he had been sitting. When he straightened up, the slim blue sandals dangled from his fingers. "Were you looking for these?" he asked with a wry lift of his brows.

Cara reached for them, and a little shock passed through her as he held them a fraction of a moment longer than necessary before yielding them to her. "Good night, Mr. Langston," she said in a voice less firm than she would have liked. Then she fled the room before she could be compelled to stay.

The next day Jeth drove Cara in the jeep out to a remote section of the ranch to give her brusque lessons in aiming and firing a .30-30 rifle. Every nerve in her was alert to the nearness of his body as he positioned the stock of the gun into the small of her shoulder and held her steady while she fired. He seemed unaffected by the closeness of her head or of his arm unavoidably pressing her breast during the demonstration. Cara was so intensely aware of him that she had difficulty concentrating.

During the drive back to the house, Jeth flicked a glance over the silk blouse and tailored slacks that she had chosen for the outing and remarked, "If you plan to be here during the winter, you'll need some new ranch clothes. Tomorrow take the Continental and go see Miss Emma again."

"You'll probably think me a coward, Mr. Langston, but I'd rather wear the rags I have than have another encounter with Miss Emma. Besides, I don't have any money."

The Texan looked at her in surprise. "What about Ryan's money?"

"That's just it—it's Ryan's money."

"Don't feel guilty about spending it now. You've earned it. If you're disinclined to spend it, consider it payment for your work while you've been at La Tierra. You've certainly earned more than your room and board. Marfá isn't the only place around here to buy clothes. You can go a few miles farther the other way to Alpine and shop. No one will know who you are if I'm not with you."

"Who will clean the stables?" she asked, more for his reaction than anything. A warm little glow had begun in the center of her heart.

"No one as well as you," he answered, surprising her still further, even though his mouth remained stern and his eyes on the road straight ahead. "However, I told you that you'd keep that job until I needed you more somewhere else. I need you in the study."

Instantly on guard, she faced him. "Doing what?"

Jeth laughed shortly. "Why, Miss Martin, what a suspicious mind you have! I want to take advantage of your skills as a librarian, not you. My library is in chaos. It's time the books and papers were put in some kind of order. Will you please see to it for the next few weeks?"

It was a command couched in a request, Cara knew, but how much nicer to tell her like that than in the high-handed fashion he usually used with her. "What about the fields? Am I still to work out there?"

"Pepe will be putting them to bed for the winter. He won't need you for that. Your talents will be put to better use in the study. You'll begin Tuesday. Take tomorrow off and take your time looking around Alpine. There's a museum there that might interest you and a fairly good restaurant where you can get a decent lunch. Write me a check for the amount you think you'll need, and I'll leave you cash for it on the hall table. Also a map of the town and my keys to the car."

He thinks of everything, Cara thought, happy for the opportunity to have a change in her routine. She had only been off the ranch one time with Jeth, and tomorrow would be an especially nice time to get away: it was her birthday.

The fall roundup was in progress and Jeth Langston had been gone from the ranch over three weeks. Cara thought about him constantly as she indexed and catalogued the valuable collection of books in his study. Her suggestion that Ryan's books from upstairs also be included had earned her a silent look of gratitude from the rancher that had warmed her heart for days. "How ridiculous!" she chided herself. "After all, I'm doing *him* a favor, not the other way around!" But she spent hours lost in the scrapbooks and photograph albums depicting the Langston family and the history of the ranch. By the time she had indexed them with the other memorabilia and documents, she felt intimately knowledgeable about every Langston who had ever been, including Jeth. He was impossible to imagine as an infant, but Cara found that indeed he had been one, and, from the photographs, held lovingly and often on his beautiful mother's lap.

Touching Jeth through the photographs, learning about him in the articles and clippings she read, made her miss him terribly, with a craving that gnawed at her heart and violated her sleep. She longed for him to return to the ranch, if only briefly, as he had during the spring roundup, leaving Jim in charge. Just a glimpse of his tall figure striding toward the house from the landing strip would be enough. She could content herself with that.

Cara was puzzled that she had not seen Jim since their broken date. The foreman had been in the mountains with the roundup for the remuda when she returned from her shopping trip to Alpine, but she thought it strange that he hadn't sought her out to offer an explanation before he left for the October cattle drive.

She was sitting in the living room playing the Steinway when she sensed Jeth's presence. Her fingers stilled over the keys, her shoulders tensed in anticipation of her joy before she turned on the bench to find him watching her, the black Stetson, now returned for the winter, pushed back on his dark head. Quietly she pulled the cover down over the keyboard. "Hello," she said, turning back to him. The interrupted notes of "Clair de Lune" hung in the air as they stared at each other.

Slowly Jeth said, "I haven't heard Debussy played like that since...well, in a long time," he amended. "How have you been?"

Lonely, Cara wanted to say, but she spoke calmly, giving him a slight smile. "Busy. The library is finished."

"I'll go up and change and then you can show it to me. We'll have a drink together." He did not wait for her to answer but left the room, the welcome sound of his black boots striking the tiled floor.

While Jeth changed, Cara decided to run out to the Feed-trough to see Leon. She had missed the dear old fellow. Like Jim, she had not seen him since her return to the ranch from her day's outing, not having wanted to interfere with his preparations to ready the chuckwagon for the roundup.

A half hour after speaking with Leon, she stormed across the ranch yard into the house to Jeth Langston's study. A small balled fist rapped sharply on the door, and when Jeth called, "Come in," Cara opened the door, not bothering to close it after her, and marched up to the rancher with blazing eyes and heaving chest. "You are insufferable!" she announced to the startled Texan. "How could you fire Jim Foster just because he asked me out!"

Jeth regarded her without speaking, all expression in the gray eyes slowly fading. Then he calmly returned to the task of pouring their drinks. "Here," he said, handing her a glass of wine. "Maybe that will settle you down." His eyes fell to the low opening of her blouse, then traveled back to her face. "You still have a tan," he observed, "and your hair is still sun streaked. What have you been doing to get so much sun?"

Struggling to gain control of her temper, Cara set the glass of wine down untasted. "I've been helping Pepe," she answered. "With so many men gone on the roundup, he needed help. This Indian summer has kept everything out there growing and productive. Now, Mr. Langston—"

"I didn't tell you to work out there," he interrupted. "You take too much on yourself, Miss Martin."

"Mr. Langston, don't change the subject. How could you fire Jim because of me? He'd been with you for years and was an excellent foreman. No wonder you didn't get away from the roundup like you did in the spring…" Cara bit her lip. She hadn't meant to say that.

Jeth's brows raised. "So you noticed?" He took a sip of his drink, considering her over its rim. "Jim meant to weave his way into your affections, Miss Martin. I don't mean to shatter any illusions you might have concerning his feelings for you, but you could have been as plain as a fence post, and he would have done the same. He had in mind to convince you not to sell your share of La Tierra to me; then he meant to put himself in charge of running one-half of my ranch."

Cara knew Jeth spoke the truth. It was all as clear to her now as the straight nose on his hard, handsome face. There had been something basically self-serving in the foreman's character, an opportunistic streak that she had dimly suspected. But what really hurt was to know that Jeth thought Jim could have succeeded. That was why he had kept her busy the evening Jim was fired. That was why he had taken her out on the range all the next day, had sent her to Alpine to shop and sightsee the day after.

Another thought struck her. Jeth had never been jealous of Jim at all! He had only been fearful that his foreman would gain an inside track on her affections, a possibility that might have cost him half of his beloved La Tierra.

Her fists still balled, Cara wanted to strike at the ruthless face that she loved with all of her heart and soul. "You didn't have to pretend that you wanted me to have some new clothes, Mr. Langston, in order to prevent Jim from seeing me after you fired him. I wouldn't have turned over Ryan's share of the ranch to him, no matter how much you'd like to believe otherwise." Tears stung her eyes. "I don't feel like showing you the library tonight. If you will excuse me—"

She was halfway to the door when Jeth's words stopped her. "I sent you to Alpine because it was your birthday."

Cara was sure her feelings were expressed in the tensing of her shoulders, the halting of her footsteps. Because she knew her face would betray her, she did not turn around. "How did you know?"

"I know everything about you, Miss Martin. The detective, remember?"

"Oh, yes." All he needed to know of her, he was saying, could be reduced to a few pages in a file folder.

The rancher had come up behind her. "Turn around, Miss Martin." When she did, he saw the sheen of tears in her eyes. "Are those for Jim?"

Let him think so, she thought. "I feel responsible. If I hadn't been here, then this wouldn't have happened."

"Many things would not have happened if you had not been here, Miss Martin. Believe me, Jim is a minor casualty."

The tears dried in Cara's eyes. She understood what he was implying. He hated her very presence on La Tierra. Well, he needn't worry that she would impose herself on him in the future. She would stay completely out of his way. He would not set eyes on her again, not if she could help it. On the day her promise to Ryan was fulfilled, she would quietly disappear. He wouldn't even know what had happened to her, nor would he care, for on that day the papers would arrive releasing her claim to the ranch, and he would be free to marry.

"I dislike you intensely, Mr. Langston," Cara said bitterly. At the moment, it was the truth.

"I am aware of that, Miss Martin. It's such a shame."

Without a word, she turned and left him standing in the middle of the paneled room, a tall, forceful figure who gazed after her long after she was gone.

As winter approached, the shorter days made it more difficult for Cara to avoid the owner of La Tierra Conquistada. Twilight came early and fell fast, halting the ranch activities that kept Jeth out of the house. Having no assigned duties and finding solace in work, Cara volunteered her now-coveted services where they were needed. She helped Homer in the stables and Leon in the Feedtrough, ignoring Jeth when he happened to appear unexpectedly. For convenience, she had to bring Lady back to the smaller stable for the winter, where Jeth's bay was stalled, and resigned herself to the anguish she felt when their paths crossed there.

Still, because he was essentially a man of routine, she was able to chart his comings and goings with some accuracy, and the two of them rarely met. For Cara, the long hours before bedtime were the hardest to fill. Occasionally she watched television with Fiona in the housekeeper's suite of rooms off the kitchen. In her own room she studied Spanish, which she was now able to speak with increasing fluency. She wrote her once-a-week letter to Harold St. Clair and read the best sellers and classics she got from the traveling bookmobile that stopped at the ranch every Tuesday.

Cara looked forward to the arrival of the bookmobile each week. She had become friendly with Honoria Sanchez, the gentle Mexican woman who was its driver. Honoria was also a librarian, and Cara enjoyed their professional chats.

Thanksgiving came and went and La Tierra began to gear itself for the Christmas holidays.

"They won't be nearly as exciting as in years past," Fiona grumbled in the kitchen one morning. "Señor Ryan is gone and El Patrón will spend the holidays in Dallas."

With the Jeffers, Cara conjectured, and why not? They must be like family to him, and with this the first Christmas without Ryan...Sympathy for Jeth lay in her heart for days before she found the nerve to go to his study one evening after dinner.

He had expected Fiona, as was evident by the surprised lift of his brows, the unblinking stare with which he regarded her entrance into his sanctuary. "Why, Miss Martin—" He spoke ironically. "To what do I owe the unexpected pleasure of this visit?" He rose languidly from the wingback chair to greet her, but not before his posture had suggested to Cara that he had been deeply sunk in his thoughts, his gaze lost in the fire that burned brightly in the limestone fireplace.

Cara's hands fidgeted at her sides. "Uh, Mr. Langston, I— I would like to discuss with you your plans for Christmas. Or rather, that is...*my* plans for Christmas."

"Sit down, Miss Martin," Jeth invited, indicating the other chair next to the fireplace. "You have plans for Christmas? I had thought you would be staying here."

"Yes, well, you see, that's what I want to talk to you about." She was acutely embarrassed. She had to moisten her lips to go on, a gesture that brought the lids half down over Jeth's eyes. "Fiona has told me that ordinarily when...Ryan was alive, you stayed home for Christmas and that the ranch hosted many festivities and parties. This year I understand that you are going to Dallas to be with your...fiancée's family—"

"My fiancée?" Jeth raised up in his chair, his expression instantly alert. "Who told you about my fiancée?"

So it is true, Cara thought, a hand squeezing her heart. "I read of your engagement in the Dallas *Morning News*," she answered, amazed to hear the steadiness of her voice. How is it possible that the dead can speak? "I'm afraid you're leaving because of me, that you'd be entertaining if I weren't here. If I go away for several weeks, your normal holiday activities won't have to be interrupted. Mr. Langston—" Cara raised an imploring hand when she saw Jeth about to interrupt. "I would like to do this for Ryan's sake. I can't bear for his brother to have to go somewhere else to spend Christmas because of me."

"Where will you go?" Jeth asked noncommittally.

"I have several places," she answered swiftly. "That doesn't have to be a concern of yours."

"Miss Martin," Jeth said on a sigh, "I happen to know that you have nowhere to go. You have no money to get there even if you did, unless, of course, you use Ryan's money, which you won't do, not if I have learned anything about you. I appreciate your consideration for my feelings, but you can be assured that I would not allow you to run me out of my home. I prefer to be in Dallas this year for Christmas. There are too many memories here of…what should have been."

He had turned his dark head away from her to resume his contemplation of the fire. It was a sign of dismissal, Cara knew, and she ought to get up and go. But his last remark held her sadly enthralled, like the hum of music when the final notes are played. The two of them were what should have been, she was thinking—not lovers, perhaps, but at least the best of friends. They had so many experiences in common. They had both been deprived of their parents at a sensitive time in their lives. They had each known the loss of worked-for dreams, deferred forever because of family obligations. And they had loved and lost in common a fine human being. Yet here they were, each sailing alone in his own ship on a sea of grief when they might have made the journey together, for a year at least.

Cara got up to go, and Jeth rose also. "Very well, Mr. Langston." She held out her hand politely. "If I do not see you before you leave, I hope your holidays will be pleasant."

His firm hand closed around hers. "When did you read of my engagement, Miss Martin?"

"Sometime last summer, Mr. Langston."

"I see. Happy holidays to you, too, Miss Martin."

Cara withdrew her hand and walked quickly from the room.

Chapter Twelve

Jeth was gone from La Tierra until the middle of an icy January. Somehow Cara got through Christmas Day, the ultimate emotional moment coming when she opened Jeth's gift to her. A week earlier, a tall Christmas tree had been erected before the window next to the Steinway, and she and Fiona had decorated it with the hallowed ornaments that had adorned La Tierra's Christmas trees for a century. But on Christmas morning, she and the housekeeper made their way to the headquarters building where another tree shone cozily in the window and around which La Tierra's resident cowhands gathered for the traditional opening of their presents.

Before Jeth's departure for Dallas, Cara had boldly slipped her present to him into his leather valise, which had been lying open on his bed. It was the foot-long piece of oak that she and Ryan had found their last day on the beach. She'd sent the piece away to be trimmed and set with the gemlike bits of bottle glass into the brand of La Tierra Conquistada.

She'd not expected to be remembered by the rancher, and so on Christmas morning when Leon, playing Santa Claus, handed her the small, exquisitely wrapped package with her name written in bold black ink on the white envelope tucked beneath the ribbon, her heart had all but stopped. She extracted the envelope first. Inside was a simple note: "I trust you will wear this with your seagull as a symbol of another land you have conquered. Merry Christmas." It was signed with the single initial, *J*. The gift had been a small gold drop in the design of a prairie falcon, exquisitely made. Cara had pressed the trinket to her breast and reread the brief note dozens of times.

She was not aware that the owner of La Tierra was home until she saw the big gray Continental parked in the garage. Her pulse rate quickened as she ran the rest of the distance to the house. Thank heavens he was home! She had just come from the bunkhouse where she had been summoned by the new foreman to look at Leon, who had taken to his bed with a high fever. Cara diagnosed a severe case of influenza and told the foreman to call a doctor.

When she entered the back door, frozen to the marrow in her jean jacket, she expected to find Jeth sitting at the table with the housekeeper, visiting over coffee. Neither was in the kitchen and Cara, knowing that Fiona had not been well either, felt a sense of alarm. "Fiona!" she called sharply.

"Out here!" came the familiar voice, and Cara ran to the passage off the kitchen that led to the housekeeper's quarters. Jeth was carrying Fiona down the hall as if she weighed no more than a doll. "Call a doctor!" he ordered over his shoulder. "She's burning up with fever."

"One is on the way," Cara said. "Leon is sick, too."

An influenza epidemic swept through the ranks of La Tierra's personnel as icy winds tore across the bleak plains, sending gray tumbleweeds scuttling over the unimpeded distances like uprooted ghosts. Jeth agreed with Cara's suggestion to house the sick men in Ryan's room to prevent the virus from spreading to the skeleton crew remaining in the bunkhouse. The entire household staff succumbed to the rampant virus, which left the caring and feeding of the dozen sick men in Ryan's room to her. Also, of her own volition, she helped Toby in the Feedtrough to cook meals for the rest of the crew who now had the added burden of herding as many cattle as they could find into the deep draws for protection against freezing temperatures. They were especially worried about the cows, swollen now with their unborn calves to be delivered in early spring.

"Get away from me, child," Leon attempted to dissuade Cara when she came near to minister to him. "I don't want you gettin' what I got."

"Hush, Leon," Cara told him gently, "and eat some of this soup for me."

Cara and Jeth reached the same conclusion about the housekeeper and cook three days after the pair had taken to their sickbeds. Raking fingers distractedly through his dark hair, the gray eyes flinty with worry, Jeth admitted, "I'll have hell to pay for this when they're well, but I'm calling an ambulance to take them to the hospital in Alpine. They're too old to fight this by themselves, and I'm not taking a chance of losing them. They're all I have."

Cara stared wordlessly at him, fear clutching at her throat, and Jeth saw something in her eyes that made him reach out suddenly and clasp the back of her neck, giving it a gentle shake. "Hey, now, don't look like that. They'll be okay, little girl. Just see that you don't get sick, too. Understand?"

She nodded, and Jeth released her as suddenly as he had touched her. Pulling on gloves, positioning the black Stetson, he said abruptly, "I'll be out on the north range if anybody needs me. Call that ambulance, will you, and don't listen to any protests from those two."

The epidemic lasted three weeks. Cara's days were filled

with washing and changing sheets, trooping up and down stairs with meals, fruit juices, and aspirin, interspersed with countless trips across the ranch yard to help Toby feed the tired cowhands three meals a day.

In the evening, though, fresh and relaxed from a fragrant bath and wearing one of the many soft wool dresses whose colors highlighted her beauty, Cara met Jeth in his study. They sat across from each other before a blazing fire and sipped their drinks while the January winds howled and fretted outside, seeking entrance into their haven of warmth and safety. Above them over the mantel, prominently displayed, was her Christmas present to Jeth, the glow of the pavé setting bringing Ryan into the room. They had thanked each other simply for their gifts, and Cara never removed the gold chain that held the prairie falcon.

They talked of many subjects, and Cara discovered Jeth to be a wonderful conversationalist, his dry humor sometimes making her double over her glass of wine in a gale of laughter. She listened, fascinated, to his stories about the ranch and Texas and was surprised to learn that his knowledge of music equaled Ryan's.

They dined late, going into the kitchen to serve their plates from the reheated supper that Cara had brought from the Feedtrough earlier. Their meals were eaten in the small dining alcove, accompanied by a newly opened bottle of wine over which they lingered until it was gone. Then together they cleared away the table and washed the dishes.

Cara began to play the Steinway for Jeth when they were into the second frenzied week of fighting the epidemic and the freezing temperatures. She was standing before a window in the living room looking out at the storm-blackened night. Jeth had not yet come down, or so she thought, until she felt his hands on her shoulders. "Relax," he said on a husky note as she stiffened. "These delicate shoulders have been carrying too many burdens lately." Slowly he began to massage her tense neck muscles until she was drowning in a delicious, euphoric bliss. Bending his dark head close to her ear, he whispered, "After dinner, play for us, Cara. We both need it."

And so, with Jeth comfortable with cigar and snifter of brandy in the chair where he had heard her play "Full Moon and Empty Arms," Cara played for them the music that had once been her life. Now their evenings ended with the chords of the Steinway trembling throughout the house. Afterward, Jeth would lead her to the foot of the stairs to say good night before returning to his study. It was always a slightly tense moment that neither prolonged. They seemed to share a tacit understanding about the folly of climbing the stairs together.

Jeth drove her several times to the hospital to visit Fiona and Leon, whose return to health could be measured by the degree of their indignation at having to remain until fully recovered. Driving back with Jeth on the last visit before their release, Cara was tensely aware of every movement from the man at her side. She was certain that, given the right provocation, she might burst apart inside. February was a week gone. She wanted desperately to clutch the days and hold them fast, for each one gone brought her closer to the last. The ranch was beginning to return to normal. The men had been released from the converted sick ward, and the household staff had returned. Already Jeth was busy making arrangements for the spring roundup.

"Why so glum?" Jeth asked. "Fiona and Leon are going to be home in a few days." Home. He made it sound like a place they shared, would always share. A sob rose in her throat, and she blinked back the unshed tears and looked out across the moonlit landscape that stretched to infinity. She sensed Jeth turning to her in puzzled inquiry. "Cara?" One of the strong hands left the steering wheel and covered hers in an inquiring squeeze. "What's wrong? And don't say *nothing*," he told her firmly, before she did.

"Just a little tired, I guess," she answered.

"And...homesick?"

In the darkness, she smiled ironically to herself. "Yes, you could say that, too."

There was a small disappointed silence from Jeth. Cara could feel it. Then he said, in a voice that was suddenly hard, "Forget about going back to Boston before the estate is settled, Cara. I want you here where I can keep an eye on you. I couldn't let you go anywhere where you might be prevailed upon to change your mind about selling to me."

Cara straightened in her seat and withdrew her hand. "You mean you still think I would?" She could hardly keep the appalled tremor out of her voice.

"Miss Martin, you are an enigma to me. You are the only woman I have ever met whose motives I cannot figure out. How do I know these last weeks have not been a ruse to get me to trust you, to let you leave without signing the papers so that when you are out of my...jurisdiction, you could run to the highest bidder? You've had plenty, you know, buyers who have tried to see you, who have called and written. They have all been intercepted and given...discouraging replies. Harold St. Clair's letters have been passed on to you intact, but none of the others. No one gets my land but me, Miss Martin. I am the only one bidding."

Slowly, a coldness crawling like a snake through her body, Cara asked numbly, "You...opened my mail...intercepted my calls? You had no right to do that, Mr. Langston."

"I had every right. You should know that I take any rights I choose on La Tierra."

"I could have *escaped* the day I went to Alpine!"

"Oh, Miss Martin, in *my* car? I would have reported it stolen, and you wouldn't have gotten out of the county."

"You—you led me to believe you let me use your car because it was my birthday..."

"And so I did. I was tired of seeing you in those butchered rags. However, that's not to say that I trusted you to come back. You were monitored the entire day."

"Are you saying that I—that I'm a *prisoner* at La Tierra?"

"Yes, Miss Martin. You have been since the day you set foot on it."

Cara contemplated opening the car door and running across the plains—anywhere to escape that smooth voice that masked such an iron ruthlessness. "I hate you," she spoke in a childish whisper through the choking disappointment that welled in her throat. "I hate you so much."

"I have always suspected it, Miss Martin, even in your friendliest and nicest moments."

Cara turned violently away from him, burrowing her head in the upturned fur collar of her coat. A wave of desolation washed over her. She had thought they could at least part friends, that her last month on the ranch would be as wonderful as the past three weeks had been, providing her with memories that she could hold in her heart and return to, time and time again, like seashells that recapture the sound of the sea. Now she knew that Jeth Langston had never begun to care for her, not even a little. His suspicions had not been allayed. They had simply been set aside while he made use of her as a nurse and cook and housemaid. He spoke of ruses. What kind of ruse had *he* used these past weeks in order to enlist her aid in helping him run the ranch, paying her off with the pleasure of his company, and worst of all, allowing her to enjoy a side of him she never dreamed existed. Weren't they ruses? Weren't they the cruelest ruses of all?

Her head came out of its collar burrow. Cara regarded the lean, wolflike profile disdainfully. Because she had been cruelly dealt with, she would be cruel. "You have names for all of us, Mr. Langston," she began, feeling her lip curl. "All of us who are self-serving. What do you call a man who tries to seduce one woman while being engaged to another?"

Cara had the satisfaction of seeing the muscle tighten along his jawline, but she was little comforted. "I would call that man a fool, Miss Martin, who, fortunately, saw his mistake before it was too late."

She had no answer for that. Indeed, she had no answers for anything, and probably never would again.

They met on the stairs early the next morning as Jeth was returning to his room before leaving the house. "Oh, Miss Martin," he hailed her in a voice that had returned to its former dispassion, "a temporary housekeeper will be here this morning. No need for you to concern yourself with Fiona's activities. And I have a new man out at the Feedtrough to take over for Leon. You're relieved of those duties, too."

Cara gave him a long, level look. "You are saying, then, that my services are not wanted."

"Not *needed*, Miss Martin. Enjoy your leisure. That's what you came here for."

From the cool measure they took of each other, Cara was thinking that those intimate, friendly evenings before the fire might never have been. The memory of them would be an exquisite torture, far more effective than his unabashed hostility would have been.

"And one other thing, Miss Martin," Jeth concluded formally. "I am afraid I will have to forego the pleasure of your company in the coming evenings. With the roundup coming, I'll be working late." He nodded dismissively and went on up the stairs. Cara's eyes followed him. She wanted to shout, "Who says the pleasure of my company would have been offered?"

For Cara, who had so much time on her hands, February passed surprisingly quickly. March brought a succession of unprecedented mild days, deceptive in their gentleness, with clouds scampering across the blue skies like fluffy lambs at play. Cara covered her garden with hay to prevent a sudden thaw, which would render her lilies and irises vulnerable to the inevitable spring freezes still to come. "Better to stay in deep freeze," she muttered grimly to the frozen ground, remembering how she had suffered under the thawing warmth of Jeth's attention.

The daffodils were up, and she collected golden masses of them for the house and cemetery. One afternoon as she laid an arrangement of them on Ryan's grave, she fell to her knees and began to cry uncontrollably, her shoulders heaving from the fury of her grief. "Why, Ryan, why? Why did I have to come here? Was it to fall in love with him? You knew he would despise me. Why did you make me come, Ryan?"

A sudden noise made her lift her head and listen, and she heard the clop-clop of a horse's hooves cantering away. Horror-stricken, she stood up to observe Jeth Langston astride his bay, heading toward the ranch. The implacable back, the indomitable shoulders, the hard set of the black Stetson told her nothing. Had her words carried on the clear, dry air? Had he overheard her crying, or had he, seeing Lady tethered below, decided to bypass the cemetery for another day? Her shoulders slumped in despair. Would March twentieth never come?

She began to plan her escape. She would have to elude Fiona, whom she was sure now, in spite of the woman's growing affection for her, had been Jeth's watchdog. Cara would have to find a way to get out of the house and off the ranch without arousing suspicion. An idea, simple and foolproof, presented itself to her. She wrote for air and bus schedules, which, when they arrived, she was able to intercept without either Fiona's or Jeth's knowledge.

Like one who knows her days are numbered, she observed the world of La Tierra with a sharper awareness, committing to memory all of the sights and sounds that she would never know again. Leon caught her staring at him on a morning when spring was still pretending to have arrived. "What ya lookin' at me like that for?" he snorted affectionately. "Ya got a funny look on yore face, like yore sad about somethin'. Pretty girl like you shouldn't ever be sad, leastways not 'cause of an ol' geezer like me. Stop worryin' that I ain't well, 'cause I am!"

She haunted Fiona in the kitchen until the housekeeper accused her of being underfoot. "Go for a walk!" she finally advised in despair. "You're as jumpy as a rabbit in a gunnysack!"

With one day remaining, Cara could not resist playing the Steinway once more. She chose "MacArthur Park." Her heart sang the lyrics while her fingers played the melody. *After all the loves of my life...after all the loves of my life...you'll still be the one...*

"Very well done," Jeth said gravely from the doorway of his study when she had finished. "You played that with great feeling." Cara froze on the bench. She hadn't known he was in his study at this hour of the day. She'd thought he would be at the roundup of the remuda. It was time for the spring cattle drive again.

She turned to him with a face as smooth and cold as marble. "Thank you," she said tonelessly, and walked from the room.

Once outside, she ran to the stable to saddle Lady. Her heart was beating frenziedly. Don't love anything out there, Harold St. Clair had warned her—no man, woman, or child; no horse or dog—not even an armadillo. How she wished she had taken his advice! Cara kept the gun Jeth had taught her how to use in the tack room, and with hurried, frantic motions, she sheathed it in the saddle scabbard. Once mounted, she urged Lady into a fast sprint even before the gentle mare was out of the corral. Cara thought she heard someone call to her, but it was only the wind that blew in her ears, she decided, only the homeless wind that knew her and called her by name.

Sometime later, Cara reined Lady to a halt, her attention caught by a flock of buzzards, the prairie's precursors of death, circling lazily in the distance. Some hapless animal is down, thought Cara, and kneed Lady into a lope. She had never had to put an animal out of its misery on the range, but she knew that it was a law among cattlemen to do so rather than let the sharp-beaked buzzards tear at the soft undersides and eyes of their still-living prey.

She found the object of the buzzards' interest a few minutes later. It wore the brand of La Tierra on its flank and lay in golden ruin at the bottom of a ravine, a blond-maned palomino whose attempted leap across the wide chasm had resulted in a fall that had snapped both forelegs. Cara saw at once there was nothing to be done. The legs lay at a crazy angle, and the weak rise and fall of the exposed side suggested that the end was very near.

She dismounted and removed the gun from its scabbard. As she descended the rocky incline, a shocking thought struck like a serpent inside her brain. She told herself not to be ridiculous, that there were dozens of palomino stallions roaming the range at La Tierra, and that the horse in the ravine was not the broken magnificence that had once been Texas Star.

The palomino's glazed eyes were open and watched her approach with a flicker of welcome in the brown depths. Cara's resolve faltered, and she knelt down and stroked the rough, dry coat. "I'm sorry, boy," she spoke softly. "I'm sorry it has to be like this." She had only to back away now, aim the rifle, pull the trigger, and be gone. It had to be done and delaying accomplished nothing for either of them. But the palomino gave a soft whinny and tried to nuzzle her hand, and a spasm of pity moved within her chest. "Don't—don't make it harder. It will all be over in a second. You won't feel a thing." And then, because she had to know, Cara brushed back the hair at the base of the mane. There, pigmented into the hide, was a perfectly formed, five-pronged white star.

The cry she hurled toward the heavens startled the predators flying overhead, but only momentarily. The rush of their wings came nearer Cara's head. She roused herself with an effort and hurled a rock at the assemblage. Then, stepping back from the horse, she released the lever, sliding the bullet into the rifle's chamber. The palomino's ears perked at the loud click, as if he remembered the sound from the days when he had carried his master across the plains. Cara raised the .30-30 to her shoulder, and quickly, before tears could distort her aim, centered the sights on the white forehead and fired.

The report carried across the prairie and sent the scavengers flapping skyward in raucous number. The recoil slammed into Cara's shoulder and stunned her cheek, but she was beyond the impact of pain. Only Bill's words from the roundup found their way into the void of her mind: "I figure the boss thinks that as long as Texas roams La Tierra, a part of Ryan does, too."

Deep in shock, Cara was barely aware of the gun slipping from her fingers, of the black-vested figure stepping in front of her frozen vision. From far away came the sound of her toneless voice. "I shot Texas Star, Mr. Langston. I shot Ryan's horse."

"It's all right, *querida*, Cara. You did what you had to do. You have always done what you had to do."

Like a robot she let herself be led out of the ravine and made to sit on the ground beside the big bay waiting for his master. Later, she did not remember being lifted onto the roomy saddle of Dancer, nor recall Jeth mounting behind her, cradling her in the safety of his arms. She only remembered, coming from somewhere, an acrid stench of mesquite smoke. It brought a sudden, quite total darkness, and she fainted.

When Cara awoke, she thought at first she had been asleep in the undulating cabin of a ship. She lay still and blinked. The soft, lapping waves receded, and her surroundings came into focus. She was in her room at La Tierra. Moonlight, cold and pale, filtered through the open blinds and across the blanket in which she was cocooned. A fire was crackling in the fireplace, throwing dancing shadows on the wall, mocking the fierce wind that whipped around the corners of the balcony.

For a merciful moment, Cara's mind was empty of all thought. Then, like the return of sensation after a stunning blow, memory of the afternoon flooded back to her.

"No!" Her denial was strangled as she fought to sit up and free her arms and legs from the entangling blanket. She must meet the returning tide on her feet—she could drown lying here like this.

Instantly a tall figure rose catlike from one of the fireside chairs and was at the bed as she sat up. "Easy, Cara, easy," Jeth Langston spoke soothingly. "The first few minutes will be the hardest."

With a total and utter sense of loss, a privation so great that she thought she would rather die than be denied this man for whom her soul craved, the realization came to her that this was to be her last night at La Tierra. After tomorrow she would never see him again. After him there would be no more lovers, no more deaths—only hers. *After all the loves of my life...*

Cara tried to say his name, but a yearning, so intense that she feared it would rupture her chest, made it impossible to speak. Instead, she lay back down, turned away from him, and began to sob.

When the tears were spent, the bed beneath her face was soaked and she had another of Jeth Langston's large handkerchiefs clutched in her hand. "That must have been coming for some time," he remarked, when Cara turned in surprise to find him still in the room.

Conscious of how puffy her eyes must look, how red her nose, she swung her legs to the floor. The bedside clock read nine o'clock. "You've been very kind to bother with me, Mr. Langston. I'm all right. Really. This is roundup time. You've plenty to do without having to bother about me."

Jeth had pulled one of the wingback chairs up so that he could prop his booted feet on the bed. Without removing them, he said, "So Ryan told you about Texas Star, did he?" When Cara wearily nodded, he said simply, "He was in love with you, Cara. Don't you know that by now?"

She raised her head, comprehension breaking over her face like a quiet sunrise. She regarded the rancher sadly. Yes, Ryan had loved her, not as the friend she had thought, but as deeply, as passionately, as she loved his brother. How naive she had been not to have known. Then why had he sent her here to be abused by the brother he also had loved?

"Are you hungry?" he asked unexpectedly. "I had Fiona keep you something warm in the oven. I can bring it up to you."

"No, I couldn't eat anything," Cara answered. "I'd rather just have a bath."

"Have one, then. I'll see you in about thirty minutes with something that will make you sleep. My mother used to make it for Ryan and me when we had a bad night coming up."

Cara watched him walk to the door. As he opened it, she said softly, "You've had lots of those, haven't you, Mr. Langston? Bad nights, I mean."

The rancher paused, hand on the doorknob. His expression was oddly tender. "No more than you, little girl. Thirty minutes."

When Jeth returned, Cara was sitting listlessly before the fire in a white, long-sleeved granny gown that covered her from neck to ankles. A shawl of pink flannel was over her shoulders, and fluffy white house shoes peeped from beneath the hem of her gown. The light from the fire played on her blond hair and in the dusky violet depths of her eyes.

"You look like a little girl," Jeth commented, handing her a hot mug of dark liquid. "All you need is a teddy bear to complete the picture of scrubbed innocence."

"But we both know how misleading that would be, don't we?" Cara said cynically as she took the mug.

"Do we?" he said, with the still expression she could never read. Then he changed the subject abruptly. "There's a freeze expected by morning. Will your garden be all right?"

"Yes. I knew a freeze would come, so I covered it with hay. Weather is like people, always vacillating between hot and cold. Tell Fiona—" She stopped and caught her lip between her teeth. She had almost said, *Tell Fiona to remove the hay when the weather warms so that the iris bulbs can feel the sun.*

Jeth asked, "Tell Fiona what, Cara?"

"Nothing. I don't know what I was about to say. I'm feeling rather groggy. This cocoa has alcohol in it."

"Brandy. Drink it up. It's better than a sedative."

Jeth had brought for himself a glass of bourbon, and they drank in silence, Cara thinking of tomorrow and Jeth's reaction when his lawyers called to inform him that Ryan's share of La Tierra had been restored to him free and clear. She had never intended to sell the land back to Jeth. Harold's letter, which she had received yesterday, had assured her that the appropriate papers would be in the hands of Jeth's attorneys tomorrow, the first day of spring.

"This is very good," Cara said. "It goes down like warm fingers soothing away the hurt. Your mother must have been a wonderful woman."

"I've only known one other like her."

"The woman you're going to marry, of course."

"Yes, the woman I'm going to marry. She is the most courageous person I think I've ever known, and I admire and love her with all of my heart."

"Lucky her," said Cara flatly, setting her finished drink down and getting up suddenly. "I think I'll say good night now, Mr. Langston—" The room began to spin like a kaleidoscope, and she thrust out her hands to steady herself. Her last fully conscious thought was of Jeth rising to catch them. After that she descended into a blissful oblivion in which she was buoyed up by something strong and swift that bore her away to a place of softness and warmth. In the dreamy depths in which she floated, she could feel Jeth's mouth, as soft as a whisper, against her lips. Over and over his lips found hers, and once she thought she felt the wetness of tears upon her cheeks, but they could only have been hers.

Chapter Thirteen

Cara awoke the next morning instantly alert. Rigidly she forced from her mind the events of yesterday, which she recalled quite clearly, telling herself that she had to concentrate on the day at hand. She was fuzzy only about what had happened when she tried to stand up last night. Jeth had been talking about his fiancée, she remembered. Obviously she had fainted again, and he'd been obliged to put her to bed. The man would probably heave an enormous sigh of relief when she was gone!

Fiona looked at her sharply when she entered the kitchen but made no comment about Texas Star. The fact that she prepared Cara's favorite omelet, heaping it high with fresh tomatoes and peppers and the special picante sauce she loved, spoke more than words of her concern about Cara's ordeal.

When she had eaten, Cara said casually, "The bookmobile will be here in about an hour. May I have a paper sack to carry my books in? After it leaves, I think I'll go for a ride on Lady. She got shortchanged yesterday."

Fiona nodded and went to the cupboard to get a brown paper sack. "You should rest today, señorita. You look too pale."

Cara thanked her and went upstairs to pack what little she planned to take with her to Boston. The paper sack, of course, was for her few essentials. She would leave all the clothes Ryan had bought her, including the sable-lined raincoat. They had been meant, she knew now, to impress his brother, and had failed miserably. She touched the twin charms at her throat. The gift from Jeth she would keep; she could not have parted with it. She opened the bureau drawer that contained the three clean handkerchiefs of Jeth's she'd never returned. The one from last night she had washed and dried in the bathroom. It was ready to be folded with the others. After she had packed the paper sack, placing on top of her things the library books she meant to return when she escaped in the bookmobile, she went along to Jeth's room with the handkerchiefs. Without glancing around his quarters, she placed them on his bureau and hurriedly left.

Cara left the sack of "books" on the hall table, then went out to the stable to see Lady. The mare, too, was part of the plan. She intended to turn Lady loose without being saddled. If Jeth came looking for Cara, finding Lady gone, he would assume she was out on a ride. He wouldn't become suspicious until nightfall. By that time she would already be in Boston, having taken a bus from Alpine to Midland Air Terminal where she would catch a plane.

As Cara made her way to the stable, she noticed a number of ranch hands ringing one of the large corrals used to pen the remuda. There was no one to see her hide the saddle or turn Lady loose in the pasture adjoining the stable. Her heart was heavy as she started back across the ranch yard to wait for the bookmobile, which would soon be arriving. Homer Pritchard saw her and called, "Come see what the boss caught yesterday, Miss Martin! If he ain't a sight to behold!"

The group of men parted respectfully as she approached, and Cara gasped at what she saw. Inside the corral, bucking and snorting in derision of his captors, was the last unconquered challenger on La Tierra Conquistada.

"Devil's Own!" she cried with such familiarity that the men turned in surprise and looked at her. The horse heard her and stood still. He gazed in her direction, ears pointed alertly.

"You two know each other?" Homer queried in surprise.

"Indeed we do." She turned angrily and addressed the men draped along the corral fence. "Don't you men have something better to do than to stand around gaping at that animal? Get off the fence!" she snapped. "Stop staring at him!"

"Cara, what are you doing?"

Recognizing the familiar voice, Cara wheeled to face the owner of La Tierra Conquistada, her eyes dilating in their fury.

"What do you intend to do with that horse?" she demanded tightly, vaguely conscious that every eye was on them and that the great black stallion was standing motionless in the center of the corral.

"Why do you want to know? What business is it of yours, little girl?"

"Don't call me *little girl*! I'm not a little girl! And I'm making that horse my business. What do you intend to do with him? Break him? For what purpose? You have hundreds of horses at your beck and call. Why do you need him?"

Jeth studied her closely. "Why is that horse so special to you, Cara? Why do you care so much what happens to him?"

"Listen to me, Jeth. Once that horse feels your saddle on his back, your bit under his tongue, he'll never be the same again. You'll brand his flank, but a horse like that...you'll be branding his heart. You may turn him loose when the roundup is over, but he would never be free again. If you can't love him, don't tame him. Isn't that what you once said to Ryan? And you could never love that horse. He's been too much of a thorn in your side."

Jeth smiled slightly. "You don't think I could love something that has been...a thorn in my side?"

Cara shook her head.

"Well." Jeth's voice was tender. Unexpectedly, he reached out and brushed a silken strand of hair out of her eyes. "We'll talk about it tonight. Go back to the house now."

"It will be too late then."

"No. I won't let it be too late." An employee had come up from the headquarters building. "Boss, there's a call for you from Dallas. Sounds pretty urgent."

Jeth gave the girl a soft glance. "We'll talk tonight."

With a hollow ache Cara watched him walk away from her and disappear inside the headquarters building. The men began to disperse, and Cara turned back to the corral. Calmly, without hurry, she lifted the wire hoop that secured the gate, swung it wide, and stood waiting for Devil's Own to register her invitation. In less than a minute the ears flattened, the tail arched, and the startled shouts of the men were too late to deter the thundering hooves. With tail high and mane flowing, Devil's Own streaked through the open gate, past her to freedom, deflecting with ease the hastily thrown ropes of the few men who had gotten them into the air.

Cara had a glimpse of Homer's ashen face before she tore off across the yard to the house. Fiona was in the kitchen, unaware of what had transpired. "I hear the bookmobile coming, señorita," she said.

Her escape was easier than she had ever imagined. She had simply asked Honoria for a ride into Alpine, and the young woman, glad of Cara's company, had eagerly granted her request. By early evening, Cara was landing at Logan

International Airport in Boston where Harold St. Clair met her.

"My God!" was all he could say at first when she disembarked carrying her paper sack. She was almost unrecognizable in the blue jeans and flannel-lined jean jacket, her short hair the color of platinum.

"Hello, Harold." She smiled and convinced him that she was really Cara. "Thank you for meeting me and for everything else you've done. My apartment really is available to stay in tonight?"

"Yes. The tenants left last week. Uh, is that your only luggage?"

"I'm afraid so. I left everything else at La Tierra."

"So it would seem. That's why we've all been awfully worried about you."

"Who is *we*?"

"Why, myself of course, and Jeth Langston, not to mention the whole ranch staff. When it was discovered that you were missing, Jeth Langston checked your room. None of your clothes were gone, and he thought something had happened to you. Apparently he must have turned the ranch and the whole county upside down looking for you, then something made him think that you'd taken a powder."

He found the handkerchiefs, Cara thought.

"He checked the bus company and found out that you bought a ticket to the airport. In the meantime, his lawyers called me to find out if I knew your whereabouts. I told them I was expecting you late this afternoon."

"Had they spoken already to Mr. Langston? Did he know La Tierra is his again?"

"He knew, all right. They got in touch with him this morning."

Cara remembered the phone call that had interrupted her final conversation with the rancher. She suddenly felt drained. She was sorry to have worried Fiona or Leon unduly. "Could you get in touch with him tonight, Harold, and tell him I'm here? I made some friends at La Tierra I wouldn't want to be worried about me."

"I'd be happy to, except that Jeth Langston seems to have disappeared, too. His lawyers can't find him, and his housekeeper has no idea where he's gone."

"Disappeared?" Cara was aghast. "With the spring roundup at hand? He probably went to Dallas to be with his fiancée." *To tell her the good news*, Cara could have added. *Now they can begin planning their wedding.*

Harold's face appeared troubled as he bit his lip nervously. "Cara...there's something I must tell you—"

Cara's heart felt an apprehensive chill. "What is it?"

"A few days ago, as instructed, I mailed to Jeth Langston a registered letter that Ryan wrote shortly after he altered his will. It was to arrive on the twentieth of March."

"Did it?"

"I don't know. I mentioned this to the Langston attorneys, who said, according to the housekeeper, the mail had arrived while Jeth was in the house. Whether the letter was among the correspondence, she didn't know. She had no idea whether he had signed for it. But he left shortly thereafter. As for his being in Dallas, he's not. His attorneys have checked. I just finished speaking with them before I picked you up. They thought perhaps he might come here."

"To Boston? What on earth for? Jeth Langston didn't come to Boston when Ryan was alive. There would certainly be no reason for him to come here now. The letter probably upset him. He's gone off somewhere to be alone."

At her apartment, Harold insisted on taking her out to dinner, at least a hamburger, he suggested, marking the clothes she was wearing and doubting whether the paper bag contained anything suitable for something more lavish. He thought of the red dinner dress with regret. Cara was not to try and put him off. She should eat, and in a couple of hours he would be back to take her out for a bite. In the meantime, while she rested, he would go back to the office and put in a call to La Tierra. As he was leaving, Cara said warmly, "Thank you for everything, Harold, especially for advancing the money I needed. You know I'll pay back every cent."

"Cara, you don't owe me or the firm one nickel. Ryan took care of any and all expenses that you could possibly have incurred this year, which weren't many." The lawyer gave her a diffident smile. "If I may say so, Cara, I am so glad you're back. I've been counting the days until you were. See you in a little while."

When he had gone, Cara took her curling iron from the paper sack. She really should try to do something to look less like a waif, she decided, looking at her straight hair and unenhanced face in the mirror. How far away and long ago was that curly-haired, golden-skinned young woman who had once been reflected in her mirror. She had been so striking in her blue party dress and high-heeled shoes. Quite possibly, Cara would never see the likes of her again.

As she bathed, she wondered about the letter Ryan had written to be delivered on March twentieth. Very probably it explained to Jeth why she had come to live for a year on La Tierra Conquistada. It would have been like Ryan to clear her name with his brother, to end that chapter without a question mark remaining. But as for her, she would never be able to understand why Ryan had sent her there in the first place.

There was a remote possibility that somehow Ryan had thought Jeth would come to care for her—though why, when he had known his brother had a perfectly suitable fiancée waiting in the wings? Surely Ryan would have known that Jeth would have found someone like her, a believed whore...intolerable. Perhaps the letter explained his reason for sending her there. Cara would never know.

She was ready by the time Harold's knock came at the door. She had put on makeup and her hair had been washed and softly curled about her face. Too bad about the flannel shirt and jeans, she thought, not really caring. Tomorrow she would get out of storage the dull, meager collection of clothes she had left behind a year ago. It was a good thing that she'd not discarded the old, brown "monk's cassock." Her jean jacket was not suitable for the rigors of a New England spring.

Cara did not even make the effort to smile as she went to the door. Her heart was too full of Jeth, of the yawning emptiness of a future without him. She threw the door open wide as a recompense.

"Hello, Cara," said Jeth Langston grimly from the doorway. Over his arm was draped the sable-lined raincoat.

For a paralyzed few seconds, Cara thought she was hallucinating. Jeth Langston could not possibly be standing at her door. But then the man in the fleece-lined jacket moved, stepped forward over the threshold, the gray eyes beneath the fawn Stetson never leaving her face, and the small, shabby room was all at once filled with the man's very real and dangerous presence.

Cara backed away, her mouth and eyes round Os of amazement. "Mr. Langston, what are you doing here? Surely you didn't come to—to get even with me for setting Devil's Own free?" In her alarm, it was the only reason she could think of.

"He's part of the reason I'm here, yes," Jeth answered, kicking the door softly shut and advancing toward her.

"You—you monster! Can't you bear to lose anything you set your sights on!"

"No, Miss Martin, I can't bear to lose anything I set my sights on."

"Well, content yourself with the knowledge that there's always another roundup. There will always be another opportunity to get your rope around that poor animal's neck!" She had retreated as far as she could go, furious with herself for letting him frighten her so. This was her apartment, her town, her land! How dare he come here and try to intimidate her!

"That's as may be, but there won't ever be another Cara Martin."

"What is that supposed to mean?" And why had he brought that coat? she wondered irrelevantly, looking up at the unforgettable face. He stood very near to her, and she saw that he didn't look nearly as ferocious as she had first thought. Jeth tossed the coat on a nearby chair.

"You'll need that," he said, pushing back his Stetson. As she waited for him to explain, he very calmly slipped his arm around her waist and drew her to him to kiss her.

"Mr. Langston, why are you here?" Cara sighed in resignation after the long, deep kiss. Naturally she had responded in spite of herself, as he had known she would, from the small, self-satisfied smile playing about his lips. She had been too surprised to struggle, and after a while she hadn't wanted to. "If you have any ideas about making hay with me, you'd best forget it. Harold St. Clair will be here any minute."

"No, he won't. I spoke to him a short while ago. Fortunately for me, he was working late. I managed to convince him that we wouldn't need his company tonight. He's a nice fellow. I'm afraid I've misjudged him, as I misjudged you, Cara."

"So that's why you came all this way," Cara said, the light dawning. "To tell me you had misjudged me." And maybe to get in a little dallying to boot, she thought scornfully, noting that the lean, wolflike face showed not the slightest trace of remorse. "Harold told me he had sent you a letter written by Ryan shortly after his will was altered. I am assuming you got it. It must have explained everything."

Jeth's brows rose innocently. "You mean this?" He reached inside his jacket pocket for a long envelope. An arm still around her, he yielded enough space for her to examine the envelope. She recognized Ryan's handwriting, then with a little catch of breath saw that the envelope was still sealed.

"But you haven't read it!" she exclaimed, looking up at him in puzzlement.

"I didn't have to. I know what it says. In a little while we'll read it together. I have an idea it's to both of us."

"Jeth, what are you saying?" Cara asked in confusion.

Jeth led her to the couch in front of the fireplace and sat her down. "We need a fire in here," he said, laying wood in the grate. When a crackling blaze was going, he took off his jacket and hat and joined her on the couch. Resting an arm on the back of it behind her, he searched Cara's face with a baffling scrutiny. "You still haven't figured it all out, have you? You still don't know why Ryan sent you to live on La Tierra?"

Cara stared at him. "How do you know he sent me? You haven't read the letter."

"Didn't he, Cara?"

Cara hesitated, then nodded slowly. The year was over now. Her promise had been kept. There was no reason now for Jeth not to know the truth.

211

The rancher reached for her hand. "He asked you to go, didn't he? Probably as he was dying, he got you to promise that you would live there for a year after his death, from the first day of spring to the next. Don't you know why?"

"Well...I have thought that maybe...he wanted us to—to care for each other. That's insane, of course. He knew you could never care for a woman you thought to be a—a whore, and especially since you were engaged—"

"Cara—" Jeth pressed a kiss on a soft wave at her temple. "He knew us both so well. Even though he knew he was sending you into a year of hell, he knew us well enough to know that we'd come through intact."

"Speak for yourself, Jeth Langston," Cara said bitterly.

"You aren't intact?" With a sharp glance, Cara saw Jeth's brows raise in irony, his lips twist in amusement. "Why not?"

To hell with my pride! Cara thought stormily. What comfort is it to me now, anyway? She looked Jeth full in the face, obstinately. "Because I did come to care for you, Mr. Langston. Lord knows why. You are the most overbearing, arrogant, intimidating—*man* I'll ever know, but as you say, Ryan knew us both better than we knew ourselves. The caring became—well, here is a collector's item for *your* vanity! The caring became love. I am now, *Mr. Langston*, in love with you—and that should be punishment enough for all the trouble I've caused. Don't think, however, that's the reason I restored the land to you. I planned to, anyway, from the very beginning. It wasn't mine. Ryan should never have left it to me. I can't imagine why he did."

"Because it was the only way he could set us up to fall in love. If he hadn't left you the land, how could he have gotten you on La Tierra? When would our paths have ever crossed?"

Cara blinked at him, trying to keep a tight lid on the hope

that was trying to bubble up inside her. "But you're not saying that you—love me?" she whispered.

"Of course I am. I told you last night after I brought you your cocoa."

"But you were speaking of your fiancée!"

"I was speaking of you, *querida*, though you obviously didn't realize it. Of the woman I am going to marry."

"What about Sonya Jeffers?" she cried. *Querida!* He called her *querida*, sweetheart!

"I haven't been engaged to Sonya Jeffers since I left you in your sickbed to go to Dallas to break our engagement. At the time, I still hadn't figured out all the puzzle, but I wasn't going to marry any other woman feeling the way I did about you."

"Jeth..." Cara's arms flew around his neck. Tears shone in her eyes. "That's what you meant that night in the car when we were on our way back from the hospital. I asked you what you thought of a man who tried to seduce one woman when he was engaged to another, and you said...you said..."

"I remember what I said," Jeth said with a wry smile. "And naturally you took the opposite of my meaning."

"But you had just told me I'd been a prisoner at La Tierra!"

"That was a desperate move to keep you there. You'd just said that you were homesick for Boston, and I was scared that you'd leave before I could undo all the harm I'd done. By then I was head over heels in love with you, and I had to keep you there to somehow salvage the damage. I should have known I couldn't scare you into staying."

"It wasn't Boston I was homesick for. I was sick about having to leave La Tierra, which by then was home to me. But you became so cold to me after that, Jeth. I thought...I thought...you'd just been kind to me during a time when there was no one else to help you. When I was no longer of use to you, I thought you had rejected me."

"Oh, honey—" Jeth pulled her tightly to him as if he were afraid she might disappear into thin air. "That was sheer self-preservation. You told me that night you hated me. I believed you. I couldn't imagine how you could even like me after all I'd done to you, much less love me. Then I began seeing some signs, and remembering others, that told me otherwise."

Cara said in a muffled voice against his chest, "Probably one of them was that time you heard me crying my heart out in the cemetery. I knew you had heard me."

"There was a message in your torment, Cara. You left me messages all year, had I chosen to read them—like that discarded calender of yours that I found a few months after you'd been at La Tierra. You had marked the days very black at first, with heavy crisscrosses that reflected your anger and desire for the year to be over. Then gradually the marks had become fainter, almost reluctant. After a while, you hadn't marked the days at all. Then you threw away the calendar.

"But the final proof I had of your feelings was the despair I heard in the way you played 'MacArthur Park.' I'd just brought Devil's Own down from the mountains. That's why I was in the study at that time of day. And then this morning when you set Devil's Own free after giving me that little speech about him, when you got so hopping mad at me for capturing him, I knew then, lovely lady, that I had you, that you were mine. You identified with that horse. You wanted him to be free, unbranded, as you never would be again. I intended telling you all of this tonight when I proposed—"

Wide-eyed, Cara looked up to interrupt him. "Do you still plan to?"

"Try to stop me. Try to say no."

"You kissed me while I was sleeping last night, didn't you?" And cried, too, thought Cara. Imagine: Jeth Langston crying!

"Yes, just like I'm looking forward to doing when you are sleeping, and I want to wake you to—" His arms tightened. "I have loved you, Cara Martin, since the day I first saw you in my attorney's office. You were exactly—the very image of the woman I had always dreamed of—the woman I wanted to marry. I thought I *was* dreaming. After I'd held you, kissed you, touched you, you were like a fever in my blood. It nearly destroyed me to think that, as much as I loved Ryan, he had gotten to you first."

"But he didn't!" Cara protested.

"Shh, I know that now, sweetheart, though it took me longer than it should have to realize it. Once I did, everything else fell into place. Even as late as the evening we were driving back from the hospital, I still couldn't believe you hadn't been Ryan's mistress. By then, I didn't care anymore. I just knew that I loved you and that after you there would never be anyone else for me."

"When," Cara asked, "did you believe the truth about me?"

"I'm ashamed to say, honey, that it was only yesterday when you were playing 'MacArthur Park.' I was sitting in the study thinking how everything I felt about you was in that song. Then it hit me like the kick of a mule that you were playing it to express how *you* felt about *me*! In that moment, I think, I saw the whole picture clearly. All along there had been two conflicting points that I could never reconcile: Ryan, I knew, would never have loved a tramp—not enough to leave her half of La Tierra. But Ryan, I also knew, could never have kept his hands off you. Being a man myself, I just couldn't let go of that idea. But then when I looked at that part of the equation from the viewpoint of a *brother*, then I knew what Ryan had done..."

Cara lifted her head to look at him inquiringly. "What exactly *had* he done?" she asked softly.

"Shortly after he found out he was dying, he met you, Cara—"

"In the library," she offered, "a little over two years ago."

"He saw in you the woman he knew I'd always wanted, needed, would especially need after he was gone. He decided you would be his gift to me, his final gift of love, to ease the pain of his death."

"Of course..." Cara whispered sadly, thinking of all those times she had wondered at their relationship, all the conversations in which Ryan had tried to defend and explain his older brother to her.

"So he spent his remaining time setting the scene, so to speak. He bought you beautiful clothes to make you even more appealing to me. He arranged a will that would force us to be together and keep us together in spite of the obstacles. And then he extracted that promise from you that would finish setting us up—"

"He told me I'd need courage," Cara murmured.

"Which you had, honey, plenty of it. God, when I think of what I did to you—how I made you suffer! But if you hadn't, Cara, I would have been without some other pieces to the puzzle. Why, I kept asking myself, would a girl like you take such abuse to simply stay at La Tierra for room and board? Why didn't you ever throw your weight around as half owner? Why didn't you ever ask to see the land, the oil, the water rights you'd inherited? Why, I asked, if you hadn't been Ryan's mistress, did he leave you half of La Tierra?

"By the time the roundup was over, I had just about decided that Ryan and you had made some sort of contract. I was willing to believe that you were telling me the truth about your never having been lovers. You were so damned innocent looking, and I was already so gone over you, and I wanted so desperately to believe you. Then you threw me that curve that day in the garden—"

"I had to, Jeth," Cara interrupted. "I had to make you not want me; otherwise, you'd have made love to me. According to the newspaper article, you were just waiting for the estate to be settled to be married. I thought you only wanted to make love to me so that you could get me to sign the papers so you could marry Sonya. I knew that I'd sign those papers. And then I couldn't have stayed at La Tierra. I couldn't have fulfilled my promise to Ryan."

Jeth let out a short, incredulous whistle through his teeth. "We called an awful lot of the shots wrong, didn't we? Still, I should have figured out the whole puzzle at Christmas when you told me that during the summer you'd read of my engagement to Sonya. I spent most of the holidays searching through the summer editions of the Dallas *Morning News* trying to find that damned article. When I did, I pinpointed its release to the day that you put on that very convincing performance for me in your garden. I hoped, of course, that it had been more than hurt pride that had made you behave that way—confess to being Ryan's mistress. But by that time, I'd abused you so...I didn't think I had a snowball's chance in hell of ever winning you again."

Cara reached up to stroke his hard cheek. "Sonya was one of the casualties you were referring to when you told me that Jim had been a minor one, wasn't she?"

Jeth nodded. "I'm afraid so. She's a fine woman. I've known her family all of my life, and I've always known how Sonya felt about me, how she was hoping someday to become mistress of La Tierra. When Ryan died, I was suddenly so—so alone.

She was there. Someone I could trust, someone I could take for granted…If you hadn't come along, I would have married her. Ryan knew that, too, of course. He knew I would have turned to her for solace."

Cara buried her face in Jeth's shoulder, feeling a surge of sympathy for the girl who had come so close to marrying the man of her dreams only to lose him in the eleventh hour. "You know now," she said gently after a while, "why Ryan didn't tell you he was dying, why he didn't go home to be with you in his last days…"

"Yes, honey, I know," Jeth said against her hair. "I would have found out about the will and taken steps to contest it. And then I would never have met you, never known you, never loved you. Ryan was so convinced of your integrity that he knew I'd get the land back anyhow." His voice broke suddenly. "But, Cara, he fell in love with you himself along the way. What that must have been like for him, knowing that he could never have you, never touch you—"

"Let's read his letter," Cara suggested, her eyes growing moist, and reached for the long envelope in Jeth's jacket pocket. She also slipped out another of the white monogrammed handkerchiefs.

"I come with a lifetime supply of those." Jeth grinned. "Not, I hope, that you'll have many occasions to use them."

Ryan spoke to them, Cara decided as Jeth read, not from the grave, but from wherever it was that he watched over them, had watched over them from the beginning. As Jeth had suspected, the letter was addressed to both of them. Tears spilled down her cheeks when Jeth's voice broke, and she stole her hand into his to comfort him. In the ironical, lighthearted banter that she remembered, Ryan explained how he had set in motion the events, when he knew he was dying, that would lead the two of them to love. "Sonya's a good girl," Ryan wrote, "but marriage with her would never fulfill you, Jeth. The girl beside you is the only one for you." The letter closed with declarations of love for both of them and the dry wish that someday there might be a noisy assortment of little Langstons to make the rooms of the big house "less like those of a mausoleum."

"Quite a man, wasn't he?" Jeth said when he had finished the letter.

"Quite a man," Cara agreed. "One to name our first son after."

"Cara—" Jeth's eyes were shining. "I love you with all my heart. The losses are over now. The tears are done. Ryan can rest in peace." And he lowered his head to claim the lips of the woman he loved.

In the sweeping tradition of the *New York Times* bestselling *Roses*, Leila Meacham delivers another grand yet intimate novel set against the rich backdrop of early twentieth-century Texas. In the midst of this transformative time in Southern history, two unforgettable characters emerge and find their fates irrevocably intertwined as they love, lose, and betray.

TURN THE PAGE FOR A PREVIEW OF

TITANS

ON SALE NOW.

Prologue

From a chair beside her bed, Leon Holloway leaned in close to his wife's wan face. She lay exhausted under clean sheets, eyes tightly closed, her hair brushed and face washed after nine harrowing hours of giving birth.

"Millicent, do you want to see the twins now? They need to be nursed," Leon said softly, stroking his wife's forehead.

"Only one," she said without opening her eyes. "Bring me only one. I couldn't abide two. You choose. Let the midwife take the other and give it to that do-gooder doctor of hers. He'll find it a good home."

"Millicent—" Leon drew back sharply. "You can't mean that."

"I do, Leon. I can bear the curse of one, but not two. Do what I say, or so help me, I'll drown them both."

"Millicent, honey . . . it's too early. You'll change your mind."

"Do what I say, Leon. I mean it."

Leon rose heavily. His wife's eyes were still closed, her lips tightly sealed. She had the bitterness in her to do as she threatened, he knew. He left the bedroom to go downstairs to the kitchen where the midwife had cleaned and wrapped the crying twins.

"They need to be fed," she said, her tone accusatory. "The

idea of a new mother wanting to get herself cleaned up before tending to the stomachs of her babies! I never heard of such a thing. I've a mind to put 'em to my own nipples, Mr. Holloway, if you'd take no offense at it. Lord knows I've got plenty of milk to spare."

"No offense taken, Mrs. Mahoney," Leon said, "and...I'd be obliged if you *would* wet-nurse one of them. My wife says she can feed only one mouth."

Mrs. Mahoney's face tightened with contempt. She was of Irish descent and her full, lactating breasts spoke of the recent delivery of her third child. She did not like the haughty, reddish-gold-haired woman upstairs who put such stock in her beauty. She would have liked to express to the missy's husband what she thought of his wife's cold, heartless attitude toward the birth of her newborns, unexpected though the second one was, but the concern of the moment was the feeding of the child. She began to unbutton the bodice of her dress. "I will, Mr. Holloway. Which one?"

Leon squeezed shut his eyes and turned his back to her. He could not bear to look upon the tragedy of choosing which twin to feast at the breast of its mother while allocating the other to the milk of a stranger. "Rearrange their order or leave them the same," he ordered the midwife. "I'll point to the one you're to take."

He heard the midwife follow his instructions, then pointed a finger over his shoulder. When he turned around again, he saw that the one taken was the last born, the one for whom he'd hurriedly found a holey sheet to serve as a bed and covering. Quickly, Leon scooped up the infant left. His sister was already suckling hungrily at her first meal. "I'll be back, Mrs. Mahoney. Please don't leave. You and I must talk."

Chapter One

On the day Nathan Holloway's life changed forever, his morning began like any other. Zak, the German shepherd he'd rescued and raised from a pup, licked a warm tongue over his face. Nathan wiped at the wet wake-up call and pushed him away. "Aw, Zak," he said, but in a whisper so as not to awaken his younger brother, sleeping in his own bed across the room. Sunrise was still an hour away, and the room was dark and cold. Nathan shivered in his night shift. He had left his underwear, shirt, and trousers on a nearby chair for quiet and easy slipping into as he did every night before climbing into bed. Randolph still had another hour's sleep coming to him, and there would be hell to pay if Nathan disturbed his brother.

Socks and boots in hand and with the dog following, Nathan let himself out into the hall and sat on a bench to pull them on. The smell of bacon and onions frying drifted up from the kitchen. Nothing better for breakfast than bacon and onions on a cold morning with a day of work ahead, Nathan thought. Zak, attentive to his master's every move and thought, wagged his tail in agreement. Nathan chuckled softly and gave the animal's neck a quick, rough rub. There would be potatoes and hot biscuits with butter and jam, too.

His mother was at the stove, turning bacon. She was already dressed, hair in its neat bun, a fresh apron around her trim form. "G'morning, Mother," Nathan said sleepily, passing by her to hurry outdoors to the privy. Except for his sister, the princess, even in winter, the menfolks were discouraged from using the chamber pot in the morning. They had to head to the outhouse. Afterward, Nathan would wash in the mudroom off the kitchen where it was warm and the water was still hot in the pitcher.

"Did you wake your brother?" his mother said without turning around.

"No, ma'am. He's still sleeping."

"He's got that big test today. You better not have awakened him."

"No, ma'am. Dad about?"

"He's seeing to more firewood."

As Nathan quickly buttoned into his jacket, his father came into the back door with an armload of the sawtooth oak they'd cut and stacked high in the fall. "Mornin', son. Sleep all right?"

"Yessir."

"Good boy. Full day ahead."

"Yessir."

It was their usual exchange. All days were full since Nathan had completed his schooling two years ago. A Saturday of chores awaited him every weekday, not that he minded. He liked farmwork, being outside, alone most days, just him and the sky and the land and the animals. Nathan took the lit lantern his father handed him and picked up a much-washed flour sack containing a milk bucket and towel. Zak followed him to the outhouse and did his business in the dark perimeter of the woods while Nathan did his, then Nathan and the dog went to the barn to attend to his before-breakfast chores, the light from the lantern leading the way.

Daisy, the cow, mooed an agitated greeting from her stall. "Hey, old girl," Nathan said. "We'll have you taken care of in a minute." Before grabbing a stool and opening the stall gate, Nathan shone the light around the barn to make sure no un-wanted visitor had taken shelter during the cold March night. It was not unheard of to find a vagrant in the hayloft or, in warmer weather, to discover a snake curled in a corner. Once a hostile, wounded fox had taken refuge in the toolshed.

Satisfied that none had invaded, Nathan hung up the lantern and opened the stall gate. Daisy ambled out and went directly to her feed trough, where she would eat her breakfast while Nathan milked. He first brushed the cow's sides of hair and dirt that might fall into the milk, then removed the bucket from the sack and began to clean her teats with the towel. Finally he stuck the bucket under the cow's bulging udder, Zak sitting ex-pectantly beside him, alert for the first squirt of warm milk to relieve the cow's discomfort.

Daisy allowed only Nathan to milk her. She refused to co-operate with any other member of the family. Nathan would press his hand to her right flank, and the cow would obligingly move her leg back for him to set to his task. With his father and siblings, she'd keep her feet planted, and one of them would have to force her leg back while she bawled and trembled and waggled her head, no matter that her udder was being emptied. "You alone got the touch," his father would say to him.

That was all right by Nathan and with his brother and sister as well, two and three years behind him, respectively. They got to sleep later and did not have to hike to the barn in inclement weather before the sun was up, but Nathan liked this time alone. The scents of hay and the warmth of the animals, especially in winter, set him at ease for the day.

The milk collected, Nathan put the lid on the bucket and set it high out of Zak's reach while he fed and watered the horses and led the cow to the pasture gate to turn her out for grazing. The sun was rising, casting a golden glow over the brown acres of the Barrows homestead that would soon be awash with the first growth of spring wheat. It was still referred to as the Barrows farm, named for the line of men to whom it had been handed down since 1840. Liam Barrows, his mother's father, was the last heir to bear the name. Liam's two sons had died before they could inherit, and the land had gone to his daughter, Millicent Holloway. Nathan was aware that someday the place would belong to him. His younger brother, Randolph, was destined for bigger and better things, he being the smarter, and his sister, Lily, would marry, she being beautiful and already sought after by sons of the well-to-do in Gainesville and Montague and Denton, even from towns across the border in the Indian Territory. "I won't be living out my life in a calico dress and kitchen apron" was a statement the family often heard from his sister, the princess.

That was all fine by Nathan, too. He got along well with his siblings, but he was not one of them. His brother and sister were close, almost like twins. They had the same dreams—to be rich and become somebody—and were focused on the same goal: to get off the farm. At nearly twenty, Nathan had already decided that to be rich was to be happy where you were, doing the things you liked, and wanting for nothing more.

So it was that that morning, when he left the barn with milk bucket in hand, his thoughts were on nothing more than the hot onions and bacon and buttered biscuits that awaited him before he set out to repair the fence in the south pasture after breakfast. His family was already taking their seats at the table when he entered the kitchen. Like always, his siblings took chairs that flanked his mother's place at one end of the table while he seated himself next to his father's at the other. The family arrangement had been such as long as Nathan could remember: Randolph and Lily and his mother in one group, he and his father in another. Like a lot of things, it was something he'd been aware of but never noticed until the stranger appeared in the late afternoon.

Chapter Two

The sun was behind him and sinking fast when Nathan stowed hammer and saw and nails and started homeward, carrying his toolbox and lunch pail. The sandwiches his mother had prepared with the extra bacon and onions and packed in the pail with pickles, tomato, and boiled egg had long disappeared, and he was hungry for his supper. It would be waiting when he returned, but it would be a while before he sat down to the evening meal. He had Daisy to milk. His siblings would have fed the horses and pigs and chickens before sundown, so he'd have only the cow to tend before he washed up and joined the family at the table.

It was always something he looked forward to, going home at the end of the day. His mother was a fine cook and served rib-sticking fare, and he enjoyed the conversation round the table and the company of his family before going to bed. Soon, his siblings would be gone. Randolph, a high school senior, seventeen, had already been accepted at Columbia University in New York City to begin his studies, aiming for law school after college. His sister, sixteen, would no doubt be married within a year or two. How the evenings would trip along when they were gone, he didn't know. Nathan didn't contribute much to the gatherings. Like his father, his thoughts on things were seldom asked and almost never offered. He was merely a quiet listener, a fourth at cards and board games (his mother did not play), and a dependable source to bring in extra wood, stoke the fire, and replenish cups of cocoa. Still, he felt a part of the family scene if for the most part ignored, like the indispensable clock over the mantel in the kitchen.

Zak trotted alongside him unless distracted by a covey of doves to flush, a rabbit to chase. Nathan drew in a deep breath of the cold late-March air, never fresher than at dusk when the day had lost its sun and the wind had subsided, and expelled it with a sense of satisfaction. He'd had a productive day. His father would be pleased that he'd been able to repair the whole south fence and that the expense of extra lumber had been justified. Sometimes they disagreed on what needed to be done for the amount of the expenditure, but his father always listened to his son's judgment and often let him have his way. More times than not, Nathan had heard his father say to his mother, "The boy's got a head for what's essential for the outlay, that's for sure." His mother rarely answered unless it was to give a little sniff or utter a *humph*, but Nathan understood her reticence was to prevent him from getting a big head.

As if his head would ever swell over anything, he thought, especially when compared to his brother and sister. Nathan considered that everything about him—when he considered himself at all—was as ordinary as a loaf of bread. Except for his height and strong build and odd shade of blue-green eyes, nothing about him was of any remarkable notice. Sometimes, a little ruefully, he thought that when it came to him, he'd stood somewhere in the middle of the line when the good Lord passed out exceptional intellects, talent and abilities, personalities, and looks while Randolph and Lily had been at the head of it. He accepted his lot without rancor, for what good was a handsome face and winning personality for growing wheat and running a farm?

Nathan was a good thirty yards from the first outbuildings before he noticed a coach and team of two horses tied to the hitching post in front of the white wood-framed house of his home. He could not place the pair of handsome Thoroughbreds and expensive Concord. No one that he knew in Gainesville owned horses and carriage of such distinction. He guessed the owner was a rich new suitor of Lily's who'd ridden up from Denton or from Montague across the county line. She'd met several such swains a couple of months ago when the wealthiest woman in town, his mother's godmother, had hosted a little coming-out party for his sister. Nathan puzzled why he'd shown up to court her during the school week at this late hour of the day. His father wouldn't like that, not that he'd have much say in it. When it came to his sister, his mother had the last word, and she encouraged Lily's rich suitors.

Nathan had turned toward the barn when a head appeared above a window of the coach. It belonged to a middle-aged man who, upon seeing Nathan, quickly opened the door and hopped out. "I say there, me young man!" he called to Nathan. "Are ye the lad we've come to see?"

An Irishman, sure enough, and obviously the driver of the carriage, Nathan thought. He automatically glanced behind him as though half expecting the man to have addressed someone else. Turning back his gaze, he called, "Me?"

"Yes, you."

"I'm sure not."

"If ye are, ye'd best go inside. He doesn't like to be kept waiting."

"Who doesn't like to be kept waiting?"

"Me employer, Mr. Trevor Waverling."

"Never heard of him." Nathan headed for the barn.

"Wait! Wait!" the man cried, scrambling after him. "Ye must go inside, lad. Mr. Waverling won't leave until ye do." The driver had caught up with Nathan. "I'm cold and…me backside's shakin' hands with me belly. I ain't eaten since breakfast," he whined.

Despite the man's desperation and his natty cutaway coat, striped trousers, and stiff top hat befitting the driver of such a distinctive conveyance, Nathan thought him comical. He was not of particularly short stature, but his legs were not long enough for the rest of him. His rotund stomach seemed to rest on their trunks, no space between, and his ears and Irish red hair stuck out widely beneath the hat like a platform for a stovepipe. He reminded Nathan of a circus clown he'd once seen.

"Well, that's too bad," Nathan said. "I've got to milk the cow." He hurried on, curious of who Mr. Waverling was and the reason he wished to see him. If so, his father would have sent his farmhand to get him, and he must tend to Daisy.

The driver ran back to the house and Nathan hurried to the barn. Before he reached it, he heard Randolph giving Daisy a smack. "Stay still, damn you!"

"What are you doing?" Nathan exclaimed from the open door, surprised to see Randolph and Lily attempting to milk Daisy.

"What does it look like?" Randolph snapped.

"Get away from her," Nathan ordered. "That's my job."

"Let him do it," Lily pleaded. "I can't keep holding her leg back."

"We can't," Randolph said. "Dad said to send him to the house the minute he showed up."

233

His siblings often discussed him in the third person in his presence. Playing cards and board games, they'd talk about him as if he weren't sitting across the table from them. "Wonder what card he has," they'd say to each other. "Do you suppose he'll get my king?"

"Both of you get away from her," Nathan commanded. "I'm not going anywhere until I milk Daisy. Easy, old girl," he said, running a hand over the cow's quivering flanks. "Nathan is here."

Daisy let out a long bawl, and his brother and sister backed away. When it came to farm matters, after their father, Nathan had the top say.

"Who is Mr. Waverling, and why does he want to see me?" Nathan asked.

Brother and sister looked at each other. "We don't know," they both piped together, Lily adding, "But he's rich."

"We were sent out of the house when the man showed up," Randolph said, "but Mother and Dad and the man are having a shouting match over you."

"Me?" Nathan pulled Daisy's teats, taken aback. Who would have a shouting match over him? "That's all you know?" he asked. Zak had come to take his position at his knee and was rewarded with a long arc of milk into his mouth.

"That's all we know, but we think...we think he's come to take you away, Nathan," Lily said. Small, dainty, she came behind her older brother and put her arms around him, leaning into his back protectively. "I'm worried," she said in a small voice.

"Me, too," Randolph chimed in. "Are you in trouble? You haven't done anything bad, have you, Nathan?"

"Not that I know of," Nathan said. Take him away? What was this?

"What a silly thing to ask, Randolph," Lily scolded. "Nathan never does anything bad."

"I know that, but I had to ask," her brother said. "It's just that the man is important. Mother nearly collapsed when she saw him. Daddy took charge and sent us out of the house immediately. Do you have any idea who he is?"

"None," Nathan said, puzzled. "Why should I?"

"I don't know. He seemed to know about you. And you look like him…a little."

Another presence had entered the barn. They all turned to see their father standing in the doorway. He cleared his throat. "Nathan," he said, his voice heavy with sadness, "when the milkin's done, you better come to the house. Randolph, you and Lily stay here."

"But I have homework," Randolph protested.

"It can wait," Leon said as he turned to go. "Drink the milk for your supper."

The milking completed and Daisy back in her stall, Nathan left the barn, followed by the anxious gazes of his brother and sister. Dusk had completely fallen, cold and biting. His father had stopped halfway to the house to wait for him. Nathan noticed the circus clown had scrambled back into the carriage. "What's going on, Dad?" he said.

His father suddenly bent forward and pressed his hands to his face.

"Dad! What in blazes—?" Was his father crying? "What's the matter? What's happened?"

A tall figure stepped out of the house onto the porch. He paused, then came down the steps toward them, the light from the house at his back. He was richly dressed in an overcoat of fine wool and carried himself with an air of authority. He was a handsome man in a lean, wolfish sort of way, in his forties, Nathan guessed. "I am what's happened," he said.

Nathan looked him up and down. "Who are you?" he demanded, the question bored into the man's sea-green eyes, so like his own. He would not have dared, but he wanted to put his arm protectively around his father's bent shoulders.

"I am your father," the man said.

About the Author

Leila Meacham is a writer and former teacher who lives in San Antonio, Texas. She is the bestselling author of the novels *Roses*, *Tumbleweeds*, *Somerset*, and *Titans*. For more information, you can visit LeilaMeacham.com.